TRAITOR WOLF

HOWLING DEATH MC
BOOK ONE

SOPHIE ASH

CONTENT WARNING

While the female main character is captured, her captor closely resembles an abusive partner, mainly with manipulation tactics and guilt trips.

This book also contains: kidnapping, imprisonment, drug abuse and addiction, gun violence, and main characters experiencing PTSD and depression

PROLOGUE
RILEY

Don't stop, I told myself. *Don't you dare fucking stop.*

I had no other options but to run.

The pain lancing through my bare feet had to be ignored, no matter how badly they hurt. Branches scraped my arms, legs, ribs, and face; but I couldn't slow down. As badly as I wanted to check, I didn't dare look behind me to see if any of them were after me. I just shoved everything, even my terror, aside and kept running for my life.

Sunlight filtered through the tree branches, but it was quickly fading. The light gave me some advantage but in mere moments, darkness would take over. And there'd be no hope of escaping the horror I was running from.

I couldn't stop, couldn't slow down, despite the pain wracking through me. I still couldn't believe I'd made it out at all.

My lungs were on fire, to the point where every inhale felt like being stabbed. My heart was a rapid drumming in my ears and chest. If I could hear myself, I was certain my breaths would be coming in wheezing, high-pitched pants.

Every step felt like the next one would bring me to collapse. Still, I kept on. I needed out of their territory. Getting off of those monsters' home turf was my only chance of surviving this escape.

Even if I didn't survive, if something else got me, that was okay. It was a better option than going back to them.

One glance up at the sky showed me how much darker it had gotten since I last looked, and the resulting panic spurred me on. How long had I been running? I thought I had two hours of daylight left. Had all that time passed already?

My body physically couldn't move any faster, but the determination willed me on a little farther.

Fuck, everything hurt so bad. And I was so cold. My chattering teeth could be equally due to the temperature or my sheer terror.

At some point, my resolve hit a wall. My brain and body just gave up. I was done, completely out of gas. My wobbling, half-frozen legs could no longer support me, and they buckled until they hit the damp forest floor.

So I crawled.

I pulled myself forward on my forearms, dragging myself through the dirt and fallen leaves while my lungs tried to suck in mouthfuls of air. The smell of earth so close to my mouth and nose reminded me of them, and I retched, my empty stomach protesting violently at the memory of my captor.

After a while, I couldn't crawl anymore either. My shoulders screamed from exertion, and I was filthy.

I was done. Completely and utterly done.

I laid my head down, hoping I had gotten far enough out of their territory so that they couldn't immediately snatch me back, or if they did, that I'd be long gone and frozen solid by then. Couldn't suck blood out of a block of ice, could they?

Anything but going back to them alive.

Footsteps crunched over leaves, and I closed my eyes. I couldn't bear to face them again if they'd found me so soon. Those steps came to a stop right next to my face, and then I felt warm fingers touch down to my neck.

"Holy shit, she's alive," I thought I heard someone say. "Oh, you're freezing, though. Poor thing. Let's get you inside."

Something heavy draped over me, and then I felt a hand on my shoulder and a woman's voice near my ear. "If you can hear me, you're safe. We're going to get you warmed up and treated, okay?"

A pair of hands started to lift me up from the ground, and the blanket that had been draped over my back was then pulled around me to wrap in front.

"Where?" I had no voice left and could only mouth the question. "Where am I?"

"You're at the western border of Vargmore, the werewolf territory."

A stab of panic shot through my chest. My captors hated the werewolves, their sworn enemies. What if my situation had gone from awful to worse?

But that final thought was the last use of my strength, and I collapsed in the arms that held me.

CHAPTER 1

SAWYER

Dusk had fallen when I pulled up to Stout & Spirit. The air was crisp and sharp, and it had been a great day for riding. Tonight would be perfect for a run with the pack. The moon wasn't full yet, but it would be in a week. Now was the time we felt the moon's magic start to ramp up, fueling our shifts and calling forth the wild animals that came out when she was full.

Already, I was antsy for the forest floor beneath my paws. To run with my brothers as a single unit, one predatory force with many faces and eyes.

But I was also human and had to deal with human responsibilities, like collecting rent, as I was doing now. Pretty fucking lame when the other half of your consciousness was a wolf. Still, it was one of the many jobs I had to do as the enforcer of Howling Death MC.

As humans, we were a motorcycle club. As wolves, we were a pack. In both forms, we ran and protected the little corner of Shyftworld that our ancestors had founded centuries ago.

I cut the engine on my Harley and stalled for a moment, keeping glued to my seat as I glanced up at the cheery tavern's front door. I was both dreading going in there and also eager to get this over with. This was my last business to collect rent from, because I'd been stalling and avoiding it all day. Time to face the music, though.

I dismounted the bike and started to pull my leather gloves off as I headed for the door, pushing it open with my shoulder. The bar's interior was a stark contrast to the cool, quiet, darkness of outside. Inside was warm, with rustic chandeliers made of barrel staves throwing light everywhere, and the place was filled with the regular crowd.

A multitude of scents hit my nose as I approached the long wooden bar separating the kitchen from the seating area. Beer, wine, and liquor were the obvious smells. The people were an even more jumbled mix to my senses. There were fellow werewolves, of course. I also picked up the earthy magic of witches and the bright, sunshiney scent of angels. Ordinary humans were difficult to pick out in a crowd because they didn't smell like anything in particular, unless they liked wearing a lot of artificial fragrance. Thankfully, no fake scents assaulted my nose as I parked my ass on a barstool.

Shiloh appeared in front of me within seconds, giving me a cautious, tight smile. "Hey, Sawyer," she greeted.

"Evening, Shiloh," I returned, folding my hands on the bartop.

"What can I get you?"

"Nothing, thank you. Just here to collect."

The witch's face drooped, which was just what I was

afraid of. It made my gut twist with discomfort. When we last saw each other two weeks ago, I had ended the fun little fling we had going on. She wanted something serious, and I just wasn't the guy for that.

When I wasn't with the pack, I was as close to a lone wolf as one could get. I didn't stay in town at the lodge like the rest of the unmated guys. Instead, I had my own place at the edge of the woods that I'd built myself. I had hammered every nail and wired every piece of electricity. I preferred my solitude, and that cabin was my sanctuary.

Shiloh was a good woman. A kind soul, shrewd business owner, beautiful, and the sex we'd had was a good time. She deserved a guy who wanted a partner to add to his life, and that just wasn't me. I gave it my best shot, but the few nights she'd spent at my place just didn't feel right. She looked damn good wearing nothing but my bedsheets, sure. But sitting on *my* couch, making breakfast at *my* stove, using *my* coffee mugs? I got twitchy about someone else in my space, touching my things. It was always a relief when she left, which was the biggest sign I had to end things.

I wanted to be honest with her, because she deserved nothing less. Still, I'd crushed her feelings, and that made me feel like a bastard. She'd done nothing wrong except fall for a guy who couldn't love her back. Shit, at this point, I was all but convinced I couldn't feel that way about anybody. I liked being on my own too much to share that much of my life.

So I'd given Shiloh some space, hoping a couple weeks of distance would ease things. God knew she was a busy woman, running Stout & Spirit. But as she stared across the bar from me now, the look on her face carried the exact same hurt as when I'd broken up with her.

Fuck. I should've let Tryn collect rent tonight like he'd offered, but I wasn't the type to send others to do my work for me.

"Look, I just want to get out of your hair and leave you be," I said. "I know we'll see each other around, but I don't wanna..." *Hurt you*, were the words I left unspoken.

I wasn't Howling Death's enforcer for no reason. I was happy to shred throats with a single-word command from my president. But when it came to women, shit, I took no joy in hurting them.

Shiloh composed herself quickly, hardening up her face. She placed one hand on the bar, next to mine but not touching. "Can I get you to stay for one drink? When I have a second, I need to talk to you about something. Not about us," she added quickly.

"I can't stay. I have plans tonight." I wanted to reassure her that it wasn't a date or having a woman over, but I kept my trap shut. She wasn't my girl, so I didn't owe her that information.

"Please." Now she put her hand over my wrist, her expression imploring me. "I think it's important. Something you might want to bring up with the club."

That got my animal senses tingling, and I leaned forward to speak quietly. "You in danger?" The vampires and dragons had left well enough alone in recent months, although that could always change. You never knew what set those assholes off.

"No. I mean, I don't think so. But I think it's something Howling Death should be aware of." She looked left and right to the packed bar. "Can I get you a beer and come back in a second? On the house. I just gotta take care of some customers first."

What she needed was more employees, but I wasn't about to tell her how to run her business. "Okay," I relented. "IPA would be great."

She poured the drink and set it on a coaster in front of me. "Be right back," she said before hurrying off.

While I nursed my beer, I pulled out my phone and opened my text thread with Derric, the pack alpha and president of Howling Death. My fingers hovered over the keyboard, wondering if I should let him know something was up or that I might be late to the pack run. After some internal debate, I locked the phone and shoved it back in the pocket of my leather jacket.

No need to raise any false alarms. I'd see what Shiloh wanted to talk about first. She seemed stressed, but that could have been because of our break up. She wasn't one to exaggerate or make false claims, so whatever it was was possibly serious. I just needed to see for myself.

I leaned back in my barstool, tilting my head back to take another long pull of beer. It was a good fucking IPA, made in that state-of-the-art brewery up in Helios City, where the angels resided. Who knew if it was due to money or magic, but those winged fuckers made some excellent fermented alcohol. Perfectly balanced, both hoppy and refreshing. Clear as liquid gold. Good thing we had an alliance with them and that this ambrosia wasn't wasted on the likes of vampires or dragons who couldn't appreciate it.

A new scent hit my nose as I tipped my head back for another swallow, and I froze. *No, it couldn't be. Not here.*

I set the beer down and lifted my head, taking another inhale while concentrating hard to filter through the many scents in the bar. That same one hit me, and a growl released from my throat. The bar patrons on either side of me immediately scooted away, as they should.

I smelled the cloying mix of blood and earth in this bar, which could only mean one thing. Shiloh was harboring a vampire.

What the fuck was she thinking? A fucking vampire? *Here*? One of our enemies on werewolf land? No wonder she had looked so distressed. This couldn't wait, though. This business had to be taken care of, now.

My barstool scraped back as I stood and my feet got moving. I cut through the crowd, following Shiloh's familiar scent through a swinging door to the back bar area. There she was, pulling a flat of glassware from a steaming dishwasher.

"Where is it?" I demanded, stepping right up to her. "In your apartment upstairs?"

She froze, her face red from exertion and also probably from embarrassment. "Sawyer, please calm down. It's not what it looks like. Well, smells like."

"Are you telling me I don't smell a fucking vampire up on the second floor? And you wanted me to *wait?*"

"I can explain!" She set down the glasses and held her empty palms up to me, like trying to calm a wild animal. In a sense, she was. "She's hurt. She's resting. I—"

Right above our heads, an anguished scream came over the hum of dishwashers and refrigerators. The bar patrons outside probably couldn't hear it over the noise, but that definitely came from Shiloh's apartment.

"And now she's feeding on someone," I hissed, marching for the back door that would lead to the staircase heading up to Shiloh's place. "How could you be so careless, bringing a vampire here?"

"Sawyer—"

"I can't believe your lack of judgment. You *know* the alpha won't allow this." Frustration roiled in me as I stormed up the stairs. Shiloh was sweet and kind-hearted, I always knew that. But I never took her to be stupid enough to allow an enemy within our borders.

The doorknob to her studio apartment turned easily when I tried it. Good, I was nearly pissed and impatient enough to break through without waiting for her to come unlock it.

The scents of blood and earth hit my nostrils hard as I entered, triggering the start of a shift, which I happily allowed. My human teeth elongated into canines, visible from the snarl on my face and amplified by the growling in my throat. It didn't matter what kind of shape this vampire was in, they were going to regret coming within even one inch of wolf territory.

My gaze swung back and forth across the room a few times, and I was temporarily confused. Where was the bloodsucker? It was all up in my nose but missing from sight. Did it hear me storm up and hide in the bathroom with its prey?

That had to be it. There was no other place to hide in this little studio apartment. I started in that direction when a flash of movement pulled at my peripheral vision, and then there was another terrified scream, followed by soft whimpering.

It was coming from Shiloh's bed.

I whipped around, gaze locking on the bump moving under the quilt. The shape was so small, I figured it was Shiloh's dog or just regular rumpled sheets at first. But there was definitely someone under there.

Cautiously, I moved toward the bed without making a sound. The quilt thrashed again, and I froze. There was that soft whimpering again. The sound fired up a different part of my wolf instincts that seemed unusual in this situation —the urge to protect, to fight off whatever was harming this distressed creature under the covers.

Quick as a flash, I grabbed the edge of the quilt and yanked it back.

CHAPTER 2

RILEY

"I don't want to do this anymore." I sounded like a broken record. A sad, exhausted, blood-deprived, pathetic broken record. "Please, let me go. I...can't do this anymore."

The monster unlatched his fangs from my wrist and laughed. "And where would you go, pet?" His wet tongue slid over the puncture marks, sealing up the wound he'd made to feed from me. "Back to the filthy streets of the human world? You have a home here, a purpose. Back there, you're just garbage. Litter on the sidewalk."

"Please, I just..."

He rolled his eyes and made a dismissive noise at my pleading. "Don't start crying. You know I hate that. It makes your blood bitter."

The cruelty of his words only made the tears come faster. After being his blood pet for so long, I could only wonder how I still had any left in me.

He cursed under his breath and grabbed my hair, yanking my head back in an angry, forceful hold. When he sank his teeth into my artery, he made sure it hurt me, and I screamed.

"Hey! Hey, wake up!"

I had a sudden sense of falling and then jolted upright, breath and heart hammering.

"Hey, you're alright. I'm not gonna hurt you."

It took me a moment to get oriented. I was in a bed, a really soft one that was piled with blankets and pillows. Not the lumpy mattress that I'd known for the past year that had given me all kinds of aches and pains.

That's right, I ran away, I remembered. The aches in my body returned with a vengeance. But I'd actually made it! Someone had helped me.

And this massive presence at my side was not my captor. But with one look at his hard face, I knew he was not the kind soul who had sheltered me.

He looked to be in his thirties, and the sharp eyes roving my face were a dark, inky blue, like a sky at dusk. Aside from his eyes, the feature that captured my attention most was the patch of pale white hair near his temple. The rest of his hair was short and mussed, as though tossed around by the wind or someone's fingers. A neatly trimmed beard covered the lower half of his face. Except for the white patch, his hair was a dark, rich brown.

He's kissed by moonlight. Now that was a random-ass thought to pop into my brain.

"You're not a vampire." Oh, so it was his voice that had told me to wake up. Rich and deep, like cozy thunder.

"No." I curled up smaller, bringing my knees toward my chest. The way he looked at me was so heavy. I felt like I was being crushed under his stare.

"You're human?"

"Yes." My throat was strained from all the screaming I apparently did in my sleep, so I cleared my throat and tried again. "Yes, I'm human."

The man turned his head to look behind him, the corded muscles in his neck twisting elegantly, and I had a random thought of biting him there.

Fuck, *biting* him? After everything I'd been subjected to for the past year? I must have been really fucked in the head.

"Can you bring some water?" he said to the person behind him. "Thanks." He looked at me again, and I froze like a deer caught in headlights. "My name's Sawyer."

I swallowed. "Are you a…" I went beyond looking at his face to the width of his shoulders. He was crouched by the bed like a predator; all lithe, powerful muscle waiting for the perfect moment to spring.

"Werewolf, yeah." He turned to accept a steaming mug from the woman he'd spoken to earlier, and even that small movement was too fluid to be human. "Thanks, Shiloh."

The woman stood behind him, looking at me with warmth and relief. "It's actually a sipping broth infused with some herbs and spices. It'll start you on getting rehydrated and healthy again."

"Thank you," I whispered, staring at the vessel cupped in the werewolf's large hands. I truly didn't know if I'd have the strength to hold the thing myself, but we made the transfer successfully.

I felt the werewolf's eyes on me while I sipped at the broth, which was the *perfect* temperature and fucking delicious, so my self-consciousness went out the window while I slurped on that heaven in a mug.

"What's your name?" he asked when I took a break to swallow a mouthful.

I hesitated before answering, but I was too mentally drained to consider why I should lie. It wasn't like I was anybody that mattered. "Riley," I answered.

"Riley," he repeated. Well, damn. Why did it sound so sexy when he said it? "And do you mind me asking why you reek of vampire?"

All the warmth from the blankets and broth were immediately sucked away by cold terror. My hands tightened around the mug to stop the tremors running through them. "Don't make me go back to them," I said. "Please, *please* don't take me back. I'd never escaped successfully before, and I just can't go back. I'd really rather go anywhere else, *please*—"

Sawyer held up an open palm in a calming gesture. "You won't go anywhere against your will. You have my word. But you're in my pack's territory, smelling of our enemy, and I'm just trying to figure things out."

It was only then that I noticed the leather jacket. And the patches. On the right side was his name. On the left, the word ENFORCER was embroidered over his chest.

Oh shit.

I shrank back until my spine hit the wall. This wasn't just any werewolf. He was dangerous. Just as, if not more so than, my captor had been. I didn't know much about club politics but had heard my captor and his minions curse and complain about this very wolf at my bedside.

Sawyer had vampire blood on his hands and not in the feeding sense. The two species didn't just feud over territory. The conflict between werewolves and vampires was deep, ugly, and personal. They killed not just each other, but humans, witches, and any innocent species residing in each others' territories. There was constant bloodshed between the two of them.

I thought I'd finally had a stroke of luck, but of all the werewolves I could have run into in this territory, this was probably the worst one. He might not turn me back over to the vampires, but his treatment of me could be even worse.

How much of an idiot could I be? To escape from one predator and land directly in the jaws of another.

Sawyer had patience and a soothing way about him that was practically nonexistent in vampires, I'd give him that. He backed away the moment I pressed against the wall, holding both palms up.

"Easy," he said. "I'm not going to hurt you. I promise you're safe."

"How do I know that?" I blurted out. *He* had told me I was safe too. It was how he lured me in and fed on me for over a year.

The wolf said nothing for a moment, then reached inside his jacket and pulled something from an inner pocket. He held the black, folded square of fabric out to me. "Take this. Wear it in a way that's visible. As a scarf, in your hair, wherever. Anyone who sees it knows you're under my protection."

I put the mug aside to unfold the fabric in my lap, revealing a bandanna with the image of a wolf skull in the center and HOWLING DEATH MC curving underneath. Along the edges, repeating in a seamless pattern, were the words PROPERTY OF SAWYER.

Some funny sensation occurred in my chest, one that I'd never felt before and couldn't place. On some level, I rejected the notion of being someone's property again. That was all I'd been as a blood pet, and part of me wanted to wad up the bandanna and throw it at the wolf's face.

But some other unknown side of me preened with pleasure at receiving this gift. Like this wasn't enslavement but an elevation of my status. A title, and one that wasn't given out often. It meant protection and a kind of symbolic ownership that wasn't degrading but full of pride.

I blinked down at the fabric, absently tracing my hand over the wolf skull. Where all these thoughts came from, I had no idea.

"How do I know you're not lying about this?" I asked, choosing to cling to the rational side of my brain.

"He's not."

Sawyer and I both looked up to the woman who had brought over the broth. She was standing in the doorway to this place, which was where I assumed she lived. Her eyes were still kind but her expression was stony, like she was trying to hold back a whole slew of emotions.

"Howling Death takes their property flags very seriously," she said stiffly. "And werewolves, by nature, are extremely loyal. That flag means he'll put his life on the line for you. You can trust him."

Sawyer faced me again, his expression a bit sheepish. "She's right. It means a lot of things, but the big thing is that you can count on me to protect you. I won't let any harm come to you."

My eyes went back and forth between the two of them. I'd have to be comatose to not notice the palpable tension between them. Was there...something going on with them? Was giving this flag to me some kind of slight against her?

A sudden possessiveness rose up in me, and I watched my hands roll up the bandanna and wrap it around my wrist. Sawyer growled so softly, it was almost a purr. I looked up and figured I must have imagined it. His expression had softened, a smile even pulling at one corner of his lip.

"Now we're getting somewhere. May I?" I held my arm out and allowed him to tie the ends of the bandanna to secure it on my wrist. "Too tight?"

"No, I'm good."

His rough fingers lingered on the black fabric for a moment, then trailed slowly upward a few inches to the mess of puncture scars dotting the skin of my inner forearm.

I snatched my arm back, and he growled again, but not like the one I had just imagined. The sound made me flinch, because that was the low, threatening growl of a predator.

"Now that our trust is established," Sawyer said. "Tell me what the vampires did to you."

CHAPTER 3
SAWYER

"Tell me what the vampires did to you." It was not a question, and if this human, Riley, had a lick of sense, she would tell me. At the same time, I also tried to keep my tone gentle, toeing the line between not scaring her and getting the information I needed.

She held her arms close to her body, looking so small and fragile. Her complexion was so pale, I could see the blue veins on her neck, and the many, many puncture marks from fangs dotting her neck and wrists. If I had to guess, I'd venture there were more over the femoral arteries on her inner thighs. Sick fucking insects, those vampires.

Dark circles surrounded wide mahogany eyes, which skittered around the room like a typical prey animal. This poor girl. Had she felt the sun on her face a single day in the past month, or even year? Somehow I doubted it. I was drawing my own conclusions from the state she was in, but she needed to open her mouth and talk if I was going to get the full picture.

"You will not be harmed, no matter what you tell me," I

said, touching my forefinger to my flag wrapped around her wrist. "This guarantees that. I promise you."

I had pulled back my shift, looking fully human so as to not scare her, but my wolf instincts were riding me hard just below the surface. For some reason, my creature was personally offended that this girl had been hurt. He wanted to run out into the woods and tear out some vampire throats *now*.

Along that same vein, he also howled with pride that she was wearing our flag, our symbol of protection. She was ours to keep safe, and he wanted to prove himself worthy of protecting her.

It was fucking distracting, I had to admit. He'd never gone bonkers like this for a woman before. Sure, he did a little howling and strutting around attractive females, but this was different. The instinct knocking around my hind-brain could only be summed up to one English word —claim.

He didn't want to just flirt and swagger in front of this human woman, he wanted to make her his.

There were not enough mental *'Down boys'* in the world for that shit. For one thing, she was only human. Second, she was a complete stranger.

"I was fed from," Riley finally told me in a small voice.

Well, that much was obvious from one look at her. But saying something was better than staying clammed up, so I did my best to ignore the possessive howling and scratching under my skin and proceed with the questioning.

"Were you held against your will?"

Her whole body started to shake, and that was enough of an answer for me. The terrified look in her eyes made it clear she wasn't up for answering any more questions, so I leaned away from the bed to give her space. As I did that, I could almost feel a resistant pull, like there was some force compelling me to lean forward and gather her up in my arms instead.

Calm. The fuck. Down. Boy.

My wolf wanted to whine as I stood from the bedside. "Everything'll be alright. I'll leave you to get some rest."

I headed for the apartment door, which had been closed but not locked. Shiloh must have headed back down to tend the bar. She was just coming toward the stairs again as I descended.

"How's she doing?" Shiloh crossed her arms over her chest, brow furrowed as she looked at me.

"Okay, I guess. Scared as hell."

"What are you going to do?"

"I don't know. She's not really talking to me yet."

Shiloh worried her lip and shifted her weight on her feet. "I feel bad for her, I really do. And I want to help. But I'm worried, with the bar so close to the border as it is. What if she leads vampires straight here?"

I had thought of that too. Getting Riley away from the edge of the territory would be for the best. If the vampires came after her, we wanted as few innocent bystanders in the way as possible. The solution left my mouth before it became a fully-formed thought in my brain.

"I'll take her to my place."

Shiloh's brows shot up. "Your place? You mean...have her stay with you?"

I shrugged. "It's secluded, away from the border. I got extra bedrooms and showers, plenty of food to spare. I'm probably better equipped to handle her recovery than you are here, and she'll be out of your hair." Shiloh's studio apartment was spacious enough for a single person and the occasional guest, but it wasn't the best option for housing a complete stranger for an unknown amount of time.

"Yeah, but it's *your* place," Shiloh pointed out. The '*as you so often reminded me*' was left unsaid. "And you're...*you.*"

I shrugged again, shoving down my oddly-possessive wolf howling in victory. "She needs help. It'll be temporary. I can deal."

Shiloh's mouth wobbled, and she blinked a few times. "You gave her your flag."

I should have been holding a pair of dumbbells so at least my shoulders could get a workout from all this shrugging. "She needs to feel safe enough to talk, and it was the first thing I thought of. I still haven't gotten much out of her, so it doesn't seem like it's worked anyway."

"And you think taking her to your remote cabin in the woods will?"

One more shrug rep. "If you got a better idea, I'm all ears."

"Take her to the pack. Just go straight to Derric, and let him deal with it."

I shook my head. "The pack will get one whiff of vampire and tear her apart without a second thought. I gotta see if that stink can be washed away first before I get her anywhere near them."

Shiloh breathed out a long sigh and looked away for a few seconds before turning back to me. "Are you trying to, like, rub it in my face that it's over between us?"

Her eyes glittered with unshed tears, and a pained ache cut through my chest. "No, why—"

"Having her stay at your place? Giving her your flag to

wear?" Her arms spread out to the sides. "Is she someone to you? Do you know her?"

Yes, she is ours! my wolf howled.

"No, she's not." I started toward Shiloh with my arm outstretched but thought better of it and kept a few feet of distance. "I'm just trying to do the right thing. It's got nothing to do with what we had."

I made sure to use the past tense and still hated the sight of Shiloh's face falling. Hurting her killed me, but I liked and respected her too much to give her any false hope. As much as it sucked to see her hurt, my chest didn't ache with the same pain I saw in her. My wolf didn't howl mournfully at the loss of our brief relationship. Hopefully soon, she would be healed and realize she deserved a guy who was crazy about her.

"Okay," she said on a shaky exhale, then wiped her eyes. "Sorry, I'm..."

"No, I'm sorry." Again, I reined in the urge to hug her, as a friend. "I made you feel like this. I—"

"It's fine." She gave a little sheepish laugh. "Water under the bridge, I get it. I just need to process it, you know?" She took another deep breath and looked at me with strength and composure. "So, when you taking her?"

"Tonight, I guess. If she'll let me."

"Thought you had big plans." When I opened my mouth, Shiloh gave me a little slug on the arm. "I'm kidding. Obviously a vampire's victim takes precedence."

"Yeah. And if they come looking for her, they'll come at night. Better to get her away from the bar as soon as possible."

Shiloh nodded gravely before her eyes trailed upward to

her apartment. "Maybe I should break the news to her. She might take it better coming from a fellow woman."

A knot of tension loosened from my chest. Getting Riley to my place and having her stay there while she was clearly afraid would be a whole other ordeal. Better to let Shiloh, not the big bad wolf, convince her that it was safe.

"Thanks," I said. "That's a good idea."

Shiloh patted my chest as she passed me on her way up the stairs. "Watch the bar for me? Help yourself to anything."

"Sure. Thanks again, Shiloh."

"What are friends for?" She flashed me a little smile as she hoofed it up the stairs, and the knot in my chest loosened some more. She'd be alright, and she was a good friend.

I re-entered the bar through the back door, crossed the back room, and emerged into the main serving area, scanning the crowd for any trouble. Everyone seemed in good spirits, however, talking amongst themselves as they all nursed drinks that were no less than half full. Satisfied, I went behind the bar and poured myself a small amount of the IPA I had earlier. Just a little taste for the road.

"Sawyer! Are you Shiloh's new bartender?"

I turned toward the familiar voice of Fallon, a fellow werewolf and former Howling Death member. He and his mate, Aria, were wrapped up in each other, their eyes bright and complexions flushed, like they'd just been on a run together.

"Just watching over it while she takes care of some things upstairs." I leaned across the bar to him and lowered my voice. "You been through vamp territory lately?"

Fallon might have been a wolf but as the Traveler, he

belonged to no pack. He was truly neutral to all our conflicts and the only one who could travel freely among the territories of Shyftworld. I knew he made some trips over to the human-only world too. That was where he'd met Aria.

The smile disappeared from Fallon's face as he angled his head toward me. "No, we just came back from Helios City. Why, something going on?"

"I don't want to bring it to the pack yet," I told him. "But a human girl turned up here, smells like a vamp, all bitten up, and scared out of her fucking mind. Shiloh is tending to her right now, but I'm taking her to my place for everyone's safety."

Aria frowned. "Poor thing. Is she a blood pet?"

"Kinda seems like it, but she looks..." I shook my head. "Battered. Terrified. I thought the blood pet deal was a consensual thing."

"Usually, but the pet can also be manipulated into it," Fallon said. "By the time they realize what it's all about, well, they're usually too weak to get out."

The growl rolled out of me before I could stop it, a visceral, knee-jerk reaction that made Fallon lean away with wide eyes. "Whoa. You okay there, Sawyer?"

"Yeah, sorry. I'm good." I threw back my small taster of beer, wishing I'd given myself a full pour instead. "It's just fucked up, what they do to people."

Fallon's mouth tightened, but it was Aria who spoke. "They're not all bad. They can't help what they are, just as much as you can't. Even vamps are people."

I held my tongue, not wanting to disrespect a friend's mate, but Aria was new to our world and didn't know the centuries of bloody history between our kind and the vampires. She believed herself to be fully human until Fallon's bite not only revealed her to be a latent wolf shifter, but also chosen for him by fate.

My wolf howled in yearning at the thought of a chosen mate, which was a big fucking news flash to me. We'd never been interested in finding a mate, our solitude was too precious. The pack was enough. Getting laid once in a while was enough.

"The vampires aren't big fans of me lately," Fallon said. "Last time we were there, we took another blood pet from them and returned her to her family."

"Huh," I scoffed. "Maybe that whole consensual thing is a bunch of dogshit. They probably say that to get victims easier."

Fallon put a hand on my forearm. "I know it's not a good look, but Aria's right. They can't help that they need blood to live. There are bad wolves out there, you know that as well as I do."

"Yeah, and we deal with them," I grunted. "We don't let them get away with holding innocent people captive and using them as chew toys."

I was getting heated and the other wolf could see this. Fallon released my arm and backed away. "They might be dealing with it, who knows?"

"Considering she ran all the way here, I doubt it."

"Sawyer."

I looked to see Shiloh poking her head out of her back room. "She's good to go."

"Good luck. We hope she recovers," Aria said to me. "And that this doesn't bring about conflict between you and the vamps."

"Thanks." I started heading for the front door. "See you

two later."

"Let us know if you need anything," Fallon called after me.

I shook off the annoyance as I made for my bike. If he really wanted to help, he'd be a spy for our pack. Hang out with those vamps and let us know how they planned to react to us keeping one of their blood pets.

But he wouldn't do that. Fallon was a peacekeeper of sorts, a thread weaving through all of our worlds. True, things had been relatively peaceful since he'd become the Traveler. But as I popped up my kickstand and started walking the bike around to the back of the bar, my wolf snapped his jaws and growled his fury.

He didn't want peace. He wanted to do right by Riley and hurt those who made her a small, trembling shell.

And so did I.

CHAPTER 4

RILEY

"How would you feel about having a bedroom and shower all to yourself?" Shiloh asked me gently after the big werewolf had left. "Somewhere safe, of course. Where you can take all the time you need to recover and get back on your feet again."

"Where?" It sounded amazing, but that was how I'd been lured to the vampire's den in the first place. He'd promised me a soft, warm bed, delicious food, and luxurious showers. The things he failed to mention were that he'd drink my blood regularly and never allow me to leave.

Shiloh played with the tassels on a pillow in her lap. "Sawyer has offered to let you stay at his place." At the fear in my eyes, she quickly added, "You don't have anything to worry about, he's a good guy. A little gruff, sure, but he would never hurt you or take advantage. I promise you, he's one of the good ones."

"He's an enforcer," I whispered.

Shiloh looked at me squarely. "He's good at his job, yes. But that's not who he is. He's a hardass about rent getting paid on time, and yeah...he deals with the werewolves' enemies, but that's to protect people like you and me." She reached for my hand and gave a gentle squeeze. "You're safer with him than any other wolf in Vargmore. That's a fact."

I picked at the wolf's flag on my wrist, pulling it around and around in a circle, and noticed Shiloh's eyes on it as I did so. "Are you and him, um..."

Maybe it was the awkward nature of the question or that my brain was still in a fog, but I couldn't force it all the way out. Shiloh got the gist, though, and shook her head with a sad smile. "Nah, we were seeing each other for a hot minute, but that's over. We're better off as friends. For a pack animal, he flies solo a lot. So I don't think you have to worry about running into a girlfriend or anything."

Just like when he gave me his flag earlier, some part of me preened happily, as if to say *'the wolf is mine',* but that made no sense. All he wanted was to find ammunition against the vampires.

He wanted information from me, and to get that, he needed me safe and calm enough to talk. To make me feel like talking, he had to show kindness and get me comfortable. I was traumatized, not an idiot. I could see right through what he was trying to do. The only question was, what would he do with me once he got the information he wanted?

One thing at a time, I guess. As long as no one was feeding from me and preventing me from leaving.

I looked at Shiloh square in the eye, trying to tap into a reserve of courage I wasn't sure existed anymore. "I don't want to be touched, ever. And I want to be allowed to leave if I want to. I won't go anywhere that I'll be held captive."

Shiloh blinked and then nodded quickly. "Of course, none of that will be a problem. Howling Death doesn't imprison people. And like I said, Sawyer is an honorable guy. He won't touch you or do anything to make you uncomfortable."

I still wasn't fully convinced on that last part. All my life, I'd had people lie to and manipulate me to get what they wanted. But I couldn't stay here, and I felt bad that I was taking up space in Shiloh's little home. There was no other place for me to go, so what choice did I really have?

Hopefully Sawyer's rooms had locks on the doors.

"Okay," I said quietly. "I'll stay with him."

Shiloh beamed a smile at me as she stood up from the bed. "I'll let him know. There's a few changes of clothes for you." She pointed to a tote bag on the bedside table. "Keep them as long as you need. Oh, let me also give you a jacket. It's gonna be cold on that bike."

"Bike?" I repeated, dread twisting in my stomach.

"Oh yeah, I should have said." Shiloh grimaced a little. "He rides a motorcycle everywhere. So there's going to be some touching for you to, you know, live."

Well shit. So much for that rule.

))))) >>>>>> ((((((

AFTER GETTING DRESSED in several layers of Shiloh's clothes for warmth, I came down her staircase to find Sawyer leaning against a massive Harley. The machine was completely black except for a few accents of silver. Kind of like its rider, an imposing figure in black leather, jeans, and boots, with only that touch of pale, moon-kissed hair on his head.

"You ever ride before?" he asked me.

I shook my head, staring at the long, powerful piece of machinery as if it might roar to life and run me over like a stampeding beast.

"Well, first things first." Sawyer offered me a round, shiny black helmet. "Gotta protect your noggin."

"Okay." I slipped it on and felt like one of those bobble-head dolls. Thankfully, I was able to find the chin strap and secure the helmet without any help from him. Although, a part of me felt pouty that he didn't get up close and put his hands on my face to tighten the strap. A shame he didn't get close enough to smell.

Hold on, since when was I into sniffing men? Damn, I really needed to replenish all the blood I'd lost over the months.

"Next thing." Sawyer turned away and threw a long leg over his bike. The way he mounted his seat was almost… sexual. He gripped the handlebars and scooted forward with a small thrust of his hips, settling into a place that he clearly knew well and had mounted many times before.

"Sorry, what?" He'd been saying something to me while I was too busy playing that thrusting motion on a repeating loop in my head.

Dark blue eyes narrowed in annoyance. Clearly, he was not one who liked to repeat himself. "I said, climb on and hold on to me. You're going to have to be close against my back, it's just safest that way. When you feel me lean into the turns, lean with me, don't fight it. Motorcycles aren't the same as cars. You use your body to ride just as much as the vehicle. Understand?"

I nodded and he must have noticed how jerky the motion was, because his expression and voice softened. "My place isn't too far. We'll be there in about fifteen minutes. Then you can rest and recover in privacy. I promise you'll be safe on the bike, alright?"

My nod was a smoother up and down motion this time. Something about his tone was utterly soothing, like being cocooned in a warm blanket. I knew I was safe, I just needed to will my body forward, until I was right up against him.

Finding my seat on the bike was more of an awkward climb than his smooth, sexy mounting, but I eventually made it and looked down to find my inner thighs pressed right up against the outsides of his.

"Arms around my waist will probably feel the most secure for you," he said. "But once you're comfortable, you can hold on to just my shoulders or whatever."

After a moment's hesitation, my arms circled around him. He was so big and broad, my hands couldn't find each other on his stomach. Rather than awkwardly patting him to find a hold, I just let my hands rest somewhere on his torso.

"Here we go." Sawyer turned a key and the bike roared to life, like a great beast awaking from a slumber. It vibrated under my body in a way that...

Oh God, why did that feel *good?*

"Hold on," Sawyer yelled over the engine. His gloved hands returned to the handlebars and I saw a confident, deliberate flick of his wrist right before we jolted forward. The motion startled me, bringing my chest to crash into his back and my fingers curling into his shirt for purchase.

"You okay?" He'd turned his head to look at me over his

shoulder, and I gave a small nod. It was kind of embarrassing to be clinging to him like a koala bear, but no way in hell was I letting go.

The bike started moving again, and this time I was ready for the acceleration. Sawyer slowly increased his speed, and I was certain it was due to me being a little scaredy cat. If it weren't for me, he'd burst out of here like a bat out of hell.

I appreciated that he went slowly though, and my white-knuckled hold on his shirt gradually relaxed. With more of my fear easing away, I found myself able to actually enjoy the ride. The dense forest whipped past us like we were flying. I looked up and gasped at the night sky full of stars and a bright heavy moon that would be full in a few days.

"About to hit some turns," Sawyer yelled at me over his shoulder. "Remember what I said about leaning."

"Okay!" I answered. "You can go faster if you want."

I swore I saw a smile right before he resumed facing forward and thought I felt the beginnings of one on my face too.

My arms hugged snugly around him as he maneuvered the winding roads with expert precision. After the first couple times, it finally clicked like the steps in a dance routine. I knew what was coming and gave in to the swaying movement with absolutely no fear. I actually started craving the turns, eager for that thrilling pull of gravity while I remained pressed to the solid safety net of Sawyer's body.

Almost too soon, he pulled up to a detached garage next to a beautiful two-story cabin with huge windows and a massive porch on the entry level. The trees came right up to the sides and back, like this house was just as much a part of the forest as they were. It looked like something out of a magazine, and I could only stare dumbly as the motorcycle came to a stop.

"This is yours?"

"Yeah. Home sweet home." He slid from the motorcycle first, then turned around and offered me a hand. "Need help getting off? I mean—fuck."

The mortification on his face made it clear he hadn't intended the innuendo, but it was enough to give me pause. And to retreat into my small bubble of suspicion and distrust.

"No, thanks. I got it."

"Sorry. I didn't mean anything like that." Sawyer ran a hand through his hair, fingers lingering on the white patch among the dark strands. "I'll, uh, I'll get the door." He turned abruptly and marched for the front door, jingling his keyring as he hurried away.

I was grateful for the space but also a little disappointed. The ride had been...fun. He had never tried to touch me once while I'd been wrapped around him. The solid, warm feel of him had been nice. I kind of hoped to ride with him again one day.

Given that he kept his word that he would leave me be, while also not holding me captive.

Steeling myself with a breath, I followed the path he made up to the front door and wiped my feet with Shiloh's borrowed shoes on the mat. Just because I didn't fully trust the guy didn't mean I'd be rude enough to track mud into his house.

I stepped over the threshold, looked up, and couldn't help the, "Wow," that left my mouth.

If I thought the outside was magazine-worthy, the inside put it to shame. The cabin was completely open, a modern design while also being cozy. A black pellet stove stood in the corner, surrounded by couches in an L-shape. Soft rugs covered the hardwood floors and the stairs running up to the second level, which looked to be an open loft.

"Guest bedroom is through there." Sawyer pointed down a short hallway past the kitchen. "It has its own bathroom. Linens and towels are clean. You should have everything you need."

He wandered to the kitchen and pulled open one of the two stainless steel refrigerator doors. "I made a big pot of soup that should last several days. You're welcome to join me for dinner, or help yourself to it whenever you'd like. Bowls are right here." He opened a cupboard and took down one of the heavy stoneware dishes.

"Um." I fingered the knot on his flag again, turning the fabric bracelet around and around my wrist. "I think I'll just shower and go to bed."

He gave a sharp nod, focused on ladling soup from the pot in the fridge into his bowl. "Goodnight, then."

I stood there dumbly for a second, as if waiting for him to argue or insist I eat with him. When I realized no angry outburst was coming, I turned and scurried down the hall before he could think I was a total weirdo. If he didn't think that already.

Once in the guest bedroom, the first thing I did was shut the door and turn the lock. It was only then that I realized he probably had keys to all the locks in his house. *Well, no shit, Sherlock. It's his goddamn house.*

Sawyer didn't seem like the type to force himself into

my room, but then again, how well did I really know him? Maybe I should move a piece of furniture in front of the door just in case?

Turning to inspect the room, I quickly saw that such a thing wouldn't be possible. The bed was a queen on a low, sturdy wooden frame. The dresser against the wall, nearly as tall as I was and just as sturdy-looking as the bed frame, was the only other piece of furniture in the room.

I went to quickly check the dresser drawers and found them all empty. Seemed like Sawyer didn't have guests over very often.

A yawn escaped me, and then my eyelids drooped. Exhaustion hit me like a warm, heavy wave. Shower. I needed a shower. Then sleep. For some reason, I didn't want to dirty up Sawyer's bed with whatever filth was still on me.

The hot water came instantly and with a pressure that almost tenderized my skin. It felt really, really damn good, and I stayed under that hot spray for probably too long, scrubbing my skin until I was pink.

After getting out and changing into a pair of loaner sleeping shorts and a tank top from Shiloh, I sat on the edge of the bed while plucking at the knot of Sawyer's flag around my wrist. Once I got it off, I unrolled it from its bracelet state and hung it on the corner of the bed frame to dry.

My last thought before succumbing to sleep's embrace was that I'd have to remember to put it back on when I woke up.

For some reason, I just liked wearing it.

CHAPTER 5

RILEY

My stomach woke me up. A massive ripple of hunger that first reached my ears and then ricocheted throughout my body. Holy shit, I was *starving*.

I rolled over, blinking at the bright sunlight streaming through the windows. Oh God, *sunlight*. Immediately awake, I sat upright in bed and turned toward the window just to bring my face closer to those delicious, warm rays. My face felt strange, and I knew it was because I was smiling.

I'd never take the sun for granted again. How any creatures could live without it ceased to make sense to me. It was so comforting, like a hug or a blanket, and my mood instantly brightened when that light touched my skin.

Another pang of hunger ripped through me, which sorted my priorities right away. I needed food. The sun would still be there in a few hours.

A mouthwatering scent hit my nose the moment I cracked open my bedroom door, and I nearly salivated. I couldn't place the scent, maybe it was just spices and cooking oil, but it had been so long since I'd smelled anything but blood that I just took a moment to pause and inhale. Sounds floated toward me from the kitchen, so Sawyer was definitely up and cooking something.

Nerves held me back, keeping my palm on the knob with the urge to shut the door and retreat under the bed covers. I was so damn anxious about seeing him. Last night had been such a blur, probably because I was still in shock that I had actually managed to escape. Now, after the most restful sleep I had in months and seeing real daylight for the first time in nearly a year, this felt startlingly real. I was in werewolf territory. Not only that but in the home of the enforcer for Howling Death.

I still might not be entirely safe. I had to remember that.

My eyes drifted over to the black square of cloth that I'd hung out to dry after my shower. Without a second thought, I grabbed it, rolled it up into a long strip, and re-wrapped it around my wrist. He'd said it was for my protection, but would it protect me *from* him if it came to that?

Hunger finally won out over my nerves, and I marched through the door, padding quietly toward the kitchen in search of the source of those delicious smells.

Sawyer stood at the island counter, chopping something with a knife. He didn't look up immediately, so I paused at the end of the hall to just drink him in. He wore jeans and a white T-shirt, the fabric doing its best to stay intact while stretched across his broad chest and shoulders. The muscles in his arms jumped as he swiftly moved the knife through the small, neat piles of vegetables on the cutting board. His hair looked a bit glossy, like it was still wet from his shower. The white patch seemed smaller, hidden by the darker strands, and I had a passing thought of running my fingers through his hair to uncover it.

He was also barefoot, one heel lifted like how a dog sometimes let its paw hover in midair. Something about that was...cute. Endearing even, and my chest loosened slightly while I watched him.

"Morning." The low timber of his voice brought me back to the awareness that I was staring. "Sleep well?"

"Uh, yeah! I mean, yes. Thank you." I swallowed, the warmth in my chest turning into flames in my cheeks. "You?"

"Well enough." Sawyer set the knife down and wiped his hands on a dish towel. "Do you like omelets?"

It took a moment for that word to conjure up a familiar image in my brain. Warm, fluffy eggs. Cheese, peppers, and sometimes sausage in the center. And a metric fuck-ton of ketchup.

My stomach answered for me, letting out an embarrassingly loud growl. A smile pulled at the corners of Sawyer's mouth while I slapped a hand over my abdomen. "Uh yeah, you could say that."

"I'll make you a big one." Before I could think of how suggestive those words sounded, he turned and pointed toward the refrigerator. "There's a few different kinds of juice in the fridge door, help yourself. I'd offer you coffee, but you probably need to get your blood sugar up, so I'm going to insist on the juice."

"Bossy," I remarked, heading for the stainless steel door. Although I was privately touched at the consideration. That strange, hidden part of me preened again, relishing the idea that this wolf wanted to take care of me.

He just doesn't want you to drop dead in his house, calm the fuck down.

"On that note," Sawyer said as he continued chopping at the counter. "I'm loading your omelet with spinach, because you probably need the iron."

The pineapple-ginger juice looked the most appealing to me, so I carefully pulled the glass bottle from the door before closing the fridge. "I'm kind of surprised a werewolf even has spinach in his house."

A soft sound drifted over from his direction. Something like a low, growly chuckle. I liked it. "Believe it or not, wolves aren't completely carnivorous. Glasses are in the cupboard to your right."

"Thanks." I brought a glass down and went to work on the opening the juice, but the fucking lid wouldn't budge.

"Here, I got it." In a single stride, Sawyer was standing right in front of me, his hand outstretched and waiting.

Damn, he was big, towering over me like a wall of impenetrable muscle. I had already figured that the Shyft-world species were bigger and stronger than humans, but only vampires had ever come this close to me before. For a split second, I felt cornered. Trapped.

Sawyer seemed to sense my fear and immediately took a step back, his chin and gaze lowering in a wordless gesture of apology. "Sorry. Just wanted to open that for you," he muttered.

I blinked, fighting the waves of shame and embarrassment rolling up. Shit, he was only trying to be nice. He was letting me stay in his house, for fuck's sake.

"Yeah, sure. Thanks." I held out the bottle of juice to him, and he took it, clamping his massive hand over the lid and popping it open with a quick, easy twist before returning it to me.

"So, uh." I turned away to pour my juice and hopefully move on from that awkward moment. "Wolves like spinach, huh?"

"Well, everyone likes different things." Sawyer thankfully returned to his chopping at the island. "But wolves are omnivores, like humans. We can eat almost anything and actually do need more than just meat to live."

"Oh, I had no idea." I returned the juice to the fridge and took a big gulp from my glass.

"Common misconception. Now cats, on the other hand, they're obligate carnivores. So you're likely to find only meat in their fridges." Sawyer went to the cooktop and turned on one of the burners. "Have a seat. I'll get you served up here in a minute."

I went to one of the barstools at the far side of the island, taking my juice with me. "Are there cat shifters in Shyftworld?"

"Not sure. I kind of doubt it, though. Wolves and dragons have been here so long, you'd think we'd run into other shifters at some point if there were any."

My juice nearly went down the wrong pipe and I coughed. "Did you say dragons? Like, *dragon*-dragons?"

Sawyer smirked at me from across the island, tilting a pan from side to side to coat the surface in cooking oil. "If by *dragon*-dragons, you mean lizards the size of a car that can fly and breathe fire, yes." He was teasing me but not maliciously so.

"So dragons are real?"

"Yep. Their territory is to the south. It's all desert and rocky cliffs down there."

"What else is in Shyftworld?"

"Angels run Helios City, the metropolis to the north." Sawyer carefully poured an egg mixture into his pan. "They're allied with us, so you might see a few around Vargmore. Although it's rare they leave their skyscrapers and shiny roads. Witches and humans are kind of spread out among the four territories. Shiloh, who you met yesterday, is a witch."

I raked my fingers through my now freshly cleaned hair, just taking it all in. It felt crazy, and wholly unfair, that I'd been in this world for a year and knew so little.

"What else?" I asked. "Fae? Orcs? Unicorns?"

Sawyer gave me that small smile again. "That's all the sentient species we know of, so far--humans, witches, us, dragons, angels, and vampires."

I watched him silently for a few minutes. His eyes were more of a deep sky blue in the daylight, and they were rapt on the pan he held over the burner, moving it around to spread the egg mixture. As his hair dried, the white patch at his temple became more prominent. He looked up at me and my gaze jerked away, mortified that he'd caught me staring again.

"I hope you're not one of those humans who refuses to eat vegetables." His tone was light, teasing as he transferred some chopped spinach, peppers, mushrooms, and cheese to the omelet in the pan.

"I will eat literally anything you put in front of me." My attention zeroed in on the food now, focusing so hard that I almost missed another soft growling chuckle rolling up from his chest. It was a low, long vibration, almost like a purr. And it was fucking sexy.

Sawyer coughed and cleared his throat, almost like *he*

was embarrassed. "That's good. We've got to get your strength back up."

I tapped my fingers on my glass on a nervous impulse. "So that I can tell you all about what happened with the vampires, right?"

He stiffened for a moment. "When you're ready, yes. But your physical recovery is most important."

That was a surprise. I'd figure he'd let me get one full meal in at most before he started grilling me about my captivity. He'd have to report me to his club, right? And they'd want to know sooner rather than later. But he made it sound like he wanted me to recover just because that was what I needed most and giving information about my ordeal was secondary to that.

It was far more kindness than I expected, and it threw me for one hell of a loop.

"Thank you," I blurted out. "For the food, letting me stay here, giving me...time to adjust. It's all just really overwhelming."

Sawyer only nodded casually, and I saw his throat tighten like he was trying to suppress another purring growl. "Doesn't seem like you've had a good meal or comfortable place to stay for a while. So it's only right."

That made me wonder if my effusive gratitude was an overreaction. He made it sound like it was no big deal at all, so maybe it wasn't. All my life I'd had people try to manipulate and take advantage of me, so maybe my barometer for basic decency was all fucked up.

Even so, he and Shiloh had shown me more care in under twenty-four hours than I had received in years. Compared to what I was used to, that was...confusing.

"Order up." Sawyer plated a huge omelet and set it in

front of me, then pointed at my empty glass with his spatula. "More juice?"

I wrapped my hand around the glass and started to slide from the barstool. "I can get it—"

"No, you sit and eat. I'll get it for you."

The command left no room for argument and held the weight of physical touch on my skin. That wasn't metaphorical either, I literally *felt* it like a caress on my neck. My body reacted as though it wasn't a creepy sensation but a welcome one. I wanted him to command me again so I could feel it and arch into it.

What the fuck was wrong with me?

Sawyer had already snatched my glass and was pouring me another drink while I tried to figure out what the hell was happening. The only conclusion I had was that I was so exhausted and deprived of blood, my body was firing off all kinds of wrong signals. That had to be it.

"Thank you," I said demurely when Sawyer placed my refilled glass next to my plate.

He only gave a sharp nod to my plate. "Eat up, don't wait for me."

I didn't want to be rude, but I was also starving. It was all I could do to not shove the omelet down my throat like an eggy burrito, but I somehow maintained enough composure to cut into it with a fork and take modest, human-sized bites.

"This is delicious, thank you." I made sure to swallow before speaking and not chew with my mouth open.

"You're welcome." Sawyer's chest puffed out subtly while he poured his own egg mixture into the pan. "Oh, I forgot. You want any toppings? I like mine with hot sauce."

He'd already done more than enough for me, but I

couldn't shake the instinct that this whole exchange was pleasing for the both of us.

"I'd love some ketchup, if you have it."

He shook his head solemnly, turning to the fridge. "Ketchup is poisonous to wolves. You won't catch me within ten feet of that stuff."

"Oh, I'm sorry! I didn't realize—"

Sawyer abruptly turned around, holding a telltale red squeeze bottle and wicked grin spreading across his face. "Just pulling your leg, Riley."

He set the bottle in front of me while I laughed and tried to ignore how hot he looked when he smiled that widely.

CHAPTER 6

SAWYER

My wolf wouldn't shut up for a single second while Riley and I had breakfast together. He was like an overexcited puppy under my skin —howling while spinning around in a circle, yipping with excitement as he tripped over his own paws, tail puffed out and going crazy. My animal side was so fucking happy.

That space where we overlapped, the human and animal mixture somewhere deep in my DNA, knew exactly why. I was taking care of Riley, protecting someone who was vulnerable and needed my predator instincts to keep her safe. And the deepest, most instinctual parts of me got so much fucking satisfaction out of that.

Riley had spent the night in my house. Slept in my sheets. And was now eating food that I provided. She was being gracious, polite, and appreciative despite the fact that she was still skittish. She accepted my food and hospitality, which meant I was a worthy protector. My wolf side wanted to stand atop a boulder and howl his lungs out for the world to hear. The human side of me wanted to beat my chest like a fucking primate.

And sweet moon, her *scent*.

The blood-and-dirt stench of vampires was mostly gone from her, with only a small amount lingering that would likely fade in time. Her human scent came through, a simple and neutral smell that, on its own, was nothing special. But there was something else layered underneath.

It was so subtle that I couldn't place it, not even sitting a few feet away from her while I ate my omelet. But the few small whiffs I caught were delicious and tantalizing. It made me want to push aside her chestnut brown hair, run my nose along her neck, and inhale her like a drug.

Which was exactly what a skittish, traumatized human didn't need from the werewolf she was staying with. I dumped more hot sauce on my food simply to give my senses something else to focus on. That scent of hers was putting all kinds of thoughts in my head that were inappropriate of a host.

"This is really good." Riley wiped her mouth and cut her fork through the thick layer of ketchup she'd squirted onto her omelet. "Spinach and all. You're quite the chef," she added with a small smile.

My inner caveman's mental chest-thumping became even more vigorous. "Thanks. I'll make sure to throw some spinach in the stew for dinner tonight."

"Sounds great, Popeye."

A laugh burst out of me, and I nearly choked on the bite drenched in hot sauce. Riley looked pleased as well as surprised. "You know who Popeye is! So you get the same TV shows over here, huh? I wondered about that."

"I've never been to the human world," I said once I

recovered. "So I don't know what we have in common, but yes, I watched Popeye on TV when I was a pup."

Riley set her fork down and looked at me, intent and focused for the first time. She'd snuck glances at me when she thought I wasn't looking, but she always seemed to avoid eye contact when we spoke. Now there was brightness to her skin and alertness in her eyes, more curiosity than fear. The skittish little human was getting braver, and I loved to see it.

"Are werewolves immortal like vampires?" she asked.

I shook my head. "It's a lie that they're immortal. We have similar lifespans, about six hundred to eight hundred years."

Riley's eyes widened. "Holy shit. How old are you? If you don't mind me asking."

"I'm sixty-five. Still a pup by elder wolf standards."

Her eyes went even bigger. "Sixty-five! That's retirement age for a human!"

"Really?" I frowned at her skeptically.

"Yes. Healthy humans can live to their eighties and nineties. Rarely into their hundreds. The oldest humans have only lived to one hundred and twenty or so."

"That is just...such little time." I rubbed my jaw in disbelief. "At what age can humans reproduce?"

"Um." Her face reddened and I fought the urge to tease her. "We go through puberty in our early teens, sometimes a little younger. We're considered adults at eighteen."

"Eighteen? But aren't you still children then? And to sexually develop when even younger! That must be...terrifying for human parents."

"Yes, exactly." She laughed a little. "Many, many humans act like children and make stupid decisions well into their twenties." Her face fell then, like that last state-ment hit a little too close to home.

"Wolves, dragons, and vampires aren't considered adults until they're thirty," I said. "We hit sexual maturity in our early to mid-twenties. No one really knows about the angels. They might actually be immortal, or at least that's what they want people to believe."

"You obviously age much slower." Riley gave me another intense, roaming look, and it made me wish her gaze could physically touch me like hands. "I thought you were maybe thirty-five at the most."

"This is how I'll look until roughly the last fifty years of my life," I said. "My president and pack alpha is about a hundred years older than me, but we look the same age."

"That's insane." Riley brought her hands to her temples. "I feel like I'm in the Twilight Zone."

"Nope, just Shyftworld."

She smiled at me broadly, showing all her pretty white teeth. A mental image flashed of those teeth sinking into my shoulder, preferably with no clothing between us. "So you've seen the Twilight Zone too?"

I coughed and picked up my coffee mug in an effort to reset my mind. "Sure have."

"How funny. I wonder how much overlap between our worlds there really is."

"I know someone who travels back and forth between them quite regularly. He could probably tell you."

Riley glanced away for a moment, worrying her lip between her teeth. "Are you going to send me back? To the human world, I mean."

I studied her, noting the reluctance in her tone and posture. "You don't want to go back home?"

She laughed, the sound humorless and even a bit sad. "It's not like I have much of a home to go back to."

"What do you mean?"

Just as she opened her mouth to speak, a heavy knock rapped at the front door.

"Who is it?" I barked, annoyed at the interruption.

"It's Tryn!" came the answer. "Just making sure you're still alive."

Relief swept over me as I went to the door. Tryn wouldn't immediately go to the club the moment he saw Riley. He was a solid friend like that.

I pulled open the door to find his dark, massive form hulking on my porch like a shadow. With the guy's shrewd eyes, long dark hair, and dark beard to the top of his chest, one had to wonder if he was a bear shifter instead of a wolf.

Tryn's hands flipped palm up in greeting. "What happened? Missed you on the run last night."

"I, ah." I scratched the beard on my jaw. "Ran into a situation at Stout & Spirit. Kind of an emergency."

Tryn's eyes narrowed. "Is Shiloh alright?"

"Yeah, she's fine. But, uh…"

"Oh." Tryn's expression brightened as he looked over my shoulder. "Hello."

I heard a soft, "Hi," and then the clinking of ceramic. When I turned to look, Riley had gathered up our dishes from breakfast and set them in the sink. She turned the water on and started rinsing.

"I see," Tryn muttered under his breath with a soft chuckle. "Didn't think you liked humans."

"It's not like that," I hissed.

Isn't it, though? my wolf seemed to ask. Not so much with words but with this edgy, possessive feeling clawing at my chest. Tryn and I had been friends since we were pups. My wolf knew he wasn't a threat, and yet I still fought back to urge to growl a warning when he noticed Riley.

The friendliness in Tryn's expression shifted into a scowl, and he lifted his nose to inhale a bit more sharply. "Sawyer, is that..."

"Yeah," I gritted out, quickly scanning the forest behind him for anyone else, even though hardly anyone came out to my place. "We should talk. You want to run?"

He stroked his beard and returned a skeptical gaze to me. "You sure about leaving her here alone?"

"Should be alright." I looked over my shoulder just as Riley set our freshly-rinsed plates in my dishwasher. "Hey, don't worry about cleaning up. My buddy and I are gonna talk outside, but we'll be nearby. You gonna be okay for a few minutes?"

Riley nodded, her eyelids heavy as she dried her hands on a dishtowel. "I just got hit with a wave of fatigue, so I think I'll lie down for a bit."

"Good, you still need to rest."

I expected her to head down the hall to my guest bedroom, but she went for the couch instead, curling up in a patch of sunlight as she pulled a throw blanket over lap. "Thanks for breakfast, Sawyer," she murmured sleepily.

"Sure thing." I gripped my front door's handle while my wolf howled with delight. "Back in a few."

The door had barely closed when Tryn started grinning. "Don't start," I grumbled at him.

"Making breakfast, huh?" He stroked his beard some more as we stepped off my porch and headed for the tree line. "You're all Mr. Romantic all of a sudden."

"Wrong," I bit out forcefully. "She escaped from

Sanguine yesterday. Shiloh looked after her at Stout & Spirit, but she couldn't stay there. I brought her home last night so she wouldn't lead any vamps to the bar."

Tryn sucked on his teeth. "Well, that explains the scent. And why she looks like she could use about ten more hearty breakfasts. What was she, a blood pet?"

"I'm thinking either that or they're kidnapping people again. But I don't know. She's skittish as a doe, and I don't want to force her to talk."

"Some enforcer you are." Tryn gave me a slug on the arm. "Here good?"

"Good as any." My house was out of view but just beyond the thicket of trees we walked through. We'd stay close but out of sight.

The two of us stripped out of our clothes and shifted in an effortless, instinctual transformation. Tryn's wolf was predominantly black with bits of dark gray, his shaggy fur making him look even more bear-like. My animal also had dark fur but with pale gray around my muzzle and on my neck and chest.

With a huff, I took off running, eager to release some pent-up energy. My wolf side was like an energizer bunny ever since meeting Riley. He wanted to do literally everything for her, from hunting food, to licking the rest of that vampire scent off of her, to guarding her day and night from any threats. He'd become a single-minded drone dedicated to proving himself worthy of her. Thank fuck I had a human side to rein him in.

Tryn loped alongside me, his tongue lolling out in a big canine smile. *You're going to have to tell Derric about her*, he told me with his mind.

I know. I was planning to wait until she told me more herself.

Tryn barked as he leaped over a fallen tree. *Better to do it sooner rather than later, just to be aware of anything the vamps might do. If she's valuable to them, they could make up all sorts of claims. Like you kidnapped her. It'd be a perfect excuse to attack us again.*

My teeth bared as I ran, picking up the pace. *If they're keeping human prisoners, we've got bigger problems than just this one girl.*

Do we?

Twisting my body through the air, I turned to face him, abruptly stopping my run. My four paws slid on the wet ground as my hackles raised and I growled at him.

You're not suggesting we turn a blind eye if they're capturing humans? That's not the consensual blood pet role they claim. If they're treating people like cattle, we need to do something.

Tryn barked softly and nuzzled my snout in a friendly, placating gesture. *Our peace agreement with the vampires and dragons was clear. Their business doesn't cross our borders and ours doesn't cross theirs. We have to protect our own, Sawyer. Unless they take* our *humans, we have no right to interfere.*

I turned away with a frustrated bark, teeth still bared. *That's how it always starts,* I said bitterly. *Then when they do come for us, no one will be around to help.*

CHAPTER 7

RILEY

"Why did you run away?" Fabian's face was heartbroken, his voice soft and laced with hurt. "Why did you leave me, Riley? We had such good times together."

At another time in my life, that kind of manipulation would have gotten to me. It would have made my chest ache, made me desperate to fix what was wrong. But I could see right through it now. "Because you hurt me, and I hate you," I spat.

His head jerked back, red eyes blinking in disbelief. "After I got you off the streets? Gave you a home and everything you ever wanted? *This* is how you repay me?"

"You lied!" I screamed. "You used me and kept me prisoner."

"I gave you a purpose," he growled. "A reason to stop decaying on the sidewalk like a piece of garbage. *I'm* the only one who's ever treated you better than garbage!"

"I'm a person! You never asked me for blood, you

always took it from me! And you made me so weak that I couldn't escape."

A rough hand clamped my jaw, his blood-colored eyes now seething with anger that was all too familiar. And terrifying. "You don't even realize how lucky you are, pet," he spat out. "Women beg me to take their blood, but I only keep *your* ungrateful ass. Maybe I should hand you off to one of the others, huh? You think you'd like Rhain better? Or maybe Thorne will teach you some gratitude?"

A bolt of pure fear struck my chest. I would never be 'grateful' for his taking me captive and leaving me constantly drained, but at least he was the monster I knew.

"No...no, I'm sorry." The words ground on my teeth as they left my mouth. He'd twisted me up in his manipulations, made me feel weak and pathetic, again. "I'm sorry, Fabian. I don't want anyone but you."

"Mm-hm." The sound he made was satisfied, but he didn't loosen his hold on my jaw. "That's more like it. You'll hold still for me like a good little pet now."

"Yes," I whimpered, bracing myself for the pain. He always made it hurt.

His fangs struck my artery, and I screamed, my limbs flailing to get away but he held me down. A sharp sound pulled my attention away. The vampire at my throat and the room I was imprisoned in seemed to be fading, almost melting into blackness. And then he was no longer feeding from me but...licking my face?

Another sharp sound made my body flail, and then I was upright and awake. I felt so warm, almost uncomfortably so, and I realized I was under a blanket and bathed in sunlight. Relief swept over me so hard, I brought a hand to my racing heart.

I heard a whimper that wasn't my own and the pressure of something touching my leg. Next to the couch was a huge, beautiful wolf. It was covered in dark fur with patches of gray around its muzzle and chest. His paw was on my leg, dark blue eyes wide with concern.

"Sawyer?" I asked, still catching my breath.

The wolf barked and wagged his tail. That bark had been the sharp sound I heard earlier, pulling me out of the nightmare.

"I was dreaming." I wiped my brow, which felt slightly sweaty. "Sorry. I...didn't mean to alarm you."

Sawyer huffed and then jumped on the couch next to me. His wolf was almost as big as his human form, and I scooted to make room for him. But he didn't seem interested in putting distance between us and laid his chin over my knee.

It was unexpectedly sweet. I reached toward his head but pulled back at the last minute. "Is it okay if I touch you? I know you're a person and not a dog."

He lifted his head and nudged my hand, licking it with a warm tongue. I took that as permission and scratched behind one of his ears. My hand was still shaking and damn, it was actually helpful that Sawyer was just sitting with me in his wolf form. If he had been a human and started grilling me, I probably would have been a lot more intimidated.

Not that his wolf wasn't formidable, not in the slightest. The creature was huge with bright, intelligent eyes, and dense muscle under that fur. But it was a different experience, sitting with an animal rather than a man. The animal calmed me just by being there. With a man, I would have felt the expectation to talk or act 'normal'. But I was in no hurry to rehash that nightmare, and thankfully, Sawyer didn't seem rushed to shed his fur for his human skin.

"Thank you," I said when my heart rate returned to normal levels and my hands stopped shaking. "You didn't have to sit with me, but I appreciate it."

Sawyer lifted his head and licked my hand once more before sliding off the couch. I watched the wolf go up the stairs to the loft level of the cabin, which appeared to be Sawyer's entire bedroom. The wolf went through an open doorway, and a light turned on a few seconds later.

After about a minute, the very human Sawyer emerged wearing a white T-shirt and gray sweatpants. "Didn't want to leave you alone," he said softly, making his way back down the stairs. "But also..." He gave a lopsided grin and... was that a blush? "We can't shift with clothes on, so..."

Oh...oh!

The heat on my face had nothing to do with the fact that I'd been napping in the sun for God-knows-how-long. So he'd stayed as a wolf so I wouldn't see him naked. Good to know.

"Uh, thanks for the heads up," I said dumbly.

Sawyer hit the bottom floor and approached me slowly. "Are you alright? You were really thrashing around in your sleep."

There it was, the piercing, knowing stare inspecting and unraveling me. I curled up small, bringing the blanket up to my chin. "Just a bad dream." Understatement of the fucking year.

He came toward the couch with slow, deliberate steps, as if trying not to startle me. When he lowered himself to take a seat, it was hard to believe he'd been there just a few minutes ago with four legs and a tail. He stuck to the far side though, which I appreciated. We both seemed to understand that having his head in my lap, his paws on my legs while nuzzling and licking me, carried very different meanings between humans and animals.

"I know your experience was traumatic," he began in a surprisingly gentle voice.

"Really, what gave it away?" I laughed mirthlessly.

Sawyer didn't laugh or even smile. "The last thing I want to do is ask you to talk before you're ready. But the sooner you do tell me, the sooner we can prepare for any retaliation from the vampires." He rubbed his palms together before lacing his fingers. "Our two species have been, uh, at odds, to put it lightly, for centuries. And if they figure out you're with us, well...we want to prevent anyone else in our territory from getting hurt."

I nodded along to what he said. It made perfect sense. Fabian considered me his literal property, and I had no doubts he'd send underlings into Vargmore to retrieve me. There could be lots of collateral damage, and it would be all my fault. Sawyer was doing his best to be patient with me, but his priority remained his territory and the people in it.

Even so, my chest felt like a sealed jar, the details of my capture locked away. This all felt so familiar. Every time I'd opened up to someone, gave them a tiny inch of trust, a pinch of vulnerability, they'd trampled all over me. How did I really know Sawyer wasn't going to toss me right back to the vampires once I told him everything? It would be the easiest solution to keep the territory safe.

"How did vampires and werewolves come to be enemies?" I asked on a whim.

Sawyer inhaled and leaned back against the couch. "They fed on my kind centuries ago, before the territories and clubs were well-established. Apparently, werewolf blood tastes especially good to them. It's like a drug, and back then, they were left completely unchecked. Kidnapping pups from schools, stalking lone females and dragging them away to feed on them. We retaliated by killing a bunch of them, and they answered by killing and feeding from us even more. It was an all-out war for years and years." His dark blue eyes hardened and got a faraway look. "My parents and grandparents were casualties of that war."

"Oh no. I'm so sorry, that's terrible."

He shrugged, as stoic as ever. "I was a small pup when it happened, and I barely remember them. Tryn's family raised me, and then we got initiated into Howling Death together as adults. But that was something our parents' generation never let us forget—don't ever trust a vampire, because their first priority is making a meal out of you."

I certainly knew that firsthand.

"How did the war come to an end?" Without realizing it, I'd scooted closer to him on the couch and my knee nearly touched his.

Sawyer sighed heavily. "I think we'd both just had enough after a while. There were heavy losses on both sides. Our populations were either decimated in the war or many had fled to the human world. They'd rather blend in, suppressing their nature to survive, than risk being killed over here. Anyway, an agreement was made about fifty years ago and the separate territories were established. With the exception of a few skirmishes over the years, we have mostly left each other alone."

"It doesn't sound like anybody really won," I mused.

He shook his head. "No one wins in war."

A quietness settled in as we both relaxed on the couch,

close but not touching. "So, there are werewolves and vampires hidden in the human world?"

I was deliberately avoiding talking about my own situation, but Sawyer didn't seem to mind. He was humoring my nosiness, at least.

"How do you think your world got its legends of us?" He grinned. "Centuries ago, it was supposedly easier to cross between our worlds, and it happened a lot more frequently. Now it's more rare. But yes, there are human descendants of Shyftworld species walking around in your world. They probably have no idea because of generations of breeding out their abilities, plus having to hide themselves."

Sawyer touched a hand to my knee, the movement so light and casual I almost didn't notice it right away. "My friend who travels between worlds, his mate came from the human world and believed herself to be human all her life. But after they met, they discovered she was a latent wolf. Her ancestors had been werewolves that crossed over centuries ago, probably during the war."

"Wow," I breathed in disbelief, feeling a pang of envy. How amazing would it be to find out you had an animal side, especially a wolf? "How many latent wolves are out there, do you think?"

"No one knows," he said cryptically. "Aria was the first real one anyone had met in recent history. The latent wolves were starting to become the stuff of legend. A whole generation of us had just up and gone, never to be seen again. People searched for the entrances to the human world, but no one could find them. Some say witches closed the portals so those fleeing couldn't be followed." Sawyer shrugged again. "Compared to your kind, there's probably not many latents. Humans are so short-lived, that must be why you all breed constantly."

"Hey, we don't *all* breed constantly!"

"Well, you certainly get an early start compared to us." Sawyer poked my knee, teasing me again. "Most werewolves don't start having pups 'til they're a hundred."

"So you've still got a few decades of being a bachelor, huh?" The remark was out of my mouth too late for my brain to catch up, and I immediately regretted it. "Sorry, that was inappropriate."

Sawyer just chuckled dryly. "Nah, it's fine. I don't know if settling down with a mate and pups is for me anyway. I like my solitude."

A crumbling sadness filled up my chest when he said that, which was such a weird reaction. I barely knew this guy. What did it matter to me if he found someone and started a family or not? Sure, I felt bad to be imposing on his space, but this deep ache was more than that. It felt so at odds with what was normal to feel that I had to rub my chest as if that would soothe it away.

"You alright?" Sawyer lifted his head from the back of the couch.

"Yeah, fine!" I dropped my hand. "I'm feeling a lot better today actually, so, you know, I'll be out of your hair before you know it."

He relaxed, letting his head fall back again. "Nah, take all the time you need here. I'm glad I can help."

Just like that, the sad ache in my chest eased into a warm, pleasant sensation. That was almost as jarring as the initial feeling. It felt so strange, like being an observer in my own body.

"Thank you," I said quietly, distracted by my own reactions to him.

"Of course."

Silence fell on us again while I looked down, my fingers playing with a frayed string on the blanket. Sawyer was being more than patient with me, even sharing openly about his own world and past. He had only asked once for me to talk, never pushing for information.

As terrifying as it was, it was only fair to give him what he wanted. If he did use the information to hurt me, at least I was prepared for it. Most importantly, I didn't want Shiloh or anyone else to get targeted by the vampires because of me.

With a deep breath, I broke the seal on the jar holding everything away.

"I was homeless in the human world," I said, my gaze fixated on the blanket. "The vampire lured me to his car, saying he had food and a spare room to sleep in." The frayed string on the blanket broke off between my fingers. "Normally, I wouldn't be that stupid to just go along with a stranger, but he seemed really sincere. We just small-talked about nothing for like an hour before. I got no creepy vibes or anything. I...felt like I could trust him."

A low growl emanated from Sawyer's throat. "Vampires are excellent at playing on needs and emotions. It was all him and not in any way your fault."

"Well, that's the thing. He made good on his promise, at first. He was really nice and respectful to me. I ate well and slept great that first day." I swallowed the lump in my throat. "Until I wanted to leave and...he wouldn't let me." I slid a finger under Sawyer's flag wrapped around my wrist, touching the first scars Fabian had given me. "He said I was his pet and that he was going to keep me as a blood supply for as long as he wanted."

"Piece of shit," Sawyer muttered under his breath.

"It really was a head fuck." I shook my head, still trying to make sense of the bizarre, terrifying time in Fabian's captivity. "There were times where I felt bad for him, then I realized it was just him manipulating me. Then I felt bad for thinking he was manipulating me because he couldn't help needing blood to live." I rubbed my forehead. "Does that make me sound totally crazy?"

"No," Sawyer grumbled out. "You sound like someone who was preyed upon. By the moon, I fucking hate vampires." He swallowed another growl, as if trying to compose himself. "How did you manage to escape?"

"I'm still not entirely sure," I confessed. "If I had to venture a guess, my captor has some kind of drug habit. I don't know what kind of drugs affect vampires, but sometimes, he'd be totally alert, and other times, completely out of it. He seemed...stoned or drunk or something the last time he came to feed from me, and when he left, he forgot to lock me in. I waited for him to come back, but he never did. So I took the one chance I had and just bolted." Remembering the cold, the pain, the fear, and the exhaustion, I stuck my hands under the blanket. "I'd never been so scared in my entire life."

"You were incredibly brave." The growl roughening Sawyer's voice had that warm, purring quality to it again. "And I'm glad you made it out."

I stole a glance up and found the deep blue pools of his eyes focused on me. "Me too," I said, glancing back down. "If it wasn't for Shiloh, I might not have made it."

The quietness that followed felt easier now that I was

no longer a sealed pressure cooker on the stove. It was truly a relief to get it out, and I was grateful that Sawyer didn't push for more details but simply listened.

"Would you mind telling me the name of the vampire who captured you?" he asked after a few moments.

"It was Fabian," I said.

Sawyer hissed in a breath. "Fuck."

"Yeah," I agreed.

He didn't have to spell it out for me. I had a feeling being captured by Blood 'til Dawn MC's vice president made things a lot more complicated.

CHAPTER 8
SAWYER

I couldn't sleep for shit that night.

Hours after Riley and I had talked on the couch and then said goodnight to each other, I remained staring at the beams in my ceiling, my brain refusing to turn off.

My wolf had been clawing under my skin the whole time she'd told me about being held by the vampires. Gone was the happy puppy eager to please and impress her. Now he was a vengeful monster who wanted to kill for her. To rip out throats until his muzzle was stained red.

She was a vulnerable human, for fuck's sake. Even for vampires, it was a new low to prey on a homeless woman from the human world. As if they didn't have plenty of groupies of all species, ready and willing to give their blood to those monsters. And none had more adoring fans and blood pets than the self-appointed rulers of their little kingdom, Blood 'til Dawn MC.

I rubbed my forehead, groaning. It didn't make any fucking sense. Fabian, the VP, of all the people in that club, surely had his pick of blood pets, second only to Thorne, the president. Why would Fabian lure Riley from the human world and keep her captive? If he had been just some random nobody vampire, I could understand. But while I didn't trust Blood 'til Dawn, they were the closest thing to honorable that vampires could be. They were supposed to keep their people in line.

On top of all that, I had Tryn's words rolling around in my skull. Humans from the human world weren't our problem. Once I went to the alpha, I knew Tryn would advocate for returning Riley to the human world. But what the fuck was waiting for her there? Homelessness again? More opportunities for predators to swoop in on her?

An involuntary growl rumbled up from deep in my chest. *She's ours*, my wolf insisted. *She needs us. She's sweet and warm and smells wonderful. She may have a beautiful wolf hidden away.*

"Stop," I muttered, rubbing my face. Sure, there was a small chance she was a latent shifter like Aria, but what were the odds, really? Shyftworld was tiny. A speck of dust compared to the billions of humans populating their world.

Regardless of how I felt, I needed to report to Derric soon. And whatever he decreed, I would have to obey.

Flopping over violently in bed, I almost missed the whimper floating up from downstairs. I froze, scarcely daring to breathe as I listened. Nearly a full minute later I heard it again—a soft, pained cry that could only be coming from Riley's room.

Another nightmare? The poor thing couldn't catch a break.

I was up in an instant, remembering to shove my legs into a pair of sweatpants as I headed down the stairs. At

Riley's closed bedroom door, I paused with my ear against the wood. I knew she didn't want to feel trapped or cornered, but damn if I was going to stand around and do nothing while memories terrorized her.

Another high-pitched cry cut through the silence, stabbing me right in the fucking heart.

Shift, my wolf urged. *Let me calm her as I did before.*

Nope. It's my turn, buddy, I thought, testing the knob. Damn, she locked it.

I went to the kitchen and rummaged in the junk drawer for the master key to all my interior doors. Riley sounded like she was sobbing when I finally found the thing and raced back over.

Once I threw it open, she wasn't so much thrashing like before as just lying there, defeated. She was on her side, her legs curled up to her stomach and her hands jerking up toward her neck, fingers curling like she was trying to grab something. All the while, she cried softly with the occasional pained whimper.

I wanted to leap inside her head and annihilate everything that tormented her. My palm ached from gripping the doorknob. One jerk of my wrist and I could have torn it from the wood, I was so wound up. But what could I do except watch? She wouldn't want to wake up from that nightmare to some strange guy in bed with her.

Riley's legs kicked out on a cry, and the knuckles of her curled hand against her throat were white.

Okay, fuck this do-nothing bullshit.

I rounded the bed to approach her from behind, thinking it would be best if she didn't see my face when she first woke up. It wasn't easy lumbering all my two hundred and thirty pounds onto the bed gently, but I gave it my best shot. I stretched out next to her, focused on her hair spilled over the pillow and her back curled up tight to protect herself. I kept on the edge of the bed, an arm's length away from her so I could provide some distance if she woke up and freaked out about my being here.

"Riley," I said, hoping my voice would reach her through the dream. " You're okay. You're safe. He doesn't have you."

There was no reaction except another kick of legs and a pained whimper of, "Please stop."

Before I could stop myself, I scooted closer and placed a hand on her arm. My lips inched closer to her ear. "You're safe, Riley. It's just a dream. No one's going to hurt you here."

I took an inhale and...oh fuck, her scent.

I'd never been this close to catch it, but it was all I could do not to bury my nose in her hair. She must have showered again because the vampire scent was completely gone, and underneath her plain human scent was something so damn sweet.

She smelled like fresh spring flowers and rain. Light and feminine and somehow so utterly intoxicating. I wanted to never *not* be smelling this. I wanted this scent filling my home at all times. I wanted her in my clothes, my sheets, everything I touched.

My bed.

While I wrestled with being drunk on her scent, Riley thrashed again. This one sent her backwards, crashing her directly into my chest. The right thing to do would have been to scoot away, putting more distance between us, and keep talking to try and pull her out of the dream. Maybe even getting out of the bed altogether.

But I just…couldn't.

My arm slid around her, pulling her flush against me while I reached up to clasp one of her hands. My mouth was directly against her ear when I said, "You're safe with me, sweet girl. Your wolf is here. No one will lay a hand on you again. Anyone who tries will get my teeth in their throat."

I meant every word too. Her scent didn't just enhance my protective instincts, it cemented them into promises. She was mine. And no harm would come to her while I still breathed.

Did I know how to explain this to her once she awoke? Absolutely not. And in that moment, wrapped around her while she battled her own mind, I didn't care.

Of course, she finally woke up a second later with a gasping breath, so I had to figure it out quickly.

I lifted my arm from her and scooted away from her back, despite the all-consuming drive to pull her into me tighter. "Hey, it's just me. You're alright."

Riley flipped around to face me, her eyes still terror-stricken while her breath came in ragged pants. "You…what are you…?" She looked toward the open bedroom door, and my gut clenched, feeling like a fucking bastard.

"I'm sorry I unlocked the door." I slid off the bed entirely, standing next to it while she peered up at me. "You were having another nightmare, and I wanted to check on you."

Her hand came to her chest, eyes bouncing around like she was still trying to make sense of where she was. "Were you…talking to me?"

"Uh, yeah," I croaked. "I didn't want to shake you or anything, so I figured that would be the best way to pull you out of it."

"I think it worked." Her eyes met mine again and then lowered a few inches. Oh shit, I didn't have a shirt on. "I heard you. In the dream, I was able to...take control."

"I'm glad." I crossed my arms, then thought that might look too aggressive and dropped them to my sides. "Well, I'm glad you're okay. I'll just go——"

"No! Please stay." Riley dropped her eyes to the bed, as if embarrassed by the request. "I'm sorry. I just...really don't want to be alone right now."

Both halves of me were crying out victoriously. She needed my protection, needed *me*. I was fully prepared to leave her be, because her trusting me was more important than the chemical reaction her scent did to my instincts. I still considered her mine, but it worked both ways. I was just as much hers, and if she wanted me away, I would leave just to please her.

I expected as much, after everything she'd been through. But to hear that she wanted the exact opposite? It was almost too good to be true.

"Are you sure?" I asked, my voice rough.

"If you wouldn't mind." She swallowed. "If you'd rather not, I understand." Her voice sounded pained, as if bracing herself for my rejection.

Which would never fucking happen.

"I'll stay," I told her more huskily than I intended. "I just want you to feel safe."

"With you, I do."

Sweet moon, my heart went crazy like my wolf was stamping his paws all over it.

"I'll stay on top of the covers," I said. "You get underneath."

Riley complied, pulling the duvet up to her chest while shooting me a curious expression. "What if you get cold?"

"Then I'll shift and use my fur." Come to think of it, I should've probably grabbed a shirt, but Riley was looking at me so vulnerably, so expectantly from the bed, that I didn't want to leave her for a single moment.

She slid down until her head rested on the pillow, watching me just stand next to the bed like a dumbass.

"Are you going to lie down?"

"Yeah." My throat felt tight, so I cleared it and tried again. "Yeah, I'm coming."

Wrong choice of words there, smart guy.

I smoothed out a spot on the duvet next to her and climbed on top of it, slowly stretching my body out next to hers until we lay side by side, facing each other. Even in the darkness, I could feel Riley's eyes on me, inspecting me with a curiosity that part of me was dying to let her indulge.

"Is it okay if I stay close to you?" she asked in a small voice. "So you can, you know, talk me out of the dream if it happens again."

That depends. Will you let me hold you again? I wanted to ask.

"Yes, of course," I said instead. "That's why I'm here."

"Thank you." There was a soft rustle of blankets as she scooted toward me. My heart rate jumped as she got close enough for me to actually feel her body heat. And those soft puffs of warm air on my face... Those were from her mouth. Fuck me, she was close enough to kiss. Close enough for me to throw my arm over her and draw her into my chest.

Yeah, staying on top of the covers was definitely the right call.

If we actually kissed, or more...I'd give her a good time, no doubt. And I was certain she'd make me feel like the biggest, baddest alpha in Vargmore.

But she wasn't an ego boost. She wasn't for me to play with. Too many people had used her already. There was a line here, one that I had no intention of crossing. And yet somehow, the more closeness she asked for, the longer she looked at me with those big, curious eyes, that line seemed to get blurrier.

"Sleep well, Riley." I tucked my hands under my pillow, as if that move would force me to keep my paws to myself.

"You too, Sawyer."

I shouldn't have slept at all. I should have stayed awake and vigilant, watching her for twitches or any other signs of an oncoming nightmare. While I had tossed and turned in my loft, however, that persistent restlessness was gone here.

My limbs and my mind finally settled, knowing she was nearby and most importantly, safe.

CHAPTER 9

RILEY

I awoke slowly from a long, dreamless, utterly *delicious* sleep. My eyes weren't ready to open yet, so I stretched first, pointing my toes and arching my back with a soft groan. Damn, when did waking up ever feel this good, like a luxury?

When I tried to stretch my arms up, I found them pinned down by something heavy and had a sudden moment of panic. My eyes popped open to find the sleeping, handsome face of Sawyer mere inches away.

He was still on top of the duvet, shirtless and uncovered, with his arm thrown over my waist. Like he'd been trying to protect me even in sleep. I still had the blankets up to my chin and was starting to hate this barrier of fabric between us. His skin looked so smooth and warm, golden-brown from the sun and stretched over the taut muscles of his shoulders and back.

And he smelled amazing.

I scooted closer, testing the durability of the duvet as I tried to inhale even more of his intoxicating scent. He smelled fresh, like Irish Spring soap and clean water, with an undercurrent of spices. Something about it made me want to put my nose right to the crook of his neck and lick his skin.

Even more, I wanted to bite into the muscle of that big shoulder.

The thought got my pulse pounding, both in my chest and between my legs. I stared at the smooth, unblemished skin, wishing he had my teeth marks in him. Sawyer was a damn sexy wolf, but he would look so much better marked as *mine*.

As my *mate*.

Whoa, what the fuck?

The rational part of me screeched to a halt, but that did nothing to calm the surge of possessive, sexual need in my body. I was fully aware of how badly I wanted Sawyer, not just to touch him but to mark and claim him. Some furious, pressing instinct was pounding against my sternum, telling me to bite this wolf before some other female claimed him.

"What the fuck is going on with me?" I whispered.

Sawyer moaned softly and stirred at the noise. His eyelids parted as slits but didn't fully open. "Y'alright, sweet girl?" he mumbled in a single, groggy breath.

"Yeah, I'm fine. Sorry to wake y—"

His arm tightened around me, pulling himself flush to me. If it weren't for the duvet between us, I'd have been blanketed in the bare skin of his torso. My heart drummed rapidly as I stared at his slitted eyes, too shocked to react. He couldn't have been awake, could he?

The hand on my back caressed up my spine to cup my nape. And then his mouth was against mine.

Holy shit, definitely not awake. Not after he had been so

careful last night, so insistent on putting this barrier between us. This man, sipping lazily at my lips and gently probing with his tongue, was not the exceedingly cautious Sawyer I knew.

And still, I couldn't bring myself to push him away, to yell or smack him into waking up. Instead, I opened to him, letting our mouths fit against each other. The taste of him was a head rush unlike any other, the potency of his scent dialed up to a hundred.

His kisses were unhurried and warm, gentle and soft. I let my tongue glide against his and soaked up every rumble of the soft moan that followed.

"Mm, Riley..." He gently squeezed my nape, his blunt nails scratching ever so lightly at the sensitive skin there.

Meanwhile, my mind was on a fucking rollercoaster. He said my name. *My* name, while sleep-kissing me! For a second, I was willing to let this go as a selfish indulgence while he dreamed of someone else. Maybe Shiloh or even no one in particular. Never in a million years would I believe he'd actually dreamed of me.

In the next moment, Sawyer's eyes popped open and the illusion shattered.

He lifted away from me with a gasp and scrambled to get away so quickly that he fell off the bed and landed on the floor with a heavy thud.

"Sawyer!" I sat up, breathless. "Are you okay?"

"I'm sorry," he called up from the floor. "Fuck! I'm so fucking sorry, Riley."

"Um, it's okay." I touched my fingertips to my lips, still feeling the heated press and friction of his mouth there.

"No, it's not."

"You were asleep!"

"And you don't need another predator putting his mouth on you without consent." Sawyer got to his feet, his eyes cold and refusing to meet mine. "I'm so sorry. It won't happen again, I swear."

I wished I was brave enough to tell him, *What if I want it to happen again?* He looked so distraught, so disgusted with himself. My mind was still processing the fact that it had happened at all, but I knew I didn't hate it.

In fact, I was pretty damn sure that I liked it. And I really, really wouldn't mind it happening again.

"It's really okay." My stomach felt like it was dropping off the edge of a cliff as I said that. "I actually, um..." When I mustered the courage to look up, I saw that I was speaking to an empty room.

He'd already left.

))))) ● ● (((((

BREAKFAST AN HOUR later was wrought with tension, and not the good, sexy kind. Sawyer was polite as always, but he made sure to stand no closer than six feet away from me. He also didn't make small-talk or crack jokes as he had yesterday. Gone was the friendliness that bordered on flirting. He was being a gracious host, nothing more.

And that stung like hell.

This feeling in my chest was completely unlike the hurt I knew well, the betrayal of trusting the wrong person. The shame and anger at myself for being played for a fool again. No, this was simpler. Sharper.

It was the straight, aching punch of rejection.

Sawyer didn't actually want me. That was why he'd looked so horrified and scrambled to get away. People dreamed about weird shit all the time. Just because he might have been dreaming of me, and acting that out, didn't mean he'd actually wanted to kiss me.

That made me feel like an even bigger fool, because the only reason I lingered in bed after he'd left was to sink into that delicious scent he'd left on the duvet. I wanted to cocoon myself in it and never emerge.

"I need to go meet with the alpha today," he said after we ate in awkward silence. "To talk to him about what you told me."

"Oh, okay." I finished swallowing my last bite of omelet and set my fork down. "Do I come with you?"

"No, you stay here." Sawyer glanced at me quickly before shooting his eyes back to his plate. "I can have Tryn or someone stay with you, if you'd prefer that."

I swallowed. "What about Shiloh?"

He cocked his head as if pondering that. I imagined his wolf doing the same gesture, and the mental image was so endearing that it made my chest ache. "You know, the bar's closed today. She might be busy with errands, but I can call her."

"Oh, good. I'd like to see her again."

He gave me a half-smile, some of the tension bleeding out of him as he gathered our plates. "She'll be happy to see you too. She's a good friend, that one." His gaze shot down as his phone rang. "Speak of the devil." He answered the call, bringing the phone to his ear. "Hey, I was just about to call y—whoa, slow down."

My ears pricked, trying to pick up Shiloh's words while Sawyer's expression morphed. First, his brows furrowed, then his mouth pressed into a frown. I couldn't make out words, but Shiloh's tone was rapid, frantic through the speaker.

"Is anyone with you?" he finally asked. When the answer came, he said, "Okay, stay put. Don't touch anything. I'll be right there." When he hung up, his breath came in angry puffs, and his eyes were wild with anger. He looked moments away from shifting.

"What happened?" I wasn't sure if I really wanted to know, but I had to ask.

Sawyer's gaze snapped to me like he was noticing me for the first time, and he hesitated a long while before answering. "Shiloh found a dead wolf pup on her doorstep, drained of blood. She doesn't know if it's a shifter or a full wolf."

"Oh my God, did you say drained of..." My balance started to escape me, and I threw a hand out onto the counter just as Sawyer rushed at me like he was about to stop my fall.

"Are you okay?" His eyes were concerned now, the warmth returning to them. "Do you need to lie down?"

"Um, yeah. Just got a little lightheaded." My heart beat erratically, and my mouth had gone completely dry, but I was mostly keeping it together.

Sawyer put a hand on my arm, the first touch since our kiss this morning. "I have to go check this out, but there's no way I'm leaving you alone here. Do you think you'd be okay to come with me? I can't call a pack member because they're all going to want to meet about this."

I pulled in a deep breath through my nose, willing it to calm my racing pulse. "Yeah, I can come."

That powerful hand gave a gentle squeeze to my arm. "Are you sure? I mean, we already know who did this."

I bobbed my head up and down in a nod. "Yes. I'm positive."

It wasn't just him I was trying to convince but myself. I was sick of being terrified of vampires, tired of always being a victim. More than anything, I wanted to take some power back for myself. To face my fear head-on instead of always cowering and letting it rule me. This would be a first step.

But I knew from the tension in Sawyer's face and shoulders, that if that wolf pup was also one of his kind, there were much bigger problems on the horizon.

"Alright." Sawyer's hand fell away. "Get dressed and meet me at the bike."

Ten minutes later, we were roaring through the winding roads of Vargmore's forest, taking the turns at what would have been a thrilling speed under different circumstances.

The mega-dose of fresh air did make me feel better, though. I was clear-headed and steady by the time we pulled up to the back side of Stout & Spirit where the entrance to Shiloh's apartment was.

She stood next to the stairs leading up to her front door, hugging her arms around herself. Next to her stood a man dressed in gray slacks, a white, collared shirt, and gray vest that matched his pants. It was a waistcoat type of vest, the formal kind a guy would wear as part of a three-piece suit.

His manner of dress wasn't what stood out though. No, it was the wings.

A pair of massive wings arched high over his head, covered in reddish-brown feathers that had a golden sheen in the sunlight. I couldn't stop staring and had to blink several times to make sure my sight wasn't tricking me.

Sawyer parked several yards away, and even as he cut off the engine and we got off the bike, I couldn't believe my eyes.

I leaned in close and tried to be subtle as I asked, "Is he a…?"

"Angel, yeah. That's Kazath, he runs the brewery up in Helios City. Must've been making a delivery."

"Am I supposed to, um, do anything?"

Sawyer's already furrowed brow knotted even deeper in confusion. "Like what?"

"Thanks for coming, guys." Shiloh approached us first, smiling nervously at me before glancing hesitantly up at Sawyer. "I didn't know who else to call."

"You did the right thing," he assured her. "Where is it?"

She turned and pointed to a folded up blanket just off the patio. "It was on the landing right in front of my door. I almost stepped on it when I went outside, and I screamed. Good thing Kaz was on his way over. He calmed me down, told me to call you, and he wrapped the body up in a blanket."

"Seemed wrong to just leave it there." The angel had meandered over, blocking out the sun with his wings off to either side of his body. "Whether it's a shifter or not." Kazath's sleeves were pushed up, revealing dark tattoos running up from his wrists.

"I should be able to tell from the scent," Sawyer said. "Stay here." He marched over to the folded blanket like he was ready to fight it. Then, when he stopped and crouched next to it, he moved slower, with reverence and care.

"At least you're looking a lot better." Shiloh gave me a tight smile. "Recovery been good?"

"Um, yeah." I rubbed my arms, trying not to stare at Sawyer lifting the blanket and bending down to inspect the dead pup more closely. "You were right. Sawyer's been a great host."

"That's a surprise," Kazath muttered. "I like the wolf, but he hovered like hell when I installed his kegerator last summer. Didn't let me out of his sight, like he thought I was gonna steal something."

"He just doesn't like people in his space, touching his stuff," Shiloh said. "I got death glares if I so much as made myself a cup of tea. You'd think I was using his grandma's urn and ashes."

I said nothing, just focused on Sawyer's broad back while he remained bent over the pup's body. He never acted that way with me. If anything, it seemed like he strived to make me feel comfortable and at home with him.

"It's not a shifter," he announced, settling the blanket back into place.

Everyone collectively sagged with relief. "Oh thank the moon," Shiloh said with a hand to her chest. "It's still terrible but at least not..."

"Yeah." Sawyer rose to his full height, his gaze locked on me. "It's still a message sent by a very bold, very idiotic vampire. He knows Riley came here and is demonstrating what he'll do to get her back." He turned to Shiloh. "I have to bring this before the alpha. Can Riley stay with you for a few hours? I don't suggest you two stay here, but if you go into town or anything—"

"Oh, yes!" Shiloh nodded eagerly. "I have errands to run in town, which would be a perfect distraction." She nudged me with a smile. "Want to do some witchy shopping with me?"

Even if I had the choice, that sounded miles better than hanging around here, so close to the vampire border, or stewing in my thoughts at Sawyer's place. "Sure, that sounds fun."

"What about a place to stay?" Kazath said. "You probably shouldn't be here until the matter with the vampires is settled."

"My cousin has a place in town I can crash at." Shiloh nodded. "And I'll keep the bar closed for a few days, or however long it takes."

"I don't expect Derric will take long to make a decision," Sawyer said. "He'll have orders for us by tonight."

"Does that include, uh." I swallowed, the nerves pounding in my chest once again. "Where I'll end up after all this?"

Sawyer paused, his eyes intense as if he was examining me. "Back to the humans is a no-go, huh?"

I shook my head. "There's nothing for me there. I won't overextend my welcome at your place, but...maybe I can get a fresh start here. In Vargmore."

"Helios City is great too," Kazath piped up. "Amazing views from any of the high rises. It's not as, uh, rustic as Vargmore. Definitely more modern."

"Watch it," Sawyer said with an undercurrent of growl.

Kazath's feathers rustled. "Or if you *like* rustic, being close to nature and all, Vargmore is perfect."

Sawyer returned his attention to me. "I'll advocate for you to stay in Vargmore. Derric is a fair alpha, and we have a small but content human population here. I don't think he will object."

"Okay." I nodded and tried to smile past my skepticism. It would be great if it all worked out, the best thing to ever happen to me, actually. Which was why I wasn't ready to believe it. "Thank you, Sawyer."

He came toward me, hand reaching out until his fingers brushed the flag wrapped around my wrist. "You're safe, Riley. Remember, no one can touch you while you have this on. Or they'll have me to contend with."

With that, he turned and headed for his bike.

CHAPTER 10
SAWYER

Riding usually calmed me. The human side of me, anyway. Once I pulled up to the HDMC lodge in central Vargmore though, I felt just as wound-up as when I left Stout & Spirit.

Everything about this situation was more fucked than I imagined. It was one thing if she'd been the captive of some nobody vampire, but it was another thing entirely since it was Blood 'til Dawn's VP. Who was apparently crazy, bold, and obsessed enough to cross into our land to leave a message in the form of a dead wolf pup.

Oh yeah, and he might also have a drug problem. Even better.

But the cherry on top? How much this little human woman was affecting *me*.

Women never got under my skin, ever. And the fact that Riley was to this extent was fucking with my head too much. I never should have spent the night in her bed. I was a fucking idiot to have done so.

That dream I had of her last night was too damn good.

The reality? Even better. And it wasn't just kissing we'd been up to in good ol' dreamland. Poor thing was lucky I woke up before I took it any farther on the real her.

She kissed you back though, some treacherous inner voice reminded me.

I cut off my engine with a growl and a violent turn of my key. It had sure felt like she did, but the lines between dream and reality were all blurred in my head. I didn't truly know what had really happened, and I sure as fuck wasn't going to ask her. She had enough going on already.

She'd be safest out of my house, away from me. That kind of distance would weaken her scent too and clear my head. I'd have to wash everything she touched, as much as it broke my wolf's heart. Which, I suppose, was also my own.

Riley's scent, her presence, everything, drove me to ache for things I'd never wanted before. I wanted to wake up every morning and see her next to me in bed. I wanted to fill up her belly with food that I made and hear her voice fill up my space. I wanted her scent embedded in my home until it was just as intrinsic as the foundation I built it on. Before I met her, my independence was the most cherished part of my life. Now I wanted her woven into every facet of it.

She didn't need that, didn't need me getting all feral and overprotective when she was in control of her own life for the first time in a year.

For her own sake, I needed that beautiful woman and her sweet, intoxicating scent gone. Far, far away.

Tryn and the alpha-slash-president, Derric, were already inside the lodge when I entered. They both turned to me, almost expectantly.

"Sawyer," Derric said gruffly, peering at me with those

ancient eyes of his. He was only a hundred years older than me but had the gaze and wisdom of an elder wolf already. It was why he made a good president and alpha. "Tryn told me you'd be coming with some information."

I glanced at Tryn, who held up his palms defensively. "Didn't give details. Just let him know you'd have something important to say."

A soft growl of annoyance left my chest anyway. This was why I liked keeping to myself outside of official pack business. No one to flap their gums about what I was trying to work through on my own.

"You want to talk one-on-one?" Derric asked, clearly sensing my mood. "Or does this concern the pack at large?"

"Yeah, get everybody here," I said. "This affects the whole territory."

Derric went to yell over his shoulder. "Hey, Ors—"

"Already sent the message, alpha." From out of the back office strode Orson, his creepy, icy eyes locked onto me. "The club should be on their way."

Whereas I was a loner by choice, Orson spent all his available time at the club's lodge, despite not being particularly close with anyone. He was our pack treasurer and communications expert. The guy had a mind for numbers and technology, but people? Not really. His personality just clashed with everyone else's, even Tryn's, who was pretty much everyone's friend and the most easygoing in the pack.

Never one to beat around the bush, Orson lifted his nose in the air and inhaled deeply. "What is that delicious scent? It's so faint, but fuck me..." His hand drifted toward his crotch, a smirk pulling at his lips as he dared me to react. "It's making me want to dive between a female's legs and fucking *feast*."

My wolf clawed to jump out of my skin, show him our teeth until he submitted. *How dare he disrespect our female!* But Orson was nothing but an attention whore, so attention was the last thing I would give him.

I turned away to ignore him, focusing on Tryn. "So, seen anything interesting lately?"

Tryn was mildly prophetic, sometimes seeing future events in dreams, or threads that connected people, for either good or bad outcomes. He attributed this ability to his grandmother, who had been a witch.

"Yes, actually," he told me in a cheery tone. "Did I ever tell you that I always see this shield around you? It hovers just above your skin, like armor."

I frowned, suddenly regretting that I'd asked. I was just trying to make conversation that preferably wasn't about me.

"No, you never told me that. Guess I never asked, though."

"Right. I interpret it as your guarded nature. You don't let anyone get close to you and protect yourself by being closed off."

I shrugged. "Pretty accurate, I guess."

Tryn's eyes brightened like he was privately amused by something. "Your armor is breaking, Sawyer."

A bolt of panic snapped through my chest. "What?"

"There are gaps in your armor, enforcer. Pieces of it are missing. Here, here..." He pointed to different spots on my shoulders and arms, finger hovering a few inches above my skin. The last place he pointed was directly over my heart. "And right here," he told me with a solemn look.

With a scoff, I shoved his hand away. "Good thing I

have more than just metaphysical armor to protect my weak spots."

Tryn clicked his tongue. "Someone's getting to you, Sawyer. Getting under your skin, as they say. And I can't help but wonder who it could be."

"No one," I barked.

Even to me, it sounded like bullshit.

)))))●●●●(((((

WHEN THE REST of the pack gathered in the lodge, half were in wolf form, the other half as humans in riding leathers. Voices, howls, and barks filled the open room until Derric took his seat against the back wall and pounded his gavel on the heavy wooden armrest.

"Howling Death has urgent news from its enforcer, Sawyer." Derric looked at me and gestured to the empty space in the middle of the room. "The floor is yours."

"Thank you, alpha," I said humbly, my head lowered as I entered the cleared-out space. I only met his eyes when I found stillness, clasping my hands in front of me to say my piece. "Three nights ago, a human woman came to Stout & Spirit at the edge of our border with Sanguine, the vampire territory."

The room immediately filled with curses, growls, and aggressive barks. Some people even spit on the floor. All of the noise ceased when Derric lifted a hand. "Continue, enforcer."

"The woman was malnourished, weak, and frightened. It was clear she had escaped some mistreatment at the hands of the vampires." I suppressed a growl rising in my throat so I could keep talking. "After she received some rest and care, she revealed that she had been a blood pet and manipulated into the role without her consent by a member of Blood 'til Dawn MC."

More shouts, curses, howling, and growls. This time, the noise didn't immediately dissipate when Derric held up his hand. He slammed a fist down on his armrest next, partially shifting to growl and bare his canines at the unruly shifters. "Silence, you fucking mutts!"

The peanut gallery eventually quieted down to a low murmur, which was the best he was going to get. The alpha's gaze returned to me, hard as steel. "Whose pet was she?"

I swallowed. "Fabian's. The vice president's."

"Fuck." Derric rubbed his forehead, lips still curling back to reveal his teeth. "How long was she his?"

"Nearly a year."

"And you're certain she escaped? That she wasn't discarded?"

"Yes, alpha."

"Where is she now?" someone called out.

I waited until Derric extended his fingers, indicating that he wanted the question answered.

"She's a guest at my cabin in the woods," I said. "I thought it was important that we led her trail away from the bar for the safety of Shiloh and other Vargmore citizens."

The part about her scent driving me so wild that she needed to stay somewhere else? Yeah, that I would talk to Derric about privately. No need for the whole pack to know she affected me so much. My wolf was steadfastly against that idea, however. He wanted to let the whole world know she was ours, and it was a Herculean effort to keep his howl clamped down.

I swallowed, fighting to ignore the prickle of my wolf under my skin. "We've already received a threat from Blood 'til Dawn."

Derric narrowed his eyes, fingers curling around the chair's armrests. "What kind of threat?"

"A dead wolf pup on Shiloh's doorstep this morning, drained of blood."

"One of ours?" someone called out amidst the shouts of horror and disgust.

"No," I answered. "A full wolf, but it was clearly a message."

"Sweet moon, fuck those vampires!"

I waited until the noise faded to a dull roar before speaking again. "If I may, alpha, I propose we send teams to guard our borders with Sanguine. I'll be happy to lead them. The vampires will be looking for a response, and I say the best one is to show we won't tolerate them stepping another toe into our territory again. Let them try, and we'll show them how much blood *we* like to spill."

A low rumble of approval sounded throughout the lodge, and I stood a little taller.

"And this human woman?" Derric asked, leaning forward in his seat. "What do you propose be done with her?"

"Be done with her?" I repeated, frowning as I pushed down a protective growl. "Nothing. She sought refuge here and wishes to stay. She doesn't want to return to the human world, but ultimately, it's her choice."

Derric's eyes went to his VP, Ruse, standing quietly off

to the side. The two of them shared a look, as if communicating telepathically. My gut twisted, a bad feeling settling into my body.

"Sawyer, you're a good, honorable wolf." Derric returned his gaze to me. "And I understand you want to do right by this human woman. However, we have to handle this extremely carefully, given that Blood 'til Dawn is directly involved." One hand curled into a fist, as if momentarily conflicted. "For the safety of our Vargmore citizens, I believe the best course of action is giving their blood pet back to them."

"*What?*" I partially shifted, my canines descending as I took a step closer.

"Hold your place, enforcer," Derric warned. "This is my verdict."

"Alpha, I mean no disrespect." I reined in my wolf and lowered my head, humbling myself again. "Perhaps I was not clear enough. This woman was terrified. She lost too much blood and begged me not to take her back. There are multiple scars on her wrists and neck from all the times she's been preyed upon. She is a *victim,* alpha. To send her back would not only kill her but prolong her suffering before it happens."

"I'm sorry, Sawyer. I understand she is vulnerable and in need of help. But as long as she stays here, Blood 'til Dawn will use her as an excuse to start a conflict with us."

"Then let them!" I bared my teeth again, letting my growl loose. "Let's show them that we protect those who seek refuge in Vargmore."

"No." Derric's voice cut like a boulder through the air. "I will not risk any more werewolf lives for one short-lived human."

"What if she was a wolf?" I demanded. "One of us."

"Then she would be worth more to me, yes. And my decision would be different."

I snarled at the blatant double-standard, the unfairness of it all. Riley couldn't help that she was human, that she was taken by our enemies. It pissed me off to no end that she was treated differently just because she couldn't shift and howl.

Ruse came forward, standing between me and Derric like he was the president's bodyguard. "Do you want to contest the alpha's decision, Sawyer?"

I fired back with no hesitation. "Yes, I want to contest it."

He angled his head, looking first to the left and then right at the rest of our pack, our club and family, surrounding us. "We'll put it to a vote then. All those in favor of keeping the human?"

The lodge fell silent, just as I'd feared. I whipped around, glaring at the men who called themselves wolves but were actually dogs with their tails between their legs. I couldn't understand the cowardice. All of us were part human too. Why didn't they see our upright, two-legged cousins as worth saving?

After a few long seconds, a soft howl rose through the quiet. I turned, surprised to see Orson, who had shifted and thrown back his head, muzzle pointed at the wood beams of the ceiling as he crooned in support of me. When he finished, eerie eyes meeting mine, I gave him a small nod of thanks. It wouldn't be enough to sway the president, but I was touched that he went against the majority.

Tryn's howl followed soon after Orson's, another surprise. During our run yesterday morning, he seemed to support giving Riley back. I wondered what had changed. Something to do with him seeing my so-called armor cracking?

Silence returned once his howl of support ended. The VP crossed his arms and looked around the room again. "All those in favor of returning the human?"

Noise broke out like a switch had been flipped. It got so loud with everyone's howling, I felt my eardrums shuddering. Even those in human form cupped their hands around their mouths and sang at the moon at the top of their lungs.

There was no question. It was just shy of unanimous. I closed my eyes, unable to believe my failure. God fucking damn it, I was so sure Derric wouldn't throw Riley under the bus. I was confident he'd be reasonable.

Really, I should have seen this coming. We were pack animals, for fuck's sake. We kept to our own kind and didn't stick our neck out for others. Riley wasn't 'other' to me, but I couldn't make any of them see that.

"The alpha's verdict stands," Ruse announced, his eyes returning to me. "And if I may remind you, enforcer, going against this decision is treason and grounds for removal from the pack."

"Yeah," I said through gritted teeth, turning to leave. "I get it."

CHAPTER 11

RILEY

"I've never seen anything like this." My eyes bounced around to all the neatly labeled jars and bottles lining the dark wood shelves. Dried herbs and flowers hung upside down over the arched doorways. One entire wall was nothing but teas of various blends. Another wall was filled with various bulk botanicals—rosemary, lemongrass, cardamom, juniper, cinnamon, and things I'd never heard of.

We were at the Manticore's Cauldron, what Shiloh casually referred to as a witch's convenience store. Before coming here, we'd stopped at a bookstore called Verbatim. Shiloh had needed to pick up some magical reference book, and I browsed the shelves while she checked out.

I could have spent the whole day in that place, flipping through pages, reading back covers, and running my fingers along the spines. Verbatim had an entire section of floor-to-ceiling shelves just filled with erotic fantasy books from publishers and authors I'd never heard of before. It reminded me of the times I worked in the charity shops that funded the homeless shelter I stayed at. I always loved thumbing through the worn-out paperbacks, reading scenes of romance and adventure to temporarily escape from my real life.

How funny that my life had come full circle to here—in a magical world filled with paranormal beings I thought only existed in books and TV shows and hiding from an enemy under the protection of a huge, growly wolf-man I couldn't stop thinking about.

What was even real anymore?

"They don't have anything like this in the human world?" Shiloh's voice cut into my spiraling thoughts as she picked up a jar that said *candied ginger* and proceeded to scoop some into a small cloth bag.

"Maybe they do, but I've never seen one. I mean, our convenience stores have sugary snacks and drinks, lottery tickets, cigarettes. Hot dogs and pizza slices." I spun in a circle, marveling at everything again. It also smelled wonderful in here. "There are a lot of parallels between our worlds, it seems. Even TV shows. Sawyer and I both knew of some of the same shows."

If Shiloh was bothered by the idea of Sawyer and me spending time together, she didn't mention it. She only gave a small smile as she returned the jar of candied ginger to its proper place. "Do our worlds parallel or overlap? Where are the portals and why can some cross over easily while others never find them? Those are questions witches have been trying to find the answers to for centuries."

"No one from my world knows anything about Shyft-world," I said. "Maybe the government does but definitely not the general public. There would be chaos if they did."

"Maybe at first. But things have a tendency to balance

out." Shiloh added her small pouch of candied ginger to the basket on her arm. "If you put aside the magic, the people with wings, fangs, and the ability to shapeshift, everyone is just trying to live their lives. I mean, look at us." She gestured to the store. "I'm running errands on a day off and asked if you wanted to come along."

"Yeah, I guess we're not so different," I mused. "Thanks for bringing me along, by the way. It is cool to see what else is here."

It went without saying that I also needed the distraction from knowing Fabian was still after me and that Howling Death was figuring out what to do about everything at this very moment.

"Oh, it's my pleasure!" Shiloh said cheerily. She also seemed pleased to have the distraction of showing me around. "If you're not going back to the human world, as you said, you might as well get to know your new home." We walked down an aisle of colorful candles on one side and crystals on the other while she doubled-checked her shopping list. "Anything you're interested in doing? You know, for a living."

"I have no idea," I admitted. "Back home, it was all about surviving until the next day. I worked odd jobs here and there but nothing long-lasting."

Shiloh picked up a tall, purple candle, sniffed it, and placed it in her basket. "Would you be interested in working for me? At Stout & Spirit?"

"Really?" My breath caught in my chest. "Just like that?"

She shrugged casually. "I could use the extra help. The bar gets busy, so you'll have to work quickly. But I can start you part time to get your feet wet and see how you like it. Then we can—"

"Yes," I cut her off. "Absolutely yes. You saved my life, took me in. I'll work my ass off for you, for free even. It's the least I can do."

"Oh don't be silly. You aren't working for free," she huffed. "You deserve a fresh start after everything you've been through. And Vargmore is a wonderful place to live. We don't have many humans here, but they're a very friendly, welcoming community."

"How do I become a witch?" I was only half joking.

"*You* can't, but," Shiloh held up an index finger tipped with a long, glossy black nail, "if you meet a man here and have a child and then your child grows up to have a child, you will be the grandmother of a witch."

"Really?" I stared at her. "That's how it works?"

"Yes. For as long as we've had recorded history here, magical abilities have shown up in the offspring of humans who have been in Shyftworld for at least three generations."

"That's fascinating. Do you know why that is?"

"The general assumption is that it takes time for the magic of Shyftworld to accumulate in a human's system." Shiloh smiled and playfully bumped me with her hip on her way up to the checkout counter. "So, think about my offer. You don't have to answer me now, but most of the humans who end up here don't want to leave."

I could certainly see why. Shyftworld, at least the werewolf territory, was beautiful and fantastical. Maybe it was the magic in the air, but this place felt so much more *alive* than the human world. The thought of staying here, building a new life and letting that magic flow through to future generations was a tempting one.

But I couldn't see myself settling down with a human

man, no matter how abstract and far off the mental image was. No, when I tried to picture the future, I saw an idyllic, two-story cabin surrounded by forest. I imagined a protective growl rumbling through the air and sensed a tall, broad body looming over anything that threatened to harm me. I heard a love song through lupine howls and felt a four-legged predator keenly guarding his territory, which included me.

He would be an ideal mate, some voice slithered along my brain.

Stop it, I mentally chastised myself. *Sawyer doesn't want you. He made that abundantly clear.*

"Ready to head out?" Shiloh returned to my side, a brown paper bag in her hand. "If Sawyer's not home yet, I'll be happy to hang out so you're not alone."

"That would be great." I forced a smile. "Thanks."

We returned to her car and she drove us through the winding, scenic road back to Sawyer's cabin. I stared out the window, trying to distract myself with the beautiful forest views. When we pulled up to find Sawyer sitting on his front porch, hunched over and scowling at the ground, dread turned to cement in my stomach.

"Want me to stay?" Shiloh asked quietly. She didn't need to mention that the news didn't look good.

I pulled in a breath, trying to release some of the tension that had taken over my body. "No, it's okay. I'll be fine."

"You sure?"

"Yeah." I gave her a smile as I opened the passenger door. "Thanks for taking me out. I had fun today."

"Me too." She smiled back. "See you soon."

I left the car and forced my feet up the path to where

Sawyer was sitting. Shiloh's tires crunched gently on the gravel behind me as she backed out of the driveway and took off.

"Hey," I greeted the large, lone wolf hesitantly.

Sawyer glanced up at me quickly, then his gaze ducked down again as he ran a hand through his hair. His white patch stuck straight up like a little snow-capped mountain. "Hey. Where'd you girls go?"

"Verbatim Booksellers and then the Manticore's Cauldron after that." I couldn't figure out what to do with my hands—first wringing them, then shoving them into my pockets. "Shiloh also offered me a job at the bar."

"Really? That's great." Sawyer's voice was flat and emotionless as a robot. He was clearly distracted by something else and not actually listening.

"How'd it go with the pack?" I couldn't stand not knowing any longer, especially with him looking as glum as he did. "Did you talk to your alpha?"

Sawyer cleared his throat, glancing up again, but his gaze didn't reach mine. "Yeah, I did." An eternity seemed to pass while I waited for what he'd say next. "I'm really sorry, Riley."

My throat went as dry as a bone. "Sorry for what?" I forced out.

"I tried. I argued the decision. But the pack outvoted me." His sad, dark blue eyes finally met mine and stayed there. "We have to return you to the vampires."

CHAPTER 12

RILEY

I shouldn't have been surprised. Everyone I had ever known broke their promises to me, so I should have expected this. But damn it, this hurt. I had actually started to trust Sawyer, to believe him when he said he'd protect me no matter what.

But I had only been led on, manipulated, and lied to again.

"No," I whispered weakly, clinging to that false hope that he could still help me. "No, I can't go back there. You *promised* I'd never have to go back!"

"I'm so, so sorry, Riley." Sawyer scrubbed a hand down his face, suddenly looking much older. "I wish there was more I could do, but the alpha's word is law."

"There has to be something," I cried desperately. "What if I just ran away?"

He shook his head. "The pack will track your scent. And even if they didn't catch you, you step one foot out of Vargmore and the vampires will find you themselves."

"What about this?" I brought my forearm forward to show his flag still tied around my wrist. "You said as long as I wore this, you'd protect me no matter what. Does this suddenly not mean anything?"

That last question felt so loaded, like I wasn't just talking about the flag but every moment since we first met. The motorcycle ride. Having breakfast together. Talking and flirting. His beautiful wolf comforting me after my nightmare. And that kiss.

Sawyer's jaw clenched tightly, his frown deepening. "It *did* mean something. I had every intention of keeping you safe when I gave that to you. If I could prevent this from happening, I would. But now...I don't run the pack, Riley. If I go against their decision, I'll be exiled and branded a traitor." He pressed the heels of his palms against his eyes and sighed. "I hate everything about this, especially the fact that I can't change it. I'm so sorry."

"How could you?" I couldn't stop my voice from rising, the feeling of betrayal overflowing in my chest. "If that's true, you must have known this was a possibility. *Why* would you make a promise you couldn't keep?"

"I don't know, I...I didn't think the pack would actually choose this. That's what pisses me off so much. They're scared. The ruling pack of Vargmore is *scared* of putting some fucking vampires in their place, so they'd rather give you back instead of fight to keep you." Sawyer's fists clenched and released, his jaw and shoulders bunched with tension. "They don't see you like I do."

How do you see me? I wanted to ask, but it didn't matter. It was *his* pack, his people, serving me up like a sacrificial lamb. He was the one who led me to believe everything would be fine and then let me down, just like everyone else before him. Sawyer was no different, and what pissed me off the most was that I still yearned to know the answer to that question.

How do you see me?

What do I really mean to you?

I was so in my own head that I didn't realize I'd started walking away until Sawyer called out, "I'll leave you alone, but stay close. It's easy to get lost in the woods."

Resisting the urge to scream back, *what the fuck do you care?* I carried on, stomping loudly through the underbrush. I had no direction or distance in mind, just...away.

My jaw ached with how hard I ground my teeth. Hot tears pricked at my eyes, my composure slipping the further away I got from Sawyer. All my emotions were on the brink of overflow, and I had to let the pressure out, preferably without an audience.

At some point, my shoe caught a fallen branch and I stumbled. It would have been easy to right myself and keep walking, but in my defeated state I thought, *Fuck it. Might as well park it here.*

I let my ass plant on the ground and, after a few ragged breaths, let it all out.

There was some screaming, sobbing, pounding my fists on the ground, and all kinds of ugly noises. Inside my head I swore there was a howling noise, but it must have been tinnitus from my screaming.

My breakdown wasn't entirely about Sawyer, although his part hurt the worst. I really thought he'd be different. I thought I finally found someone I could trust. But he was just part of the same repeating pattern of disappointment.

Even a place filled with shifters and magical creatures couldn't change that.

But mostly, I hated that I let myself keep falling for it over and over. That I never learned and gave people too many chances. That I took what people said at face value instead of stopping to consider what they would gain from being nice to me.

When I quieted down because of how much my throat ached, I wondered in the ensuing silence what exactly Sawyer's angle would be. Others said he preferred being alone and got touchy about company in his place, so what would he have to gain by letting me stay? He didn't let me clean, and he certainly wasn't interested in having sex with me.

My mind felt clearer, quieter after purging all of that hurt and frustration, and the answer that came to me was as simple as it was obvious.

Nothing.

Sawyer had no ulterior motives.

I felt that deep in my gut to be true, and that feeling hadn't changed since I first met him. He was sincere, and while my anger *at* him dissolved with that realization, somehow that made the ache cut even deeper. Sawyer had every intention of keeping his promise to me. The outcome just wasn't in his control.

Plus, there had already been a death because of me.

Yes, the wolf pup had been "just" an animal without a human form. But what would stop Fabian from escalating to actually murdering people? Getting what he wanted, which was me.

I closed my eyes, the resolve settling like dead weight on my shoulders. Rising to my feet, I stood as tall as I could while carrying that burden. Of course, I never wanted to go back. I knew I would likely never leave the vampire territory again. But the brutal truth of the alpha's decision hit me right then, and I fully agreed.

I was not worth the price of more dead werewolves.

Sawyer was still sitting on his front porch when I emerged from the woods. His elbows rested on his knees, his shoulders were hunched, and his gaze stared blankly toward his shoes. He looked just as beaten down as I had been moments ago. As I slowly ascended the steps, his posture didn't change. He really was blaming himself for how this had turned out.

"It's okay, Sawyer," I said, reaching out to put a hand on his big shoulder.

He flinched as if my touch had burned him. "Nothing about this is okay, Riley. How can you say that?"

"I mean, it's not good, but I thought it through, and I understand now. Your alpha made the right call."

The werewolf stared up at me, inky blue eyes hard and intense. "He did fucking not. You're innocent in all this, and he wants us to treat you like an extradited prisoner. I can't fucking believe him."

"It's not about *me*, Sawyer. You know that dead wolf pup was just a warning. How many more until Fabian actually kills one of you? Until another war breaks out? I can't be the cause of that. I *won't* be."

He shook his head, then lowered his forehead to his hands. "You don't deserve this. It's so fucking unfair to you."

"Yeah, well. I'm kinda used to getting the short end of the stick in life."

He barked out a mirthless laugh as he lifted his head.

"That doesn't mean you should." His eyes landed on me again, his gaze unreadable. "I don't even give a fuck about the pack or the territory right now. I just hate that I failed you."

"You didn't," I protested. "I'm so grateful to you, Sawyer. Not just for letting me stay and, you know, being there for me during the nightmares and stuff..." Because I definitely wasn't going to say kissing me. "But I think you're the first person who actually intended to keep a promise to me instead of lying to get something they wanted."

Sawyer only snarled at that, his shoulders bunching up tighter. "I only did the absolute bare minimum, which you should never, *ever* settle for."

"You might call it that. But you and Shiloh showed me that good, honest people exist. That's a priceless gift, and I'll never forget that."

He only snarled and shook his head again. When several moments of raw silence passed between us, I asked, "So, when do I go back?"

Sawyer inhaled sharply like he was going to argue, then stopped himself, as if he changed his mind. "Tomorrow night," he said. "The alpha has already arranged it with Blood 'til Dawn. We're meeting with them at a pre-arranged spot on the border."

I nodded numbly, like he'd just told me our dinner plans for tomorrow rather than sending me back to the hell I just escaped from. That gave me just over twenty-four hours of freedom left. How would I make them count?

Despite knowing it was the last thing he wanted, all I could think about was burrowing into Sawyer's warm, clean scent.

"Okay. Well, you know where to find me."

I walked past him into the house, heading for the guest bedroom.

CHAPTER 13
SAWYER

I stared at my ceiling, no closer to falling asleep now than when I went to bed three hours ago. Riley had gone to her room before the sun even went down and hadn't come out. Not that I could fucking blame her. I wouldn't want to face me either.

"Fucking idiot." I flopped violently to my side for the hundredth time that night. Like a change in position was the ticket to getting some goddamn rest.

All of this could have been avoided if I just hadn't been an idiot. If my dumbass hadn't latched onto her and made a bunch of promises I knew I couldn't keep. When did I become that fucking person? The whole reason I broke it off with Shiloh was because I didn't want to lead her on. Then this human girl comes along and I'm giving her my flag within minutes of meeting her, something our MC members usually reserved for making a woman their old lady. A long-term, permanent thing.

Like some kind of sap, I promised to protect Riley with my life before thinking the whole situation through. I'd never been so short-sighted before, never allowed my words to be so meaningless and empty.

And still, I knew the reason why I couldn't sleep was because my instincts were telling me to follow the hell through. *She is still ours,* my wolf said. *You can still do right by her.*

I could, but doing so would implode my position in the pack. I'd be cast out, branded a traitor and never welcome in Vargmore again. I might as well send the vampires a handwritten invitation to start kidnapping werewolves like they had in the old days. And then I certainly wouldn't have the resources to protect Riley, if she even wanted to be with a lone, exiled wolf.

The whole situation was completely fucked, but no one would suffer more than Riley.

I flopped over again to my back, exhaling so loudly that I almost missed the soft click of Riley's door knob turning. Curious, I held my breath and glanced at the clock next to my bed. It was near 3am, but those were definitely her soft footfalls leaving her bedroom. Was she going to run? No, she was barefoot and didn't seem in a hurry. Getting a midnight snack, maybe? Nope, her footsteps bypassed the kitchen.

My sharp hearing picked up the soft rustling of fabric and I frowned, sitting up to listen harder. It sounded like she was settling on the couch with a blanket, but why?

Curiosity got the better of me, and I brought my feet to the floor, pulling on my sweatpants before walking over to the railing of my loft. "Couldn't sleep?" I called down softly to her.

Riley's head snapped up, poking out of the mass of soft

blanket wrapped around her. "Sorry, did I wake you? I was trying to be quiet."

"Nah, you didn't." I leaned over the railing. "Want some company?"

Why did I even bother asking? Obviously I was the last person she wanted to hang out with, but she was too nice to tell me to fuck off. I should have just said goodnight, gone back to bed, and left her in peace.

"Um, sure." Riley pulled the blanket tighter around her. "If you want to."

Nah, you know what? I'll leave you alone, was what I should have said. Instead, I gripped the railing and vaulted over it, landing softly in a crouch on the floor below. It wasn't until I stood to full height that I realized I had forgotten to put a shirt on. Again.

"Fancy moves," Riley said with a soft laugh. She scooted over on the couch, as if to make room for me.

"It's thanks to all the spinach I eat."

Riley laughed louder, the sound genuine and musical as I parked it on the edge of the couch.

"So, what are you doing out here this late?"

She shrugged, though her shoulders barely seemed to move under the weight of the blanket. "Started feeling claustrophobic in that room. Thought I'd enjoy your open floor plan while I still can, you know?"

My mood instantly soured, all pretense of just hanging out with this woman on the couch gone. In a matter of hours, it would be like she was never here. That lovely laugh and her delicious scent wouldn't fill up the space in my home again. And she would be nothing but a pet for a blood-sucking asshole.

Riley sensed the shift in my mood and scooted toward

me, her hand stretching out from under the blanket. "Sawyer, none of this is your fault. You did what you could for me."

My head shook from side to side, refusing to pass the burden onto someone else. *I broke a promise. I* considered her mine and failed to protect her. Therefore, it *was* my fault. And this fragile little human was accepting the outcome so calmly, so bravely. It just made the fact that I couldn't do anything to help her even more infuriating.

She would make such a fine wolf. An excellent mate.

My wolf clawed, barked, and howled so insistently at that thought, he brought a tangible, burning pain to my chest. I rubbed the spot just over my heart, remembering that the full moon was in a mere four days. He was nearly breaking through my human surface already. Once the full moon's magic pulled him forth, there would be no stopping him. No rational human mind to bring him to heel.

Riley definitely couldn't be around for that. My wolf could hurt others when trying to protect her. Or worse, he could bite her to try to force a change.

But fuck. What kind of mental gymnastics was I doing? Trying to convince myself she'd be better off with *vampires?*

"Sawyer?" I felt pressure on my arm, something warm and soft. Riley had put her hand on me, her brow furrowed with concern. "I don't want you to blame yourself for this."

"There's no one else to blame," I grunted out. "You trusted me, and I hate that I lied to you. I hate...everything about this."

"You didn't intend to—"

"Intent doesn't mean shit." I scrubbed a hand over my face and hair, feeling so utterly exhausted despite my brain refusing to shut off. "This is so wrong, and you deserve better. I just wish there was a way to fix it."

Riley pulled her hand back, making it disappear under her blanket. She sank into the knitted throw that my grandmother had made, the fabric reaching her ears and covering even her chin.

"You like that blanket, huh?" It was the same one she had fallen asleep under that day she took a nap in the sun. She looked damn cute bundled up in it, with only the top of her face peeking out.

Riley nodded, her shy smile a warm contrast to the intense conversation we were having just moments earlier. "It's the softest one I've ever felt. And I love how it smells."

A kicking sensation hit my chest as my heart went into overdrive. I'd had that blanket for nearly twenty years. My scent was just as embedded in it as those yarn fibers were. That was *my* scent she wrapped around herself, buried her nose in. She associated *my* scent with safety and comfort.

And tomorrow night, I'd be handing her over to our enemy.

Damn, how cruelly ironic and fucked up could life be?

Oblivious to my inner turmoil, Riley extended her arm, opening the blanket in my direction. "Want to share? It's yours, after all. I probably shouldn't hog this."

"You're not hogging anything." I scooted toward her anyway, accepting the offered blanket because I'd take any excuse to get closer to her. "I like seeing you wrapped up in it."

"Really?"

"Yes." I closed my lips, intending to hold back the next words on the tip of my tongue, but then thought, *Fuck it.*

This is our last night together. "I like you using my things, draping yourself in my scent."

Riley froze, a look of shock on her face before she slowly leaned toward me and inhaled deeply. "That *is* you, isn't it?"

"Yes." *Don't say it, don't say it...Again, fuck it.* "And your scent is just as pleasing to me. I wish I had something of yours to hold onto after..." *After I deliver you right back to the people who hurt you and held you captive.* Fuck, I was such an unworthy wolf.

But Riley didn't seem focused on what would be happening tomorrow. She scooted closer and leaned into me. Any closer and she'd be in my lap. She looked happily drunk, or high in the best way possible.

"Why do I just want to..." She trailed off, cheeks flushing as she licked her lips. "I've never felt like this just from smelling a man before."

"The full moon is in a few days," I explained, my throat tight. Goddamn it, she was close enough to kiss again, lips and nose hovering just over my skin as she inhaled me like her favorite drug. "Everything about us is more...potent around that time." I should have moved away, but I stayed still as a fucking rock, silently praying she touched me somewhere, anywhere, with that sensual mouth.

"It's like everything I feel, everything I want to do, is enhanced times a hundred." She met my gaze with hooded eyes, lips parted and wet.

"What do you want to do, Riley?" File that question under the list of things I shouldn't be saying but stopped giving a fuck about. "What are your instincts telling you?"

She hesitated for a long while, which was the perfect chance to get up and away from her. But I only waited with bated breath for her answer. I would have waited ten years to hear what she wanted.

"I want to finish what we started," she said.

"What do you mean?" I stared at her lips, hypnotized by their movement as she spoke.

"The other night, in bed." She licked her lips again. "When you kissed me."

A rough growl left my throat, one that was pleasure and frustration in equal measure. "That shouldn't have happened."

"But it did." Riley's scent bloomed in the air, her need calling to me like a beacon. "And I...wouldn't mind if it happened again."

"Yes, you would. You don't want me to do that again."

She frowned. "Why not?"

"Because I wouldn't be able to stop at just kissing you."

Her frown spread into a very intentional smile, slow and sultry. Her scent was so thick in the air, my nails bit into my palms from clenching my fists so hard. My last thread of control was moments away from snapping while she teased a knife along those weakening fibers.

"I thought you didn't want me like that."

"Fuck, I do." For some reason, I believed she needed to know that more than my rational brain needed to voice that this was a bad idea. "You have no idea how bad I'm struggling to hold back right now. But you've been my guest. Under my protection." I felt fabric under my fingertips and looked down to see that I was stroking my flag around her wrist. "It's not right for me to take advantage of that."

Riley cocked her head, much like a wolf would. "Well, neither of those things will apply anymore, right?" She shrugged. "Throwing the rules out the window sounds like a fine send-off to me," she said.

"Riley—"

"Sawyer." Her expression got serious, eyes bright and clear as she stared at me. "Tonight is all we have, right? The future...it's a big question mark. My time with you has been so good, the best of my life, and I just..." She stabbed her fingers through her hair, raking the strands back with aggressive hands. "I feel this pull to you that practically *hurts*, it's so strong. And I don't want to fight it anymore. Not while I'm still free."

Riley's eyes dropped, and she curled in on herself, looking so vulnerable that the need to wrap her in a protective embrace had me growling again.

"If you really do feel the same way, please don't hold yourself back because it's improper or whatever. I'm tired of being cautious, of always questioning everyone's motives." She looked up, eyes wide and bared as open windows. "For once, I want to be with someone else who wants the same thing I do."

"And that is?" I asked roughly.

"I want to feel good because I can. No expectations, no ulterior motives." Her eyes were begging me, and I didn't have the strength to say no. "I want one more good memory with you, Sawyer."

Snap. Just like that, my control was gone.

I unwrapped the blanket from where she held it in front of her and let it fall away from her shoulders. In its place, my hand stroked along her nape, her shoulders, and her upper back.

My voice was somewhere between a growl and a purr. "I can't fight this anymore either."

CHAPTER 14

RILEY

I wasn't any colder when Sawyer pulled the blanket away from me. When he caressed the back of my neck, staring at me so intensely as he leaned in, the opposite happened. I was absolutely burning up.

His kiss landed with so much gentleness, but that didn't lessen the electricity strumming through at the contact. Locking together like a puzzle, it was like we were two electromagnets made to fit.

I let my mouth fall open, gliding my tongue out to meet his and urging him to deepen the kiss. I was only mildly aware that my legs were splitting open in much the same way. My mouth, my body, all of it was an open invitation to him. Instinctively, I knew he was cut from a different cloth of all the men I'd known before. His actions of kindness, care, and respectful distance only reinforced those instincts.

Although he was a dangerous wolf, Sawyer would never use or hurt me. And that made me want to get ravaged by him all the more.

He met my tongue caresses with a rough moan, and under the weight of him, I felt the gentlest falling sensation as I reclined on the couch. My fingers curled, digging into the broad, tight muscles of his shoulders. I had a passing thought of wishing I had claws so that I could really grip him, hold on while he mounted me and give him a taste of pain with his pleasure.

"You taste like how you smell." Sawyer's lips moved roughly against mine as he spoke. "So sweet. So good."

It was the same on my end. He tasted clean and masculine, woodsy with a hint of spice. His scent surrounded me like a cloud, intoxicating and making me desperate to feel him moving inside me. I wanted to lick that scent from his skin, feel his bite and hear his growls of satisfaction.

My hands slid from his shoulders to around his neck, the thick muscles there strong and corded like bridge cables. The instant I thought of his bite, the aching pleasure in my body bloomed to a new height.

"Sawyer," I moaned when his lips broke away for air. "I...I want you to bite me."

His body froze, face pulling back until our eyes met. They were still dilated and filled with lust, but there was something else in his expression too. "What did you say?"

"Bite me," I begged. "I don't know where it's coming from, but I want you to bite me so bad." I traced his bearded jaw, letting my fingers fall to stroke his throat. "Fuck, I want to bite you too."

"No." Sawyer lowered to kiss me again as he traced my mouth with his thumb. "You keep those teeth behind these pretty lips, got it?"

"Why?" I whined. The need to bite was pressing, aching in a way I couldn't explain. Like it was the one thing I needed to orgasm, even though that was crazy. I'd never had the urge to bite someone or be bitten in my life.

"Too risky," he murmured. "I'm a werewolf, remember?"

Yeah, and?

"What would happen?" I asked breathlessly. "Would I turn into your kind?"

"I don't know. We don't interact with humans much." His mouth slid over to place a smoldering kiss on the edge of my jaw, and the desperate need to feel his teeth in my neck made me want to weep. "It could also just hurt you for no reason. Or get infected. So I'm not doing it."

"But I…I *need* it, Sawyer. I need it from you."

"Riley." My name came from his throat as a ragged moan. "This is all about you, and I'll please you until you're completely wrung out. But I am not biting you. Ask me again and I'll stop everything right now."

"But—"

"Shh." Sawyer's mouth returned to mine, his tongue lightly teasing along my lips. "Choose your words carefully, sweet girl. I would hate to stop."

So would I, damn it.

I paused for a few moments, saying nothing while I tried to figure out how distracting this biting urge really was. How strange for it to pop up right now. Was it some kind of psychological trauma-turned-kink from the vampires? I'd always hated being bitten before, so what the fuck?

After some seconds ticked by without giving in, the urge didn't exactly fade, but it kind of shifted priority in my current hierarchy of needs. I met Sawyer's eyes and became reinvigorated to touch and kiss him. To feel his hands on me and see what kind of pleasure he intended to give me as a final send-off.

Right, because this was our last night together. I had to remember that. Some deep instinct told me a bite would be long-lasting, linking us forever. To do that tonight would only ensure more pain for us in the days that followed.

And I wanted none of that, especially for him.

So while the need to bite him remained ever-present as my eyes trailed from his face down the length of his body, I felt better about controlling it. As long as I remembered this was the one and only time this would be happening.

"Riley?" I had no idea how long I was silent for, but it must have been a while for Sawyer to prompt me again.

"I'm good. No biting, I promise." With my arms still around his shoulders, I pulled myself up to kiss him. All tongue, no teeth.

Large hands slid around my back, holding my torso flush to his as he let out a deep groan of satisfaction. He licked inside my mouth, dominating the kiss in dizzying pulls and sucks that had me wondering why the hell I needed air to breathe when I could just be constantly tasting him.

Not constantly, I reminded myself. *Only for tonight.*

"I want to make you come until you physically can't anymore," Sawyer growled. "You good with that, sweet girl?"

"I want to do the same to you." My hands slid down his torso, traveling over hot skin and solid muscle to his sweatpants, until he stopped me at the waistband.

"No." I was getting really sick of that word, even though his lips scraped mine as he gave a small shake of his head. "I'm only giving to you tonight, not taking anything."

"But I—"

"Too much has been taken from you already." He dropped a kiss on my throat. "If I give you a dozen orgasms tonight, it'll only be a fraction of what you deserve."

"Sawyer..." My teeth came down on the inside of my cheek, a realization hitting me like a cold splash of water. "I...don't know if I can. I never have. I mean, not with another person before."

He didn't seem disappointed, or even surprised, really. If anything, the soft growl rising from his chest sounded pleased. "But you have by yourself?"

"Um, yes."

"Then guide me." He took one of my hands from around his neck and ran it softly down my own body, dragging my fingertips between my breasts and over my belly, pausing only when we reached the juncture between my legs. Then I let out a gasp as he pressed my fingers to my clit, the spark of sensation making my hips rock up.

"Show me what you like, sweet girl. You might find I'm a quick study." Sawyer's grin was confident, if even smug.

He was full of shit, and we both knew it. The man knew exactly where to go and what to do. When it came to a woman's body, he didn't need to learn a goddamn thing. Still, he paused. Waited for me to take over.

My heart kicked a frantic, exhilarated beat in my chest as my fingers began to move, tilting from side to side of that small bundle of nerves. His fingers remained directly on top of mine, following my movement while adding a touch of extra pressure. The weight of his hand seemed to make the pulse between my legs beat even stronger.

Rather than watch what was happening between our bodies, Sawyer's eyes remained locked onto mine. I couldn't look away, not even as I began to squirm underneath him, the toying of my clit over my leggings becoming more urgent as the pressure built.

"How am I doing?" he whispered roughly, fingers not slipping from mine for a single breath.

"Can't you tell?" Breathing was getting harder, my pulse rapid at every sensitive point in my body.

"I want to hear you tell me."

Holy. Shit.

Unlike me, Sawyer remained completely still except for from the wrist down. Aside from the huskiness in his voice and his rapt attention on me, he barely looked affected. "Good?" he prompted, fingers keeping up with mine even as my rhythm grew fast and frenzied.

"Be better if you'd kiss me," I panted.

He lowered to me, and that inky blue stare disappeared behind my closed eyelids as I just tasted and felt him. Felt us.

Oh. And he *was* affected.

He leaned to one side while our fingers still worked in tandem on my clit, and I felt the thick length of an erection on the outside of my thigh. Sawyer groaned into my mouth and his hips rolled, the heat of him like a brand on me even through my leggings and his sweatpants.

Pleasure coiled inside me, kinetic energy pulling back like bowstring while he dominated my mouth. "Riley," he groaned against my mouth.

The energy released all at once, exploding in a bright rush from my nerve endings. And as I pressed my palm down over my clit to ride out the orgasm, Sawyer was right there, following my slight movements to help me wring out the last of it.

But I was far from done.

I rolled onto my side, facing him. His arm went around my back as we kissed with warm, satisfied indulgence. "Your turn," I whispered, running a hand over his ribs to the waistband of his sweatpants.

Again, he stopped me. Taking my wrist, he brought it back and over my head, the restraint rolling my languid body to my back again. "Not done making you come," he said, nipping at my lips.

That deep, instinctive need for biting returned, but I forced it back by focusing on what Sawyer had just said. "I hope you intend to do so with that thing." My eyes fell to the bulge in his pants, which seemed to have gotten even bigger in the last minute.

"Nope. Keep your hands where I can see 'em."

I didn't know whether to laugh or whimper with need. He sounded like a cop in a TV show, but it was so hot when he gave me commands like that. Biting back a grin, I obliged, bringing my wrists together above my head.

"Good girl."

My teeth sank further into my lip as he said that, and then he yanked my leggings from my hips, peeling them down my legs and off my feet with practiced efficiency.

"Let's see if I can apply what I've learned," he purred, sliding a hand between my knees to gently part my legs.

The damn wolf spent a few good long minutes far away from where I wanted him. He turned into a masseuse all of a sudden—kneading, rolling, and squeezing my inner thighs. Just touching me with every part of those sensual hands. It felt amazing, don't get me wrong. But it was like torture, so good without getting me anywhere.

"Sawyer, please…" I reached for him, desperate for a

rough grab or a kiss, any kind of other stimulation to get me further.

"Keep those hands where they are," he ordered.

I flopped back down, hands above my head again. "This is not what I taught you," I said petulantly.

"I'm getting there, sweetness," he said in a low, throaty chuckle.

When he finally did touch me at my core, oh *fuck.*

I nearly jackknifed up off the couch from the sudden sensitivity. It was like being electrocuted in the best way.

"Like this?" The smugness returned to Sawyer's voice as his hand explored me, gently stroking my lips, rubbing my sensitive flesh, and making casual swipes over my clit hood like he was just going for a stroll in the park.

"Cut the shit," I laughed. "You didn't learn a thing from me."

"Oh, but I did." He bent down and placed a kiss next to my navel. "You have no idea how much."

He stroked a finger inside of me before I could respond, kissing along the edge of my ribcage as his other hand slowly pushed my shirt upward. I wanted to help him along and whip the suffocating thing off my head, but I had a feeling he'd bark at me to keep my hands still again.

And I really, really liked being his good girl.

Sawyer's hand was a well-coordinated instrument. Two fingers now pressed inside me, and while he stroked them against my inner walls, his thumb played my clit in a tireless rhythm, circling and pressing as his mouth kissed higher up my body.

When the undersides of my breasts peeked out from under my shirt, he let out the hungriest growl I'd heard from him yet. He shoved the shirt up to my neck, exposing my nipples to the cool air. I didn't even realize how sensitive and aching they were until he drew one into his mouth. He laved generously on the tip with his tongue, gently running the edge of his teeth along it until I whimpered.

That same sensitive ache echoed between my legs, where his hand continued to work me tirelessly. His two forefingers were inside me up to the last knuckle, curling and stroking to increase the friction while his thumb carried on with my clit like a happy little soldier.

While I arched to press more of my breasts toward his mouth, I bucked against his hand, constantly greedy for more, more.

"Fuck, Riley." Sawyer's beard rubbed the underside of my breast, the sensation both tickling and arousing. "I fucking need to taste you."

He dove down in the next instant, his wide shoulders pushing my legs further apart. The next thing I felt was my world getting rocked by that filthy, delicious mouth on my clit.

"Oh fuck, Sawyer!" I could only grab onto his hair for purchase, and his mouth was too busy to tell me where to put my hands.

His fingers withdrew from me, quickly replaced by his tongue. He groaned against my flesh, saying something, but his voice was too muffled to understand. My werewolf licked and sucked at me like a starving man, and all I could do was hold on for the ride.

When his mouth returned to my clit and his fingers stroked their way back inside me, I was already moments away from my second orgasm.

"Don't stop," I begged. "Please, just like that..."

I knew it was useless to give him instructions, but he

seemed pleased by them, moaning against my body as his fingers drove into me and his mouth worked magic over that bundle of nerves.

Sawyer's hand pumped against me once, twice, three more times before I came apart. The moment I did, he kept his fingers deep inside, giving the rhythmic pulses something to squeeze and hold onto as my pleasure crested and ebbed. Once they slowed and faded, he gently withdrew his fingers from me and kept that dark stare on me as he brought them to his mouth and sucked.

Fuck, he was so beautiful. So considerate. So giving and selfless. What had I ever done but take from him?

Hot tears pricked my eyes in a sudden rush, like the orgasm had laid my heart and emotions bare.

"Riley?" Sawyer's expression morphed to concern as he leaned over me. "What's wrong? Did I hurt you?"

"No." I tried to laugh it off and wipe my cheeks casually like it was nothing, but that only brought them on harder.

Sawyer didn't hesitate to slip in next to me. It was a tight squeeze, the two of us lying side-by-side on the couch, but his arms went around me, holding me against his chest and safe from rolling to the floor below.

"What is it?" He kissed my forehead with such tenderness, it drew a sob from my chest.

After a few shaky breaths, during which he rubbed my back and waited patiently, I let out the aching dread that sat on my chest like a boulder.

"I wish tomorrow never had to come."

Sawyer caught a tear on his thumb before bringing my head to his chest.

"Me too."

CHAPTER 15

SAWYER

The next evening, Riley rode with me one last time through the woods. She hugged tightly around my middle, arms and legs pressing against me, her cheek against my upper back. My whole body was so fraught with tension that my teeth ached in my jaw. Even so, the shape she made with her limbs around me seemed to fit perfectly. Like vines curling around a tree trunk, she held me in an embrace that was both soft and unyielding. It was a mirror of how I held her last night after giving her those two orgasms.

I'd tried to convince myself I was being selfless by focusing on her. But watching the pleasure wring out of her, being the cause of it, satisfied and stroked my ego like nothing else ever had. I wanted to give her ten more orgasms, just because I could.

Her crying made all of that come crashing down, however.

It hit me like a brick to the dome while I held her, never wanting to let her go. Long after her tears had dried, she fell asleep with my chest as her pillow. That was her first experience being pleased by another person, with no expectation for something in return. And now I was dumping her off with her abuser. No wonder she got emotional. What a headfuck that was.

What a spineless wolf I was.

Derric and Ruse were both riding ahead of us, their tail lights like a pair of glowing red eyes on the dark road. Tryn, Orson, and a few other supporting members of the pack would show up to the meeting place in wolf form.

The northwestern border between Vargmore and Sanguine was invisible to human eyes, but my wolf senses picked up the magical barrier instantly. I felt a prickling in my nose, and the telltale scent of earth and blood.

On impulse, I let out a growl and brought a possessive hand over Riley's hand resting on my stomach. I was loath to let her go. Nothing about this was right. And bless her, she laced her fingers through mine and squeezed. Like it was her job to reassure *me*.

The bikes ahead of me slowed to a stop and I pulled alongside them, keeping my ride idling. Glowing eyes, long snouts, and soft growls slowly came out of the woodwork —four wolves emerging from the brush to stand guard alongside us.

"This is your pack?" Riley asked softly over my shoulder.

"Some of them," I muttered. It seemed pointless to make introductions, so I didn't bother.

We've scouted the area, Tryn's wolf reported to Derric and the rest of us. *Their scents are old. No vamps have been here in months.*

"Should be an easy hand-off then," Derric said. "They're not trying to pull any tricks on us."

I bit back my growl. Nothing about this would be easy. Not by a long shot. Especially now that I knew Riley's scent intimately, had tasted her directly from her center and wished she could be on my tongue and in my nose every day. What the hell was I thinking last night?

It wasn't long before we heard the sound of motorcycles in the distance coming closer and saw several glowing red tail lights a few hundred yards away. Riley's breath sharpened and her fingers curled around the edges of my cut. It was all I could do to not turn tail and get her the fuck out of there.

"I count seven," Ruse said.

The wolves slunk in closer to our bikes, heads lowered and hackles raised at the approaching riders. It was just a precaution, but we weren't about to take any chances.

The leading motorcycle came to a stop roughly twenty feet away from us, flanked by three more bikes on either side. Unhelmeted, their faces were lit up by headlights and tail lights, making them look exactly like the monsters of nightmares.

Thorne, the Blood 'til Dawn president riding in front, smiled cruelly as he popped his kickstand and dismounted his bike. The vampire to his right, his VP, Fabian, followed suit while the others stayed on their rides. As the two leaders walked up to the space between us, I felt Riley tense and shrink away behind me.

"Nice to know you dogs can still fetch toys." Thorne stuck a dark cigarette between his lips and lit it, sucking in his cheeks before exhaling a cloud of blood red smoke.

Our wolves snarled and snapped their jaws in response, prompting chuckles from the vampire president and his VP.

"We don't want to be here any more than you do, Thorne," Derric said. "Don't give my wolves a reason to bite you, and we won't have any problems."

"Let's get this over with then." Fabian's lip curled, revealing his long fangs. "Where's my pet?"

Derric and Ruse turned to look at me. I returned their stare defiantly, barely holding back my own growl. *She's mine*, my instincts screamed. *They can't have her.*

"Enforcer." Red smoke wafted around Thorne's head, making him look like a demon with a morbid halo. "You've had your fun with my VP's toy. Time to give her back."

"Better not have had *too* much fun with her," Fabian growled.

It took all my strength to hold back from lunging at the vampire and tearing his throat out with my teeth. He had no claim, no fucking right to have her. Riley had only known fear and pain with him. With me, she found safety, comfort, pleasure. Why the fuck was this meeting even happening?

"Sawyer." Derric said my name with the sharp edge of a growl, the command clear. But I couldn't. Fuck no, I just couldn't.

While I stayed frozen, Riley initiated the descent from my bike seat, her arms sliding around me as she touched one foot to the ground and then the other.

"It's okay, Sawyer," she said in response to my choked-up silence. "I could never make you choose between me and your pack." She gave a tight smile as she stepped away from my bike. "Thank you again for everything."

By the fucking moon, I was physically trembling with the effort to hold myself back from snatching her to my chest and keeping her there. My throat was on the verge of exploding from everything I wanted to tell her, from wanting to tell Thorne and even Derric to shove this agreement so far up their asses that it would never see the light of day again.

"Oh, I almost forgot to give this back." Riley turned up the inside of her wrist and started picking at the knot of my flag still tied on like a bracelet.

I reached out to stop her, holding tight to her hand one more time. "Keep it," I said hoarsely. "To...remember me by."

Riley let her hands fall to her sides and the contact between us was broken. "How could I ever forget?" She smiled once more before turning toward the vampires.

I watched her go to them, frozen and struck dumb by how brave she was being. This was her worst nightmare come true, and she was handling it with all the grace and poise of, well, a wolf.

"There you are, pet," Fabian crooned as Riley approached. "I've missed you." The moment she was in reach, he snatched her arm and yanked her into his side. It looked painful, and she yelped as the momentum carried her until she pressed into him.

The growl left my throat before I even realized it, and Fabian met my eyes with a possessive glare. *He will never be worthy of her!* my wolf cried out.

"If that's all," Thorne remarked drolly, flicking ash from his cigarette. "I suppose we'll be on our way—"

"Wait," I snapped.

All heads turned to me as I got off my bike. My wolf rode hard beneath my skin, dying to claw his way out and slice these bloodsuckers to ribbons for mistreating *my* female, but I held him back. Barely.

"Sawyer." Derric hissed out my name in warning as I walked past him, not stopping until I stood toe-to-toe with our vampire enemies. Thorne's red smoke burned the inside of my nose and made my eyes water. It had to be some kind of powdered blood concoction he was smoking, but I tried not to think about it.

"Just a suggestion, but you might want to rethink your whole blood pet thing," I said, my stare level on Thorne's.

The vampire president's cheeks hollowed in as he took another drag on his cigarette, red smoke slowly releasing from his nostrils. "And might I suggest to you, werewolf, that you keep your nose out of my kind's business."

"See, when your blood pets run starving, malnourished, and terrified into our land, then it becomes *our* business," I replied. "If this keeps happening, it means *you've* got internal issues that need fixing. So do something about it." I bared my canines, which had lengthened to the point of being unable to close my mouth. "Or we'll fix it for you."

Thorne was the perfect image of calm, if even cold. The only sign of tension in him was a shortened inhale on his cigarette. "We'll keep our pets under control." He looked past me to Derric. "Given that you dogs stay on your side of the fence."

"We'll respect the agreement as long as you do," my president answered. "But if we smell one whiff of any werewolf blood pets, or any more escapees from your territory to ours, we will act accordingly."

"I would expect nothing less." Thorne pulled on his cigarette down to the filter before tossing it to the ground and crushing it under his boot. On *our* side of the borderline, of course. The disrespectful piece of shit. He smiled tauntingly, flashing bright fangs before backing away toward the bikes. "Always a pleasure, dogs."

I watched, utterly helpless, as the vampire VP pulled Riley to his bike, setting her on the seat first before climbing on himself. Her eyes locked onto mine over his shoulder until the last possible moment when the vampires turned the bikes around and drove off into the night.

I failed you, Riley. The words I said to her yesterday repeated like a haunted echo in my brain. I'd had over a full day to think of something, anything, to keep her safe. Hours upon hours in which I could have acted. Smuggled her away into the woods, done *something.* But I didn't, and now it was too late.

Those red tail lights grew smaller as they rode away, and I could only remain rooted to my spot. To cross the border and ride after them would be an act of war. It would undo the years of carefully protected peace we'd created in Vargmore and give those leeches the perfect opportunity to kidnap and feed from us again. It would ensure that the sacrifice of my parents, and countless others, had been in vain.

For Riley, I still wanted to say fuck it all and get her back anyway.

"Sawyer." Derric's bark of my name cut through the air like a knife once the vampires were gone.

"Yes, alpha," I said absently. My focus wasn't on him but on that empty dark space where Riley had been.

Derric must have known this, because he stepped directly in front of me and shoved roughly at my shoulder, forcing me back a step. We were of equal height but due to his age and status, he likely had the upper hand in strength.

He'd had to fight to become alpha of the pack, a bloody brawl that many wolves didn't survive. His place as our leader didn't come from inheritance or well-played politics. He proved himself by battling tooth and nail for it.

That had been before I'd joined the pack, but I wasn't enough of a fool to challenge him now. My head was all fucked up, and besides, his crown was not one that I coveted.

"You're stepping out of line, enforcer." Derric leaned in close, talking quietly even though we both knew all the nearby wolves could hear. "You don't provoke our enemies. You don't give them 'suggestions' on how they handle their business. You make sure our laws are followed, and carry out the consequences when they're not. That's it. What the fuck is wrong with you, Sawyer?"

I continued looking straight through him, not focusing on the squared-up, pissed-off male in front of me but on the image of Riley in my head. So brave and sweet. Giving herself over to the enemy because she didn't want me to make enemies in my own pack.

Well, look at me. Doing the damn thing anyway.

"Respectfully, alpha." I looked at Derric for the first time. "The question we should be asking is, what the fuck is wrong with us to be sending a victim of abuse back to her abusers?"

Derric's eyes narrowed, a low growl rumbling in his throat. "I know you're attached to the girl, Sawyer. Anyone with a nose can smell it. But you know what I can't get out of my head? That dead wolf pup on Shiloh's doorstep." He pulled back, examining me critically. "We're lucky it wasn't one of our own, but what if it was? You think the vampires took care to examine if it could shift into a human child?"

His voice had raised, practically echoing against the trees before he leaned in close to whisper to me again. "If it were one of our children, would you still choose a human woman over them? Do you want *that* death on your conscience, Sawyer? Because that's what it would have come to if we hadn't given her back. *Our* kind, slaughtered. Just like back in the old days."

"Everything you're saying," I shook my head, "is all the more reason we shouldn't have given her back. I agree they're that cruel, Derric. They're bloodthirsty enough to kill us, our animal brethren, humans, anything innocent with a heart. So why are we delivering innocents directly to them like free meals?"

Now Derric shook his head, turning away to head toward his bike. "This conversation is over but take this last piece to heart, enforcer. As alpha of this pack and protector of Vargmore, I have a lot of shitty decisions to make. Am I happy to send a human back to the vampires? No. But know this and fucking remember it." He stabbed a finger in my direction. "When it comes to choosing between werewolves and any other species, I will choose *us* every single time."

He gave me one last, hard look before finally turning his back to me. "And by the fucking moon, Sawyer, I hope you will too."

CHAPTER 16

RILEY

I held tightly onto Fabian's waist, only because of how quickly he took the turns winding through the woods. His body felt solid and strong, which meant he must have fed recently. The realization sent anger striking through me. Why the fuck did he want me back so badly if he had another blood source already?

The forest became more sparse as we headed toward the heart of vampire territory. Trees were more spaced apart and covered in spindly, near naked branches, as opposed to the dense boughs in the werewolves' homelands.

My heart held a fierce ache for Vargmore's beautiful forest. The wild, untamed beauty of it all felt like home, even though I'd only spent a matter of days there. I'd miss the fresh air in my nose, all the sounds of animals in the woods surrounding Sawyer's cabin. And of course, I'd never forget that wolf who opened his home to me. For a moment, I had the wild, thrilling thought that Sawyer might open his heart too.

But no, this turn of events was almost laughably predictable. I was back in the world of lies and manipulation that was as familiar as my own name. Sawyer hadn't wanted or intended to send me back to the vampires, and that alone was more kindness than I could have hoped for. The fact that he gave me food and shelter on top of that were enough blessings to last a lifetime. And last night, how he pleased me so thoroughly with his hands and mouth. For however long I had left to live, I knew I'd never feel such skilled, selfless touches from a man again.

Memories were my souvenirs of that brief, happy time. They'd stay with me forever, and I'd take them out to cherish that time whenever I needed it most.

Fabian slowed his motorcycle, and I lifted my head to see that the vampires had come to a stop at a crossroads. Thorne and the others were positioned to ride straight, but Fabian had angled his bike to turn left.

"I'll meet you back at the lair before dawn," Fabian said, his grip flexing on the handlebars.

Thorne didn't look especially pleased with that statement. He signaled the other vampires to continue onward. When it was just him, Fabian, and me, the Blood 'til Dawn president pulled back the sleeve of his leather jacket to examine his watch. "Dawn is in four hours."

"I know. I'll be quick."

"I thought you were weaning off that shit," Thorne grunted.

"I am," Fabian insisted. "This is just a quick errand for Des."

Thorne shifted his ruby gaze to me as he stuck a cigarette between his lips. "Want me to take your pet home? So nothing happens to her while you're out...doing your *errand*."

"No," Fabian growled. "She stays with me."

"She'll be safe with us."

"She's safest with *me*."

The argument was so absurd that I wanted to laugh. Like I was safe with either of them?

Thorne didn't continue arguing but lit his cigarette, his expression saying, *I'm not so sure about that,* as the red smoke exhaled from his nostrils. "Remember, you're my VP," he said finally. "You have a responsibility, not just to the club, but to me."

"I'm aware," Fabian shot back. "I told you, I'm just running an errand. This isn't like before."

"Right. Before," Thorne repeated, his tone dripping with skepticism. "A whole few days ago when your damn pet ran away."

"That won't happen again." The VP growled and flexed his wrists, making his bike engine rev loudly into the night air. "My head's on tight, Thorne. Seriously. You just have to trust me."

"I did." Thorne bared his fangs, wisps of red smoke curling around his teeth and lips. "I once trusted you with my life, Fabian. But you're slipping, and I don't like what I'm seeing."

The two of them talked like I didn't exist, and my gaze bounced back and forth between the two vampires like I was at a tennis match. I'd never seen my captor interact with his fellow club members before, and it was jarring to see them going at it like this.

Fabian was defensive, his posture stiffening the longer he argued with his president. Thorne looked frustrated, the conflict in his expression painfully clear. Fabian had fucked up somehow, presumably having to do with my escape, but I got the sense that it didn't begin or end there.

"You're my president and my best friend," Fabian said. "But you're not my babysitter. I don't have to check in with you everywhere I go, okay?"

"You're right," Thorne huffed. "So if I find out you're fucking me over again, it's not gonna be a slap on the wrist this time. There's going to be *real* consequences, you got that?"

"Loud and clear." Fabian brought his feet up, driving the bike onto the left fork in the road. "I'll see you before dawn," he called over the engine as he hit the gas on our new path.

In the mirror, Thorne's form became increasingly smaller as we drove away and headed somewhere completely unknown.

))))) ● ● ● (((((

FABIAN DROVE for a minimum of two hours, by my estimate. If my guess was in the right ballpark, we'd be cutting it extremely close to dawn by the time we returned to Blood 'til Dawn's lair. The sun might even rise before we got there, and then where would that leave us? If Fabian burned to a crisp, that was perfectly alright with me. I knew some vampires had daywalking abilities but wasn't sure how.

I kept silent as we rode, and Fabian didn't try to make conversation, not that I expected it. If he wasn't feeding from me or trying to make me feel worthless, I might as well not exist. At least that was nothing new. He'd never taken me out on his bike before, though. And certainly not on a long road trip away from his club's territory.

After a long stretch of nothing but the road and flat terrain, I saw tall formations on the horizon. At first I thought they were mountains, but the shape wasn't quite right. They were roughly shaped like columns, jutting straight up into the air with flat tops. I didn't get a sense of how truly big those formations were until we got closer. They loomed over us like giants. I wondered if this was how ants felt when they came across Stonehenge.

Light flickered atop several of those massive stone columns, like candles in the darkness. Only with how big the surface area had to be, those were probably bonfires rather than candles.

More light brought my gaze down to in front of us where a large fire roared in a clearing at the base of one of the stone formations. Fabian pulled up next to the fire and stopped, bringing his kickstand down but keeping his engine running.

The fire burned in a stone circle roughly the size of a car. The fuel in the center stretched tall over my head. All the branches and wood piled up in a neat pyramid was probably the equivalent of an adult oak tree. The heat was almost stifling, and I could feel myself starting to sweat under my clothes.

"What are we doing here?" I asked after a few minutes of Fabian just sitting on his bike near the fire.

"Nothing you need to be concerned about," he snapped. "Just running an errand like I told Thorne."

"Is it okay if I stretch my legs?"

"Fine. Just stay close."

Like I had anywhere to go. A memory of Sawyer hit my chest as I slid down from the bike. His home, his warmth and safety, felt so far away now.

I played with the flag still tied around my wrist as I walked a lap around the crackling fire. *I should burn it,* I thought. *Just toss it in the fire.* It was a morbid thought, one that came from a place of pain, even though my memories of him were good ones.

The fact was, thinking about him hurt, even though my return to Fabian wasn't his fault. Throwing his symbol of protection into a fire felt like a retaliation for all the promises that never came true. The thing was useless now anyway. He couldn't protect me anymore.

But I couldn't bring myself to do it. Across the fire, where Fabian couldn't see me, I held my wrist to my chest, pressing it right above my heart. Then, following a random impulse, I brought the flag to my nose and took a deep inhale.

God, I could smell Sawyer as clearly as if he was standing right next to me. That wild, fresh woodsy scent couldn't even be overpowered by the smoke and flame burning right in front of me. If I closed my eyes, I could even pretend the fire's heat was from his body, holding me in a tight, protective embrace. Some deep part of me wanted to cry out in some kind of mourning song, a howl. It felt like we'd lost something, even though there was barely anything to be had between us.

It wasn't healthy, wasn't going to help me get over him anytime soon, but I clasped my opposite hand over my covered wrist and held on tight, like I could trap Sawyer's scent in there forever. Holding onto him like this might not help me in the long run, but right then, it was a distraction from the hell that would surely come.

"Where the fuck are you?"

I started moving at the muttered curse, circling the fire back toward Fabian's bike, only to realize he was talking to himself and not to me. The vampire was restless, twitchy. He'd gotten off his bike and started pacing back and forth, looking up at the rocky formations that surrounded us. It seemed like he was waiting for someone and growing more impatient by the minute. I knew better than to ask questions and just stayed nearby.

In the distant horizon, I noticed the sky beginning to lighten from the almost black coverage of night to the deep, inky blue of pre-dawn light. The color of Sawyer's eyes.

Fuck, there would definitely be no getting over him soon. I pictured how dark and hungry his eyes had been, even when lit up from sunlight. I thought of the patch of silver hair near his temple and wished that I'd had more time to run my fingers through it.

One thing was abundantly clear, though. Fabian and I definitely weren't getting back to Sanguine before dawn.

A sudden gust of wind howled, whipping my hair around my face and sending a shower of sparks flying from the bonfire. With a curse, Fabian jumped out of range just in time. The gusts of air started coming rhythmically, like a giant fan waving over us.

"Fucking finally," Fabian muttered, looking skyward.

I followed his gaze and nearly screamed, but was too shocked to make a sound. A huge, winged creature the size of a pickup truck descended toward us. The beat of those wings were what had created the gusts of wind. It looked reptilian, covered in gold scales, with four legs that ended in fearsome claws and a tail that whipped around behind it. The creature had a long neck, a slender face with a headcrest and spikes that reminded me of an iguana or bearded dragon.

Wait...weren't dragons the other shifters in this world?

Holy shit. Was I staring at a motherfucking *dragon?*

It landed lightly for such a huge creature, using its wings to give a bit of lift and hover before touching those claws down. Eyes the color of melted gold stared at me as the creature transformed, its features becoming humanoid as it shrank down to the size of a man.

I recalled Sawyer mentioning dragon shifters and how I almost didn't believe him. There was nothing else this man could be. His shift stopped when he was more human than dragon, but those molten gold eyes remained, as did patches of scales on his neck, arms, and chest.

"Vampire," greeted the dragon shifter in a low, raspy voice, bending down as if to pick something up. Heat that had nothing to do with the fire hit my face at the realization that this man was naked and that he was putting on a pair of pants.

Of course. Sawyer mentioned that about shifting too. I swore I wasn't looking for it, but it also seemed like those gold dragon scales continued down onto his—

"You're late, Aran," Fabian bit out, his arms crossed as he approached the shifter.

"Mm, no. You're early." The dragon shifter finished buttoning and zipping up, flashing a smile that showed fangs rivaling a vampire's. "The sun has not even woken up to greet us yet. It's very early indeed."

"I need more dray before I go frolicking in the sun with you," Fabian said. "You got it?"

"You got payment?" the dragon shot back.

Fabian produced a piece of paper from his pocket. It wasn't folded to hide anything, but the writing on it only looked like nonsensical letters and numbers to me.

The dragon shifter took it and read the information, clicking his tongue a moment later. "These coordinates are awfully close to Vargmore. You sure this is good?"

"It's still within Sanguine's borders," Fabian said. "The boundaries are clear. That territory doesn't belong to the werewolves."

"Would your president agree?" When Fabian didn't answer, the dragon's mouth ticked up and he ran his tongue along the exposed fang. "Thorne doesn't know you're here, does he?"

"He does," Fabian insisted. "But as nice as it is to catch up with you, Aran, I do need to get my dray and head back."

"You haven't even introduced your guest." Golden eyes shifted toward me, that smile widening. "Greetings, little human."

Fabian stepped in front of me, blocking the other man's view. "You don't talk to her. Your business is with me."

"I was only being polite," the shifter drawled. "Something you vampires could stand to learn."

"Whatever. Do you have the stuff or not?"

The dragon ignored him, taking a deep inhale and then humming curiously. "How interesting. She's certainly human, but also smells a touch...wolfish?"

"She's my blood pet," Fabian snapped. "The wolves took her from me and I've just now gotten her back. Now, can you *please* give me what I came here for?"

With an annoyed huff and roll of his eyes, the other man reached into the back pocket of his jeans and tossed something at the vampire, who nearly missed catching it. "You junkies are no fun."

Fabian flinched at the statement but otherwise didn't comment as he held up his prize to the firelight. It was a small bottle with a squeeze dropper lid and liquid inside. He shook the bottle and held it up higher, where golden flecks shimmered and danced in the suspended liquid.

"Not that I'm complaining, but," Aran, the dragon shifter, rubbed his jaw, "you've been going through each supply faster than the previous one. Might want to pace yourself if you don't want Thorne catching on to your addiction."

"Mind your business, you big lizard," Fabian hissed as he twisted open the top of the bottle.

"I am. Supplying dray to you vampires *is* my business. It's one thing to be a wholesaler to your kind's retail operation. It's another thing entirely if the Blood 'til Dawn VP himself is making a sizable dent in the supply."

Fabian only ignored him as he leaned his head back and pointed the tip of that dropper directly at his left eye. He didn't even blink as he squeezed the top end, allowing a steady stream of the liquid to fall directly on his eyeball, then repeated the motion on the other eye.

"Jesus," Aran muttered. "It's worse than I thought. You're supposed to work up to three drops per eye, max."

"Unless you've been cheating me and making the solution weaker." Fabian still had his head tilted back, catching any excess liquid and rubbing it on his eyelashes like he didn't want to waste a milligram of the stuff. "Wouldn't put it past you to stretch out your profits like that."

"It's the same concentration as always," the dragon huffed. "You're just developing a hell of a tolerance, which is concerning." He shrugged, crossing his arms over his chest. "For you, anyway. As long as I'm getting paid, it's no scales off my back." The shifter winked at me and smirked, like we shared a private joke.

"I'm sorry, what is it?" I asked him, my curiosity getting the better of me.

"It's called draitrium, little human." Aran took a few steps toward me, which Fabian didn't seem to notice as he was still trying to absorb it all through his eyes. "It's a mineral found only here in the home of dragon shifters, the Shadowburn Cliffs."

"And you sell it to vampires, why?"

Aran cocked his head, his pupils narrowing to slits. "You're a blood pet and you don't know about draitrium? How odd." At my shrug, he carried on explaining without sounding judgmental, which I was grateful for. "In its purest form, and at a certain concentration, draitrium enables vampires to withstand daylight. Great for those who work shifts that cut it close to dawn or to have in case of an emergency, right?"

"Oh." A lot of things started to make sense in my head, dots connecting and pieces clicking into place.

"But it can become, well, habit-forming. And that, my little human," he nodded at Fabian, "is a full-blown dray addiction."

"What the fuck are you talking to my pet for, Aran?" Fabian hissed, finally straightening as he shoved the bottle in his jacket pocket. His normally-red eyes were different now, paler, like the color was draining out of them.

"Just stargazing while you're doing your thing over there," the dragon returned cheerfully. I was just showing her Zyrnas, the dragon god who guides all his children home." Aran moved to stand behind me and pointed to one of the few constellations still visible, his arm level with my eyes. "You see those six stars in an arc? That's his wing."

"Um, yes." I hadn't even noticed that the sky was brilliantly lit with stars. Since the sun was rising soon, this was probably only a fraction of its starry potential. But it was breathtaking, and the six bright stars Aran pointed out stood out clearly. I quickly scanned the dark expanse and realized I couldn't find any of the familiar constellations from the human world. What did that mean? Was Shyftworld on a different planet entirely?

"We are sun-worshipers, the dragon shifters," Aran said, his voice above and slightly behind my head. "We love heat and fire. Zyrnas watches over us at night, standing guard when it's dark and cold."

"I don't like you standing so close to my pet," Fabian growled, his fangs elongating and eyes taking on a sickly yellow color. "Back off, Aran."

The dragon shifter stepped away, and as he did so, whispered, "Zyrnas guards all beings who seek his protection. All one has to do is find him in the sky."

CHAPTER 17

SAWYER

I was distantly aware of riding up to Stout & Spirit, going through the front door, and shoving my way through the crowd to the bar. I might have shoulder-checked people, stepped on some toes, I didn't fucking know. It was like I was outside of my body, watching some other guy be a rude asshole.

Shiloh approached me, her movement slow and cautious as she likely sensed my mood.

"Let me get a pitcher of the IPA," I said before she could greet me. "Don't need a glass."

She jerked back, brow furrowing. "We don't do pitchers of that. The alcohol content is too high."

Trust me, it ain't fuckin' high enough.

"Can't make an exception for me?" I shouldn't have been pushing her. We were no longer an item, so I had no sway with her. She also had enough on her plate without a werewolf seeking to get obliterated as fast as possible.

Shiloh put her hands on her hips instead, not budging. "What's going on, Sawyer?"

"Riley's gone."

She blinked. "What do you mean, gone?"

"We gave her back to the vampires last night."

"What?" She planted her hands on the bar, leaning forward aggressively. "Sawyer, how could you do that to her?"

"Wasn't my call. It was Derric's."

"Oh my God, that poor girl."

"Yeah." My gaze shifted to the tap handles mounted behind the bar. "So, how about that pitcher?"

Shiloh sighed and rubbed her forehead. "Find somewhere to sit. I'll bring it over in a minute. Hell, I might even join you."

I wasn't going to say no to that. Misery sure as fuck loved company. "Thanks."

I pushed away from the bar, moving with a bit more awareness through the crowd toward a booth in the back. I slid behind the table and dropped my heft into the worn but comfortable seat. Without realizing it, I'd placed myself directly across from a couple, bantering and macking on each other like no one else existed.

They were a pair of newly mated werewolves, made evident from the fresh bite marks peeking out from under their shirt collars. There was so much touching, nuzzling, soft laughter from private jokes, and starry-eyed gazes full of the other person in front of them.

Normally I'd roll my eyes and thank the moon I didn't have a mate to be all up in my business. I could shift and run where I wanted, when I wanted. There was no one to hog my blankets or bed space. No one to fight me on my decisions like what to make for dinner, how strong to make the coffee, or what kind of cleaning products to use.

No one, no one, no one.

Those two simple words now felt like a cold, empty void instead of freedom like they usually did. Somehow, a lost little human had changed it all for me.

"This for you?"

I looked up to see Fallon, the Traveler, standing on the other side of my table with my pitcher of beer. "Shiloh just got a rush of customers, so she asked me to send it over to you."

"Yeah, thanks," I grunted out.

He set the pitcher down but didn't leave. Instead, he held on to the back of the chair on his side of the table. "Is this a pity party or cause for celebration?"

"Don't you have a mate to annoy?" I pulled the pitcher toward me, careful to not let the beer inside slosh around too much.

"She didn't feel like going out. Wanted some alone time."

"That's a thing, huh?" I tilted the pitcher carefully toward my mouth and took my first deep swallow.

"Yeah, it's great actually. We're still individuals, even when we're mated. Space and a little distance is healthier than being attached at the tail all the time." A dreamy expression, complete with a dopey smile, crossed his face. "I miss Aria when we're not together, but that's kind of the point. It makes seeing her again that much better."

"Well, aren't you quite the relationship expert now?" Damn, could I sound any more bitter? Whatever. I just needed to drink more.

Fallon's sharp eyes missed nothing though, and they narrowed shrewdly as his grip tightened on the chair. "You mind if I sit?"

I was mid-drink when he asked and waved my free hand in invitation. Even if I'd said no, I had a feeling he'd invite himself to sit anyway. Rumor had it that was exactly how he'd first started talking to his mate.

"So, what's going on, Sawyer?" The other wolf leaned back, his body language open. He and I were cordial but not particularly close. We'd never had a heart-to-heart about any serious topic before. He must've been bored without his mate around.

"You know what, Fallon? I envy you," I said, taking a breather from the pitcher.

"And why's that?"

"You're free from pack restrictions." I rubbed my palms together, hardly able to believe they'd been holding Riley, catching her tears, mere hours ago. "The alpha's decisions don't apply to you, and you can go wherever you want."

The Traveler's fingertips drummed on the table. "Derric did something you don't like, I take it?"

"He did something I find abhorrent," I admitted.

Fuck, I wasn't even drunk and my lips were loose enough to sink an entire navy's worth of ships. That wasn't like me. I kept to myself, kept things tight. But whether it was Shiloh to hear me out, or Fallon, or anyone else most likely, it seemed I was desperate to unload onto a listening ear.

I spilled everything while polishing off my pitcher of beer—from the moment I first saw a malnourished, terrified Riley in Shiloh's apartment, to moving her to my place, Derric's decision in the lodge and my being outvoted, to last night. The night we delivered her on a silver platter to the same predators who'd mistreated her.

"I'm really sorry," Fallon, who at some point had gotten a beer of his own, said. He sounded sincere, which I appreciated. "It seems like you grew fond of her," he hedged.

I nodded, the booze loosening me up even more. "We got close the night before I had to give her back. We spent the night together. It wasn't all-the-way sex, but...intimacy, you know? I wanted to make her feel good before sending her back to a nightmare. But shit, man, I didn't want to let her go at all."

"That's fucking hard." Fallon looked at me sympathetically from across the table. It was honestly a relief that he wasn't trying to give advice like, *Oh you'll find a hot new wolf and forget all about her one day,* or some bullshit like that. The guy was just listening, letting me vent. And I appreciated that from him.

"I still feel like a fucking dirt bag." I shook my head. "Even though I was all about her that night, it's such a dick move to mess around with someone when you know it'll be the last time you see them. I shouldn't have done it, but I wanted her so bad too. Just thinking with the wrong head."

"I'm sure she doesn't think of you like that," Fallon said. "Sounds like she was just as willing and eager to spend that time with you."

One particular memory stood out and pulled a wry smile to my lips. "You know what she was begging me for?"

Fallon smirked. "What?"

I wasn't one to spill private sexual details, but this, at least, wasn't too graphic. "To bite her."

The other wolf's eyebrows shot up. "Yeah?"

"Yeah, and she wanted to bite me too. It was wild. Hot. Especially coming from the mouth of a human." I lifted the pitcher before remembering it was empty and set it back down. "Shit, I almost forgot she was human. Had me thinking for a second she was one of our kind."

Fallon, who had been leaning back in his chair, suddenly pitched forward, all the humor gone from his face. "Did you want to bite her too?" He asked the question in a rush, with a serious edge that gave me pause.

"Um, yes." I stared at him, confused by the shift in his behavior. "But I never would. She'd been with vampires, for fuck's sake. Poor thing's already been traumatized to hell and back."

"But did you really, *really* want to? Like the urge to bite was instinctual, a *need*. Like the thought of it feels as good and right as, you know, sliding inside." Fallon was out of his chair now, leaning across the table toward me, eyes burning and his palms flat on the table.

"Yeah, it was all of that."

A prickling heat rushed over me as I remembered those moments on my couch. That pressing need to bite Riley, to mark and claim her, was so strong that it was honestly why I avoided kissing her neck. And with the full moon being so near, the timing of it all made it damn near unbearable. I didn't trust myself to *not* mark her. It was also a small part of why I went down on her. Aside from wanting to thoroughly taste and please her, I knew the need to be gentle on the most sensitive parts of her body would override the drive to mark her with my teeth.

"And did you want her to bite you just as badly?" Fallon pressed.

"I mean, yeah. Where the fuck is this coming from?" I leaned away, letting my head rest on the wall behind me, because he'd gotten really damn close.

The Traveler scratched his jaw, his eyes focused some-where else while the wheels in his brain turned. "Is it possible this woman is like Aria? A latent wolf."

I narrowed my eyes. "What are the odds of that?"

"I don't know. Pretty low, probably. But it's got to be possible, right?"

"Seems far-fetched, but I guess."

"That dead pup found here the other day. That was the vampires, right?"

"Word travels fast," I muttered. "Yeah."

Fallon splayed his hands on the table. "It would explain why they want her back so badly, why they would take a risk like that. If she's got werewolf ancestry, her blood must taste like a gourmet meal."

A growl left my throat before I could stop it. Riley's appeal as a blood pet to those insects was the last thing I needed on my mind.

But Fallon had a point.

And if she was a wolf, Derric's reason for sending her back was absolute bullshit. If she had been one of us from the start, he would have rallied all of Vargmore to keep her safe. If the vampires wanted a fight, he would have brought them one. But because she was fully human, she wasn't worth the effort, in his eyes.

But if she had a wolf lying dormant within her...

"How would we find out?" I asked.

Fallon brought his hands together and gave me a sorrowful look. "Aria and I found out by biting each other. I'm not sure if there's another way."

"Fuck."

"Yeah. Sorry, man." He cocked his head, as if another thought occurred to him. "Has she mentioned anything else besides the biting? A heightened sense of smell? She wants to howl, run through the woods, she feels there's another presence inside her; anything like that?"

I shook my head. "If she has, she never told me." Not that I blamed Riley. It was hard enough for her to open up about being homeless in the human world and the circumstances of her capture. And me being a closed-off prick probably didn't help.

"My theory is that being around other wolves is the trigger that starts waking up the latent wolf." Fallon gave me a hard look. "And those instincts come out especially strong when the wolf senses someone they want to mate with."

"I'd mate her in a heartbeat." The moment those words left my mouth, my wolf wanted to let out a victory howl because *finally,* my human side got with the program. "Fuck, doesn't matter if she *is* fully human. Riley is mine."

Fallon froze, his eyes widening. "What're you gonna do, Sawyer?"

"Tell me something." I laced my fingers together, resolve settling over me as a plan began to form. "Do you miss being part of the pack?"

The Traveler shrugged. "Sometimes. It's not in our nature to be solitary, you know? Before I met Aria, I had occasional thoughts of joining another pack or starting my own. Being on the road all the time, the days ending by myself, never being surrounded by the same people. It was all starting to get to me."

I saw where he was leading, and my heart jumped in anticipation. "And after you met her?"

That dreamy, dopey smile returned. "She's all I need.

It's hard to describe, but once you have your mate, abso-lutely nothing can top that."

Well that fucking settled it.

I slid out from the booth, taking my empty pitcher with me. "Thanks, Fallon. Good talking to you."

The other wolf whipped around in his chair. "Wait, Sawyer. What are you going to do?"

"Probably best if you don't know."

I headed for the bar, flipping through scenarios in my head on my way over. If Riley was a wolf, there was a chance I'd be able to stay in the pack. Derric would be pissed about my disobeying an order, but hopefully he'd be able to see the bigger picture of me saving one of our own.

And if she wasn't? Well, an exile would suck. No other pack in the region would want to take me on after hearing I'd been a traitor to Howling Death. But I'd have my mate...right?

I stopped dead with the realization that all of this was hinging on Riley *wanting* to be my mate, and that was a hell of an assumption. Wolf or not, she was completely new to this environment, to real freedom and new opportunities. If she was a wolf, being in a pack would be the healthiest thing for her. She'd need community and support, not an exiled mate.

Shit, no wonder I was so terrible at the relationship thing.

"Please don't tell me you want another one of those." Shiloh's voice cut through my spiral of thoughts, and she nodded at my empty beer pitcher.

"No." I set the thing down on the bar and resolved myself to focus. First and most important thing, I needed to get Riley out of vampire territory. Everything else would fall into place later. "I do need a favor, though. I'll owe you big time, but you know I'm good for it."

Shiloh's stare was unwavering as her hands came to her hips. "What kind of favor?"

"The kind you're best at," I said. "I need a magic spell."

CHAPTER 18

RILEY

Fabian and I returned to Sanguine long after dawn. The sun was bright in the sky as we rode into the vampire territory, and despite watching him take a megadose of draitrium, I secretly hoped he would burn to a crisp.

No such luck, though. But I was used to that.

The vampire city looked so odd in the daylight, desolate and abandoned. Except for the rumble of Fabian's motorcycle, it was completely silent and still. Not a single other soul was outside.

Most of the buildings were squat, single story brick structures. The few windows I saw were small and had thick curtains pulled over them. The place where Fabian had kept me all last year felt like a basement—no windows, and the only way out was up a flight of stairs. Now I got to wondering if the majority of the city was underground.

Fabian pulled up to one of the nondescript buildings, this one only made unique by a metal garage door on the left side. He pulled out his phone, tapped on an icon, and the garage door began to slowly lift.

As he waited for it to open, he turned in his seat and grabbed my chin in a rough hold. "I want to drink from you in the daylight, pet." He jerked my head to the side, exposing the blood vessels in my neck. "How will you taste when mixed with sunshine, I wonder? God, I can't wait to find out."

Fabian's eyes had gone fully yellow, like that of the dragon shifter we'd met, only duller and more unfocused. His pupils were like pinpricks, like his eyes knew how unnatural it was for him to be outside right now and they wanted to let in barely any amount of light at all.

I didn't respond, and he turned back around to drive forward once the garage door was fully raised. The sun revealed an entire fleet of motorcycles parked in the garage, and Fabian pulled into an empty spot. The walls were windowless and concrete, with one door on the far wall and a ramp leading down into a dark, unlit area I assumed to be the underground facilities of the Blood 'til Dawn clubhouse.

With another tap on his phone to close the garage door, Fabian wasted no time in jumping off his motorcycle and dragging me along with him by the hair. I hissed in pain, following along to ease the stinging in my scalp.

At least the werewolves are okay, I told myself. *Sawyer still has his pack. He'll be alright.*

The junkie vampire was pulling me toward the door at the far side of the garage, but someone beat him to it. I heard locks unlatch and then creaking as the heavy door swung open. "What the *fuck*, Fabian?" someone boomed from the other side, and it wasn't Thorne.

"Oh hey, Rhain." Fabian pulled up short, which allowed me to get a good eyeful of the hulking vampire in front of us.

The guy was muscled-out like a bodybuilder and stupidly tall, to the point where he had to duck under the door frame to step through. He also had classic vampire looks with long, straight black hair and a deeply angled face. He wasn't ugly, exactly, but erred on the side of too scary to be handsome.

"Don't '*oh hey*' me, you dumb fuck." Rhain flashed long canines, both in his upper and lower jaw. "What the fuck are you thinking opening the garage door in broad daylight? What if someone was in here?"

Fabian squared his shoulders, clenching his jaw. He was not a small guy by any means, but Rhain was a giant compared to him. "First of all, is that any way to talk to your VP? I could have you demoted, Rhain. Secondly, I knew nobody would be in here at this hour. So chill the fuck out."

The other vampire let out a menacing growl with a slow shake of his head. "You won't be VP for long at the rate you're going. How much dray did you take this time?"

"Mind your own business, asshole. I rode a long way to get my pet back from those flea-infested mutts. I had to take precautions, okay?"

"Right." Rhain's eyes, a deep shade of maroon, flicked toward me before returning to Fabian. "And if I ask Thorne, I'm sure he would say the same thing."

"He would," my captor insisted. "Now run along and tattle on me, since you're Thorne's bitch and all. By the way, does he know you're after my job?"

I couldn't decide if Fabian's bluffing was clever or stupid. Thorne clearly didn't approve of the draitrium usage, if what he'd said earlier in the night was any indicator. And when Rhain stalked off with a growl, fangs still bared, it was clear that not all was well under the Blood til Dawn roof.

It was eye-opening, to say the least. Over the past year of my captivity, Fabian was the only vampire I'd seen. Sometimes I could hear the other vampires in the club through the walls but never enough to get a sense of the relationships between them.

I mentally filed away that Thorne seemed near the end of his rope with his VP and that this Rhain guy seemed to flat-out despise him. Not that I expected either of those vampires to help me—they may have treated their own blood pets the same, or even worse. But if there ever came a time to leverage their frustration with Fabian's addiction, I would use it.

Once Rhain was gone, Fabian re-tightened his hold on my hair and dragged me inside. The room was dark, with only a single dim ceiling light to illuminate anything. It looked like some kind of man cave from what I could tell, with several couches, a bar, and a stripper pole in the center of the room.

Fabian took me to a couch against a far wall, where he flipped a switch. An electric whirring sounded, and light began to fill the room as a set of shutters began to fold into themselves, uncovering the window.

"Fuck yeah." Fabian blinked several times, squinting at the sunny window. "That's so damn good. My kind might be nocturnal, but if we could withstand daylight too? We'd be fucking unstoppable. I don't know why Thorne and that fucking meathead Rhain can't understand that."

He was talking to himself, clearly not looking for any

input from me as he stared out the window. He stayed like that for a while, to the point where I wondered if he'd spaced out and forgotten I was there.

I shifted slightly on the seat, just barely making a creak on the leather cushion, but that was enough to get his attention. Fabian's head snapped toward me with a hiss, and he grabbed my arm to pull me directly into the sunlight.

"Yes," he muttered to himself, pushing on my face to stretch my neck and expose the artery running up the side. My pulse raced and I knew he could smell it, hear it. "This is what I've been waiting for."

My eyes slammed shut as two points of burning pain hit my neck, and I screamed.

)))))●●(((((

I GROANED at the stiffness in my limbs, trying to roll over to a more comfortable position, but I barely had the strength to move. How long had I been here? Days? Weeks? Another year?

My head was beyond foggy. I could barely stay awake most of the time, and when I did, I was so disoriented, confused, and weak. Sometimes there was sunlight. Other times there was darkness. I had more chest pain than I ever remembered and knew my heart was constantly working in overdrive to pump blood throughout my body.

Fabian was keeping me thoroughly drained, even more so than before. He wanted to ensure I would never escape this time, so he opted to keep me barely alive.

Eventually, my heart would give out. My body would shut down. And then it would finally be over.

"Sawyer..." The name left my lips on a whisper, and I struggled to hold on to the memories of the wolf who'd saved me. My brain was just so exhausted. I remembered inky blue eyes that crinkled with laughter. Something about spinach and Popeye?

I tried to remember the best kisses I ever tasted, the reverent way he touched me and made my body feel, but I couldn't bring any of it forward. My body felt too numb, too cold.

Maybe he and Shiloh had gotten back together and they were happy. Or, if he had missed me at all, maybe some pretty female werewolf had been able to comfort him and help him forget all about me.

Our time together had been a gift, no matter how brief it had been. And every time my mind slipped into the dark void, not knowing if I'd come out again, I fought to hold on to what little I could of the werewolf I'd fallen in love with.

CHAPTER 19

SAWYER

F our weeks.

It took four fucking weeks for Shiloh to concoct a potion that would make me invisible as well as cover my scent trail. She was a damn good alchemist but had never attempted something like this before. There were countless dud mixtures that did nothing, ingredients that wouldn't react together correctly, and side effects that were too risky by her standards.

It was four long weeks of testing, measuring, experimenting, swapping ingredients in and out of various proportions and so on. But moon bless her, she did it. And that woman worked tirelessly, pouring over ancient tomes and consulting other witches to get it done. All so I could get Riley back.

Shiloh was going to be an incredible partner to some lucky male one day. And if the bastard mistreated her, I'd be the first in line to tear him a new one.

The full moon had come and gone, and now the next one approached in roughly three days. Even during the forced shift of the last full moon, when I went on the night run with the pack, my wolf felt like a shadow of himself. The time apart from Riley hadn't eased anything, but instead had made missing her unbearable. She was our mate, even if the bites hadn't been exchanged yet.

I did what I could to help Shiloh over the past four weeks. Mixing the potion when she was exhausted, running all over the territory to gather the ingredients she needed, but it never felt like enough. It never would be enough until Riley was safe with me again.

Naturally, I didn't breathe a word of it to anyone in the pack. Fallon offered to come with me before Derric with the theory of Riley being a latent wolf, but I nixed that idea. Better to ask for forgiveness than permission, I figured. And forgiveness was more likely after we already had proven she was a wolf.

If she was one.

Moonlight prickled over my bare shoulders as I stood at the border between Vargmore and Sanguine—the exact same place we gave Riley back to the vampires. Dawn would be approaching in a few hours, which would help in addition to the invisibility spell. There were rumors of more vampires abusing draitrium lately, but even if there were daywalkers around, they'd likely be too stoned to notice anything unusual.

I pulled the slender glass bottle from the back pocket of my jeans and stared at it for a moment, my throat already closing up in anticipation.

Since the potion was custom-tailored to my height and weight, and made with ingredients that wouldn't interfere with the moon magic that fueled my shifting, I had been the sole guinea pig for every single version.

Some of the early concoctions had been truly awful. In one of them, it turned out I'd been allergic to one of the herbs and had broken out in a stinging rash. Shiloh insisted on swapping it out for something else, and I relented after she said I could possibly pass the rash on to Riley. I was willing to tough it out but to make her suffer even more? Absolutely not.

Most of the time though, the potions just tasted awful. And the final winner was the worst of them all.

The container was roughly the size of a hot sauce bottle, and the potion inside could have passed for salsa verde. Too bad it was anything but. I'd happily drink hot sauce over this shit.

With a sharp inhale to steel myself, I unscrewed the cap and dumped the potion down my throat on an exhale through my nose. Once that breath finished, I pinched my nose shut, desperate to not gag and waste any of the stuff that would get me in and out of Sanguine undetected.

Once the potion hit my stomach, the effects began immediately. When I looked at the now-empty bottle, my hand and forearm were partially transparent. I wiggled my fingers in fascination, watching the muscles and tendons under my skin move before they slowly faded away.

I waited until the potion completed its work before shifting. It was trippy as fuck to feel my four paws on the ground but only saw a slightly distortion in the air when I looked down. After a quick check behind me to make sure I was invisible from nose to tail, I took off running. The border magic barely registered over my fur, I was that much of a single mind.

I had six hours to find Riley and get her out. If I ran at top speed, it would take me two hours to reach the Blood 'til Dawn clubhouse. If Fabian was keeping her somewhere else and I ran out of time? The potion would wear off and I was fucked.

The thought of what kind of shape she may be in after four weeks only pushed me harder, sending my invisible paws flying faster over the ground. I only hoped it wasn't too late.

)))))◗◖((((((

Dawn was just breaking over the sky as I came upon Sanguine's central city, which was Blood 'til Dawn's home-base. And it was a fucking ghost town.

Only a handful of humans milled about—locking doors, pulling blackout shades over windows, closing up shop for the day. I guess when the species in charge was solidly nocturnal, everyone else followed suit. One dragon shifter woman hugged a human goodbye, smiled and waved as she walked away, then shifted and took to the air. Heading home to Shadowburn Cliffs, no doubt.

I slunk along the sides of buildings and cars, making sure the coast was clear before moving. Even though no one could see or scent me, I didn't want to be reckless. As the sun rose, I stuck to the long shadows cast on the ground, and put my nose to work.

Vampires all smelled the same to me, like dirt and blood with little variation, and I couldn't catch much else. The occasional human or dragon, sure. But none of the human scents stood out to me as Riley's.

I had expected that. It had been four weeks, after all.

But I held out hope that I'd pick her up closer to the clubhouse. I'd never seen the building in person before, having never gone this deep into vampire territory, but we had maps of Sanguine, so I knew the general vicinity. And it was impossible to miss once I spotted it.

One of the largest of the squat, square buildings with a roll-up garage door on one side. That could only be the place.

A new scent hit my nose as I pressed myself to the shadowed wall, something metallic but not blood. It had a spicy, gingery quality to it too, growing so strong it made my eyes water as I approached a door.

Draitrium, I realized.

If I was smelling dray this strongly, one of Thorne's men was so hooked on it that the stuff was seeping out of his pores. That was surprising, considering we'd heard Thorne didn't tolerate its use within his club. Allegedly, he hated the stuff and only allowed the sale of it in Sanguine at all because it propped up the economy.

I turned away from the door, holding back a sneeze as I circled the building in the opposite direction. The door would certainly be locked, and no vampire in their right mind would answer a knock at sunrise.

A vampire high on dray might, though.

I filed that information away as I checked out the perimeter of the building. A frustrated huff left my mouth as I picked up nothing of Riley's scent. Of course the building would be locked up tight during the day. And if she was kept prisoner, never allowed to go outside, it only made sense there wouldn't be a trace of her around the building.

That was if Fabian even stayed at the clubhouse. For all I knew, he had his own place, like me, and kept Riley there.

Damn it, I was running out of time.

I circled the concrete building a few more times, trying to pick up anything, trying to decide if I should stay here or find another place to check out. Backup would have been great on a mission like this, but there was no way I could drag any of my packmates into this mess. Hell, just by my being here, they probably weren't going to be my pack-mates any longer.

Where are you, Riley? I projected the thought in despair. If she was a wolf, she could hear me and answer. If she was still alive, that was.

No, don't think about that. I shook out my entire body from head to tail. Fabian wouldn't go through the trouble of getting her back just to kill her. A blood pet was only useful as long as they had a heartbeat.

Soft whines started to leave my throat as I circled the building again and again. Panic and desperation started riding my wolf instincts. Time was slipping away, and I had no way in, no plan. I could potentially wait until nightfall when everything opened up, but I wouldn't have the advantage of invisibility then.

Not to mention, even if I succeeded in getting her out after dark, the vampires would ride after me once they figured out she was missing. As strong and fast as I was, one wolf was no match for a fleet of motorcycles.

I circled the building once more, this time with my nose pointed up, looking for any potential weaknesses in the tiny, reinforced windows. They were ten feet off the ground and almost certainly made of the strongest, thickest glass available. Likely tempered by the vampires' buddies, the dragon shifters.

One window made me pause to stare at it. The pane itself was impenetrable, but at a certain angle, it looked like the inside curtain was slightly askew.

That tiny spark of hope sent my tail wagging as I lifted up, placing my forepaws on the concrete wall to judge the distance from the ground. It was high, yeah, but just maybe...

With renewed determination, I turned and trotted to about thirty feet away from the wall, then turned to face it again. After only a second to hone in on my target, I broke into a run. My eyes stayed locked on that window as I built up speed and momentum, heading straight for that wall. At the last possible second, I didn't slow down but directed energy to my back legs and jumped straight up.

I ran vertically. Two beats of paws up the wall, and I was eye-level with the window. I hovered there for a second, at the crest of my momentum before gravity pulled me back down. And fuck yeah, I saw through a tiny crack in the curtain.

In the split-second I had to look through the glass, I saw the knob of a closed door inside, and some sense of *knowing* hit me before I even touched the ground. Riley was in there. My *mate* was in there.

I ran around to the opposite side of the building, remembering something I'd seen but hadn't registered in my mind until now. The ground sloped downward on this side, partially exposing the underground level of the structure. And there had been...yes, there it was!

A grate covering some kind of air duct.

It was way too fucking small for me to fit, but what other choice did I have?

I shifted to human so I could try to loosen the screws with my hands. Thank fuck the invisibility spell was holding up fine and no one got an eyeful of naked dude trying to break into a building.

The screw heads weren't budging, however, since they'd likely been settled in place for decades, if not longer. So I pulled back, balancing on my hands and bare ass as I brought my foot up and aimed a kick at the grate.

It took several tries, and my foot hurt like a bitch, but the thing finally gave way. I set the now bent-up metal scraps aside and stuck my head through the hole.

"By the fucking moon," I cursed under my breath.

It was actually a crawl space layer between the two floors. I felt claustrophobic just looking at the narrow space, and it was filthy, with dust and exhaust hoses every-where, but goddamn, I just might be able to get to Riley.

Definitely not as a human through. My shoulders couldn't even make it through the opening. But my wolf, although big, was a sleeker, more streamlined shape.

I shifted back to my animal form, put my front paws together, pulled my ears back, and started crawling forward on my belly.

CHAPTER 20
SAWYER

Claustrophobic was the fucking understatement of the year.

In my wolf form, I squeezed through the hole in the side of the building, barely. And now the floor and ceiling of the crawl space pressed constantly into the fur of my back and belly. The air was stuffy and years' worth of dust irritated my nose.

I hated every second of it, but I knew it didn't hold a candle to Riley's suffering. So I soldiered on, dragging myself toward the general direction of the door I saw through the window.

My movements were agonizingly slow, impeded by the lack of space for my four legs and the simple breadth of my body. I could barely take a full breath with the crawl space pressing in on me.

Don't think about this place collapsing. Just don't go there.

Wolves were instinctively not okay with tight spaces. Places like this crawl space were against our nature in every way. We cherished open spaces and fresh air, miles in every direction to hunt and run. Right then, my sense of self-preservation was telling me to turn tail and get the hell out, but the drive to find my mate kept me going.

It didn't matter if it took me days, weeks, or months. I was not leaving this territory without her.

It felt like I'd been down here for hours and had only crawled forward a few feet, when the tiniest echo of a familiar scent hit my nose. Fresh wildflowers and spring rain.

I'd barely caught it, but it was enough to send my tail thumping. My throat choked with the need to let loose a howl, but I had a sinking feeling my mate wouldn't have been able to answer me.

I pressed on, inching forward on my belly and paws, jutting my nose forward and trying to pick up that lovely scent amidst all the dust and vampire clogging up my senses.

After what seemed like an eternity later, I got a whiff of her again. Slightly stronger this time, and I knew it wasn't the sheer will of my imagination hoping she was here. My mate *was* here.

Riley! I'm coming, Riley. Hold on.

Inch by inch I crawled, my legs starting to cramp and strain from how little I could move. I ignored it all and pressed onward, for her.

I stopped at an air duct attached to a vent in the floor of the crawlspace, which meant I had to be in the ceiling of the floor below. Faint as it was, her scent was strongest here. She had to be in the room directly beneath me.

Shifting to my human form was a no-go here, so I had to remove the duct with my teeth and paws. Tearing away the flexible hose was easy enough, the hard part would be taking off the grate underneath.

I looked through the slender holes of the air vent just to see what I was dealing with, and just about lost my shit.

There she was, pale and unmoving on a mattress against the wall, with only a thin sheet to cover her. If she was breathing, it was weak enough that her chest barely moved.

Riley! I screamed in my head, pawing furiously at the metal grate. *Riley!*

The barrier needed to be pushed or punched free, and that would be noisy, but I had no other choice. Pawing at the thing for several minutes was no use, not even when I put all of my animal weight onto it. I needed human dexterity for this.

I stared at where my paw was, only to see nothing. Fuck. Being invisible would only make this extra difficult.

Partial shifting with control was a lot like wiggling your ears or folding your tongue. Some people had a natural talent for it, others couldn't do it at all, and some could get close with lots of practice.

As a pup, I'd been a natural. I'd clowned around by running on all fours while keeping my human hands and feet. Or I'd be in human form with only my wolf's head and tail. It annoyed the adults and cracked up the other kids. But I hadn't done anything like that in decades.

Hand, arm, and shoulder, I thought. *All I need is a hand, arm, and shoulder.*

If the rest of me went human, I could very well fall through the ceiling and alert the vampires, or worse, injure Riley. Or if the crawlspace held, I would be truly stuck and unable to breathe.

Closing my eyes, I pictured my right paw, which would become my dominant hand, and willed the moon's magic to only that area of my body. *I don't need much. Only enough to save my mate.*

The digits of my wolf paw elongated into fingers, but I still wiggled them just to make sure. I fought to not lose focus while the shift continued to my wrist and forearm, then traveled slowly up my bicep.

Just a little more, I willed. *I need my shoulder to punch through this fucking thing.*

I felt the change through my shoulder joint, and then I abruptly stopped the shift, panting hard through my wolf's mouth. Because I didn't have sight to go on, I tested my range of my motion, first rotating my shoulder, then bending my elbow and rolling my wrist.

Holy fuck, I did it.

It felt so damn weird. A human arm was not meant to be attached to a wolf's body in any configuration, but it would serve my purpose.

I balled my fingers into my palm, deciding to hit the grate with the side of my fist because of the limited movement I had.

Again and again, I hit the damn thing, focusing on the corners where I knew the screws kept it in place. Every once in a while I paused to listen, just to see if any of the vampires had roused. It was broad daylight now, and most of them had to be in deep sleep. Even so, that draitrium I smelled earlier meant someone might still be up.

One of the corners finally started to budge, and I let out a bark of victory, almost losing my partial shift. It was the work of a few moments to loosen up the grate enough so that one firm hit to the center sent it crashing down to the floor.

Despite every cell in my body dying to jump through and see to her, I paused, ears pricked and alert for any sound of movement in the clubhouse. When none came, and I could no longer stand it, my arm shifted back to a wolf's foreleg and I started to wiggle my canine body through the opening.

It wasn't badass like an action movie, or even graceful, by any means. If Riley had been awake and able to see me, I was certain she'd be laughing her ass off at this wolf squirming like a caterpillar through a hole in the ceiling until he plopped onto the floor. But all that mattered was that I'd made it through. I'd reached her.

In one long stride, I was next to Riley, my front paws on that piece-of-shit mattress as I sniffed all over her to assess what was wrong.

Her color was completely gone, her skin not so much pale as it was gray. She smelled strongly of vampire and draitrium, which worried me. Had they been giving it to her? What kind of effect did it have on humans? She did have clothes on, thank the moon. I was in a mood to massacre this whole club if there was any sign of sexual assault on her.

I shifted to human. She still couldn't see me, but I needed to know if she could respond to my voice.

"Riley?" I touched her cheek, smoothing back her hair which had gone dull and limp. "Riley, it's Sawyer. Can you hear me?"

"...Sawyer?"

Her head turned in the direction of my voice, and while I was overjoyed she still had life in her, the mess of bite marks on her neck made me see red. The wounds were open, which had to be intentional. If they wanted to, vampires could close up bites on their prey to prevent them from bleeding out.

"Fuck! My sweet mate, what did they do to you?" I smoothed a hand over her forehead. Her skin felt too cold, too thin. She needed nutrients and care. The red, inflamed skin around the bites concerned me too. I'd bet my hide they were infected.

"...miss you, Sawyer..." Riley's fingers stretched out, as if she was reaching for me.

I clasped those cold fingers in my hand and kissed them, rubbing the icy digits in an attempt to bring warmth back into them, but she needed so much more.

"I'm here, Riley. I'm getting you out." I pressed her palm against the side of my neck as I looked around the small room. There was no way she was coming up the crawl space with me, so I had to figure out the best way to get her through the door.

Her eyelids fluttered once before settling closed again. "...it's like you're really here..." she mumbled.

Of course, she couldn't see me. She probably wouldn't be lucid enough to realize what was happening until I got her home and the invisibility potion had worn off. I just hoped her condition didn't take a turn for the worse before she was safe.

Come on, you meathead. Think of something.

I could just carry her out, but would be much slower in human form. Not to mention, the potion would wear off well before I reached Vargmore, and that was trouble I could not afford. Wolf form would be better, but I didn't trust that she had the strength to hold onto me while I ran.

The bundled sheets on the mattress gave me an idea, though it was still risky. While vampires' sense of smell wasn't as keen as ours, they'd be able to follow a scent trail if it was familiar enough to them. And Riley's scent was all over that sheet.

Fuck it. What else was there?

I pulled the sheet out from under Riley, who seemed to have fallen asleep. With a loud *rrrrip*, I tore the sheet in half until I had two pieces. While rolling up the two sheets into thick ropes, I kept frantically checking her pulse and listening for her breathing. She was so pale and still that it was fucking scaring me.

Once I had my sheet ropes, I brought Riley's wrists together, pausing for a moment when I saw my flag still wrapped around the left one. The thing was tattered and bloodstained, like she'd never taken it off in the four weeks she'd been here.

I'd tell her all about how much that meant to me when she was safe at home with me. But now I had to do something mildly questionable to get her out.

I wound the length of the bed sheet around her wrists and tied them together.

"Sorry about this," I murmured as I took hold of her shoulders as gently as I could to sit her up. Then I kneeled in front of the bed, turned to face away from her, and brought her arms around my neck until her bound wrists rested at my throat.

Reaching behind me, I carefully maneuvered her legs until they extended on either side of my waist, and used the other sheet to tie her ankles together in front of my stomach. Once Riley was secure in her bound piggyback as I could make her, I shifted and landed as lightly as I could on all fours. Her weight was slight on my back, and thankfully she didn't slide around to my stomach. I could only hope she stayed put while I ran like hell out of this place.

Returning to my human form, I double-checked the ties at her wrists and ankles before testing the doorknob. Locked but not otherwise reinforced. It was the work of a moment to yank the thing free, and then I was poking my head out into the room beyond and nearly gagged. The smells of vampire and draitrium were near toxic levels to my senses.

Across the room was the window with the askew curtain, letting a sliver of sunlight into the otherwise pitch-black room. I froze in the doorway, because what I had failed to see from outside was the vampire slumped on the couch directly under the window.

Fabian was passed out cold, his face directly under the sunlight that was usually forbidden to his kind. A red mark crossed his face, one that looked like a bad sunburn, which was still nothing compared to the immediate burning of flesh that vampires usually experienced when exposed to sunlight.

A growl left my throat before I could stop it. So the piece of shit who abused Riley was also the club's draitrium addict. My teeth sharpened, and I felt my claws lengthen at the end of my hands.

It would be so easy to kill him right now, a simple tearing of his throat would do it. Let him see what it felt like to be drained of blood. Vampires weren't undead, contrary to the old human myths. They could die and be killed like anything else.

But this vampire, right now, was so fucking pathetic. Passed out and drugged up, he wouldn't be a worthy kill. I'd get no satisfaction from ending his life in this state. No, I'd want him fighting and conscious. I'd want him fully aware that I was ending his life and avenging someone he treated so poorly. I'd want to see that awareness as the life left his eyes.

A waste of space like Fabian wasn't worth the energy and certainly not worth letting go of my precious cargo to deal with.

Besides, how humiliating would it be to have lost his blood pet a second time? How would it make Blood 'til Death look to the entire vampire population? Or even all of Shyftworld? Knowing this pathetic leech would be shamed and forced into a hole of humiliation for the rest of his life was almost more satisfying than killing him would be.

Fabian's eyes snapped open.

"Oh fuck." He sat up abruptly and rubbed his eyes. "What a trip. Never seen shit like this before."

That was our cue to leave. He was seeing Riley suspended in some weird position midair and hopefully believed himself to be hallucinating from the draitrium. I went for the front door, yanked it wide open to let daylight fill the dark cavern, then shifted to all fours and hauled ass.

Distantly I heard Fabian bitching about the sunlight, but fuck him. If some other vampires got burned to ash before he could find his ass from his elbows, good riddance.

I ran so fast, my invisible body created dust clouds. My heart pounded with anticipation, adrenaline. I was ready for a fight if it came for me. But the town remained as sleepy as ever. Only the wind rushed over my ears, not the sounds of motorcycles on my heels.

Hold on, Riley, I prayed.

Her head hung to the side, leaning against my shoulder

blade as I ran, arms and legs pulling at me with each long stride hitting the ground, but her restraints seemed to be holding. And damn, it felt so good to be out of a confined space. But I couldn't celebrate yet. Not until we both crossed that border into Vargmore.

Oh, what have we here?

The telepathic voice rocked me so hard that I stumbled. It felt like getting punched in the side of the head, and the momentum sent Riley sliding up my body. Her arms nearly slipped up and free of my neck, but I grabbed her bound wrists in a light hold between my jaws and settled her back into place.

Once she was righted, I circled around, snarling, in search of who had spoken. Only shifters could speak tele-pathically, and that definitely wasn't a wolf. That meant it could only be...

Something blocked out the sun, casting a large shadow over the ground. Two long wings spread out to the sides, catching the air like sails as they swept forward in a leisurely, rhythmic beat.

My fur stood on end, hackles raised as my lips pulled back from my teeth in a growl. *This doesn't concern you, Aran,* I said to the hovering dragon shifter. *Leave us be.*

I didn't realize I was preventing you from going anywhere, wolf. His reptilian jaws opened with an amused huff of breath from which a small fireball emerged.

He was maybe fifty feet in the air, and I could still feel the heat of that fire singe the tips of my fur. This creature only had to breathe and Riley and I were fucked. Wolves and dragons had no personal beef with each other. We probably shared an ancestor, considering we were both shifters. But centuries ago, the dragons chose to align themselves with the vampires, likely because of what they could gain from selling draitrium, which could only be mined in their territory. And that alliance automatically made them our enemy.

Cool invisibility spell, by the way, Aran drawled. *Too bad it's starting to wear off. Nice intestines you've got there.*

I looked down and sure enough, the bones of my paws were becoming clearer by the second, as were the blood vessels, muscle, and other tissue between them. Shit, I could not afford to waste another moment of time in enemy territory.

This human on my back is my mate, Aran, I said in a rush. *I know how protective you dragons are of your females. She may have belonged to your allies originally, but they've mistreated her. Just look at the shape she's in.*

Yes, I have eyes, wolf, Aran mused. *And I had the pleasure of meeting the little human weeks ago.*

You did? It hit me a moment later. *When Fabian bought draitrium from you.*

Yes. I had half a mind to steal her from that idiot myself. Certainly would have been easier than sneaking in with an invisibility spell. But that wouldn't have been very smart of me, would it?

I had to tread carefully. Dragons were fickle creatures, and there was an equal chance that Aran was leading me into a false sense of security as there was that he truly sympathized with me.

She's lost a lot of blood, and her wounds are infected, I said. *I need to get her home as quickly as possible, or I'll lose her. If you let me pass...I won't forget this, Aran. I'll be in debt to you.*

Hmm.

The dragon landed gently from his hovered position

and stalked toward me on those four scaly legs. He was a sight to behold, a creature of myth covered in golden scales, horns, spikes, not to mention those wings now folded on his back. I fought not to raise my hackles again as he approached. I didn't want him anywhere near Riley.

A debt to a dragon cannot be promised in words, Aran informed me smoothly. *We need tangible proof of purchase. A receipt, if you will.*

Anything, I answered. *As long as I can take her home.*

Give me your paw, werewolf.

I lifted my—now fully visible—left front paw as though offering to shake. Aran moved faster than I could blink, scoring the top of my paw with a long black claw. It burned like a brand, the pain so sudden and blinding that I let out a short howl of pain.

The wound immediately darkened and blistered to a raised black stripe, but it did not bleed. If anything, it looked as though Aran *had* branded me. As if his claws burned just as hot as the fire he breathed.

When I call on you for payment, werewolf, he snarled as he took to the sky. *You will not hesitate. You will not refuse. You will come when I call.*

He flew higher and higher, beating those great wings until he was a speck in the sky. I didn't have time to think about the consequences of the deal I'd just made, and frankly, I didn't care.

With a sore paw and my dying mate on my back, I ran home.

CHAPTER 21

RILEY

t was torture, waking up from the most delicious dreams about Sawyer. His low, rough voice saying my name so close to my ear. The warmth and weight of his hands had felt so real. I swore I even heard him crack a joke about putting a bunch of spinach in a soup for me. The absolute last thing I wanted to do was wake up on the mattress in this tiny room with Fabian's blank yellow eyes staring at me from the doorway, waiting to drink from me until I passed out again.

I wasn't sure how much longer I could last.

Before my lids cracked open, I realized I was warmer than usual, practically sweating. Usually, I was never able to get warm enough. Shoving back the sheet, I stretched my arms above my head but kept my eyelids closed, focused on the fantasy of my werewolf behind them.

I felt...alive.

Sleepy and stiff, for sure. But I felt more energetic now than in seemingly forever.

"Sawyer, she's waking up."

The sound of a female voice got my eyelids working, and a soft groan left my mouth as I started to let the world in. Sunlight. Windows. An open space with high ceilings and dark wooden beams.

Wait, what?

I shot up in a panic, only to find myself faced with the same man I'd been dreaming about. Sawyer stared at me from where he knelt by the couch, inky blue eyes sharp and watchful. A beam of sunlight hit directly on the patch of white hair at his temple.

The werewolf gave me an easy, pleased smile. "Hey, sweetness. We've got to stop meeting like this."

I opened my mouth, but my voice wasn't getting with the program, so I could only whisper what I desperately needed to know. "Are you real?"

His smile faded as he reached for my hand, capturing the whole thing between the warm embrace of his palms. "All of this is real, Riley. We got you out. You're safe, and you're never going back there."

The relief and joy shuddered out of me in an ugly sob as I threw my arms around Sawyer's neck. How long had I been there? He seemed so much bigger. Or maybe I was just smaller. His palms ran over my back and I felt his fingers trace the edges of my ribs and spine. Jesus, I had felt so close to death for *so* long. Maybe I had finally died and this was heaven.

But no, my wolf was warm and solid as he held me. And holy shit, he smelled *amazing*. Despite having literally just woken up and likely in need of water and food, I wanted to wrap my legs around his hips and grind against him. I wanted to bite his throat, listen to his grunts and growls as he—

"Riley." Sawyer pulled away, physically removing my arms from his neck with an intense expression. Something inside me howled with hurt at the rejection. "There's a lot we need to talk about. But eat something first. You've been in and out of consciousness for three days."

"Three days?" I echoed. So those hazy visions of his voice and hands may not have been dreams after all. "How long was I with the vampires this time?"

Sawyer's face hardened before he answered. "Four weeks."

Was that all? It felt like I had been there for years.

"I'm sorry I couldn't come sooner." Sawyer's palms tightened around mine. "I wanted you back the moment I saw you get on that bastard's bike."

"Your pack," I blurted out as more memories flooded my brain. "Did you convince them to take me back? Was that why it took several weeks?"

Sawyer pulled in a deep breath, his thumbs rubbing the backs of my palms. "That's part of what I need to talk to you about. But first, food. Anything you're craving?"

His non-answer and change of subject made me worry. "Sawyer, you…you didn't go against your alpha's orders to get me, right?"

He tried to shoot me another easy smile, but his mouth was full of tension. "There's a lot that's happened, but the important thing is that you're here and safe. And Riley." His eyes became sharply focused again. "I will not break a promise to you again. I swear on my ancestors, no vampire will ever touch you again and live to speak of it."

Sawyer pulled away and stood. As his hands fell to his sides, I noticed a long, dark scar on the back of his palm that hadn't been there before.

"Shiloh and I have been spoon-feeding you broth for the last three days." He placed his hands on his hips, taking no apparent notice of the scar. "You should probably have some solid food now that you're lucid. Want to try an omelet?"

"Um, sure. Thank you." I ran a hand through my hair and realized how limp and oily it felt. "I think I'll take a quick shower."

"Of course." Sawyer held out a hand, and I accepted the help off the couch. Before I could react, he brushed my cheek with his knuckles and leaned down to kiss my forehead. "Don't worry about anything," he said softly. "It's all going to work out."

Immediately, his scent invaded my nostrils and hit my brain like the most addictive drug imaginable. I wanted to grab the front of his shirt and pull him down for a proper kiss, then climb him like a tree until I settled into the perfect position. My core pulsed with a hot, greedy ache. It was near painful to not have him between my legs.

Fighting every instinct screaming at me, I stepped away from him with what I hoped was a smile, even though it felt like a grimace. Once further away, I could think a little more clearly.

Shower. I needed a shower. I needed Sawyer to fuck me against the shower wall. Nope, shut up. Just a good old-fashioned shower. That was it.

I found my way to the bathroom of the guest room I'd stayed in before and turned on the hot water. Despite what Sawyer had said, my stomach churned with anxiety as I waited for the spray to heat up.

There was plenty to worry about. I heard it in everything he avoided saying to me.

And I had a sinking feeling this was only the start of it.

)))) ❱ ❱ ◗ ● ◖ ❰ ❰ (((

AFTER A LONG SHOWER, I somehow wolfed down a three-egg omelet. Sawyer didn't fill it with much, in order to not upset my stomach, but it was exactly what I needed. A little bland but perfect to fill my belly and start me on track to getting stronger again.

Shiloh hung out while I ate, chatting my ear off while she sipped a cup of tea. It turned out that she had stayed over the last three days and nights helping Sawyer nurse me back to health. Some deep part of me grew irrationally jealous at that. Almost violently so.

The intensity of those feelings surprised me, because I had no claim on Sawyer. We had physical chemistry, and we were...*something*, but not anything I could think of a label for. It seemed I was important enough for him to rescue, but what did I really mean to him?

And all this time, Shiloh had been a good friend to me as well as him. It was clear to me they had no lingering feelings for each other. She didn't touch Sawyer or get physically near him unless it was necessary, nor did she flirt or look at him for extended periods of time. So why did I want to bite her head off just for being in his house? Just because they had history? I had known that before though, and didn't feel this way back then.

"Well, I've got a bar to open up." Shiloh went to place her mug in the sink, then she and Sawyer embraced quickly. Platonically. I could see the friendly affection for what it was with my own eyes, and yet I wanted to grab her by the hair and toss her out through the kitchen window for touching him.

"Thanks for everything." Sawyer's gaze swung right over to me as he said that, and I wanted to purr with delight.

"Any time." Shiloh gave me a smile and squeezed my shoulder as she walked past me. "Great to have you back, girlie. Come see me after you've had more time to recover."

"Will do. Thank you." I smiled back even though I wanted to rip her hand off my shoulder.

The silence hung heavily, like a chain around my neck, when it was just Sawyer and I.

He cleared his throat and busied himself with washing dishes. "So, how are you feeling?"

"Kind of out of the loop, to be honest," I said. "What happened? How were you able to get me out?"

"What I mean is, um." Sawyer shut off the sink and dried his hands on a towel. "How are you feeling physically? Anything strange or different?"

Well, I want to fuck you into next week and brutally murder any woman who gets within ten feet of you. Does that count?

"I don't know. I mean, I felt barely alive for the past four weeks. Today is the first day I've felt strong enough to shower, eat, and have a conversation."

"Right." Sawyer rubbed the dark beard on his jaw. "That was probably a dumb thing to ask."

"What is actually going on, Sawyer?"

He sighed and looked up toward the ceiling before bringing his gaze back to me. "Tonight is the full moon."

That struck a chord within me, lighting up something

deep within my consciousness that I didn't understand. "Okay?"

"And if you were feeling...different, or maybe feeling things more intensely than normal, it's possible the moon phase is affecting you."

Confused, I waited for him to elaborate further, but he said nothing. "Why would the full moon affect me?"

He blew out a long breath and rubbed his face. "I talked to my friend, Fallon. His mate came from the human world, you know. And we think there's a chance..." He returned to staring at me. "That, like her, you may be a latent werewolf."

You could hear a pin drop in the cabin with the silence that followed.

"A werewolf? Me?"

Sawyer nodded slowly. "If you're latent, it means you had werewolf ancestors who suppressed their abilities to hide who they are. They likely fled to the human world to escape our war with the vampires. Over several generations of intermixing with humans, their wolf nature became quieter, more dormant." His gaze intensified. "But it's still there. And being in our world, among other werewolves, possibly awakens it."

My mind flickered through everything I'd felt, sensed, and wanted since meeting him. "How would I know?"

"There are symptoms that present themselves. An enhanced sense of smell. Urges and desires that you never had before. A feeling like there's another presence inside you, part of you but also separate." Sawyer paused, as if unsure if he should continue. "If you find someone you're, you know, physically compatible with, you'll want to bite them and have them bite you." He lifted his hands. "But it's not a blood thing with us, it's a claiming thing. Mated wolves will mark each other to signal that they're off-limits to others. When we're human, the marks are usually in a visible spot. As wolves, our scents change when we're mated."

I stared at his neck, his arms, his hands, fully aware I was inspecting him for just such a mating mark. "What's that?" I asked, pointing to the puffy, dark scar on the back of his palm.

He chuckled sheepishly, turning his hand over to look at the scar. "Not a mating bite. This is something else."

"What is it?"

Sawyer licked his lips, hesitating before speaking again. "I made a deal with a dragon to get you out of Sanguine."

I froze. "Is that...bad?"

"Probably. They're allied with the vampires. He should have torched us, but he let us go instead. So now I'm in his debt. When he wants something from me, I have no choice but to follow through." Sawyer shrugged like it was no big thing. "I'll deal with it when it happens."

"Does your alpha know?"

Sawyer cleared his throat. "I don't want you to worry about pack business. Just focus on recovering."

"He doesn't," I said as I realized that. "Does he even know you went back for me?"

Sawyer's expression and his silence told me all I needed to know.

"Oh my God, Sawyer." My hand flew to my chest, the sudden acceleration of my heartbeat making my breath shorten into pants. "You went behind his back *and* made a deal with an enemy? What does this mean?"

"It means you're alive," Sawyer growled. "It means

you're safe, you're healing, and you're where you should be."

The raw possessiveness in his voice delighted *something* within me. Some deep part of my consciousness wanted to...howl? Was that what that was? I wanted to cry out with victory that he chose *me*. He sacrificed for *me*. All I needed was his mark to make it official.

He risked everything to get me out, which spoke volumes of how much he cared about me. But on the surface, I was so *so* worried.

"A bite is also the final key to waking up your wolf so that you can shift, assuming it works like it did with Fallon's mate," Sawyer went on. "If you choose to do this and we find out you *are* my kind, Derric's reason for returning you is baseless. He made the call to return you based on you being a human, not a werewolf."

The dots started to connect, even with what he wasn't saying.

"So, if I am...like you," I said. "There's a chance you won't be labeled a traitor to the pack?"

"Maybe, but," Sawyer held his palms up again, "I don't want you to base this decision on what could happen to me. This is the rest of *your* life, Riley, which could extend by seven hundred years if you *are* a werewolf. Only you can decide if that's a life for you. Or if you want to stay human, that's perfectly fine too. I've made my decisions and I'm ready for whatever consequences will come. I don't want you to feel pressured one way or the other."

I stared at my hands in my lap while I began to think it over. A small laugh left my mouth because the answer came to me in under ten seconds. It was a no-brainer.

Being human sucked for me, literally. Only when I had

met this werewolf sitting across from me did I find life to be joyful and freeing. I already knew, deep down, that I was a latent wolf. All the symptoms Sawyer had mentioned made so much sense, like he was in my brain with me.

I hadn't been able to defend myself from the vampires or anyone else before. I didn't know what exactly Sawyer wanted with me and had no idea where we would end up. But even if I ended up alone, it was about damn time I armed myself with teeth and claws.

"You can take all the time you need to think." Sawyer's gaze slid to the window behind me. "But the full moon will rise in a few hours and I won't be able to control my wolf then. Actually I should leave soon before I—"

"You smell like the forest and spices," I blurted out. "And your scent makes me want you, crave you inside my body like nothing I've ever felt before. I want your bite in my flesh because I swear it's going to give me the most explosive orgasm I've ever had."

Sawyer was like a statue, frozen with his eyes wide and mouth slightly agape. But his scent filled the air and grew stronger with each passing second. It only encouraged me to keep going.

"I wanted to throw Shiloh out the kitchen window by her hair earlier," I admitted. "When she hugged you, I wanted to kill her because I see you as...as..."

"What, Riley?" Sawyer demanded. "What am I to you? Tell me."

A growl of frustration left my throat, anxiety clamming me up. "What am I to *you*?" I shot back. "You rescued me. Risked your life and your place in the pack for me. You... pleasured me. But why, Sawyer?"

The werewolf rubbed his chest as the hum of his growl

filled the air. "My kind believes our animal sides have wisdom that our human brains can't comprehend. This wisdom comes from a deep, instinctual place. Our wolves sense absolute truths, the ways of nature that are never wrong."

I could almost feel his scent on my skin like a touch, and my body only ached for more. "And what is your wolf telling you?" I asked through a tight throat.

Sawyer's gaze was rock-steady on me. "You're my mate, Riley."

CHAPTER 22

SAWYER

"My wolf knew, practically from the start, that you were my mate. That's what you are to me, Riley." It felt like a motorcycle that had been sitting on my chest was now lifted. The two halves of me were in sync now, and it felt incredible for my animal and human sides to be aligned. Now, all I needed was for Riley to accept me as hers.

She looked pleased, although not surprised. Her small hands roamed over the kitchen island's surface, like she didn't know what to do with them. "I felt so...aggressive toward Shiloh hanging out here. Which was crazy because she's a friend. And I know there's nothing between you two anymore."

"Nothing at all," I echoed. "The whole time she was here, it was just to help you. It took her four weeks to make an invisibility potion for me to sneak into Sanguine. Everything she did was to help me get you back. She's an incredible friend, but that's all it is."

"I know all that. Honestly, I do." Riley's lip curled like

she was trying to bare canines that weren't there. "And I still wanted to rip her throat out."

I couldn't help the wolfish grin that spread across my lips. "Because?" I *needed* to hear her say it.

"Because you're *mine*." A growl roughened Riley's voice and it was the sexiest sound I'd ever heard in my life.

"That's right." I rounded the counter, closing in on my mate. "I'm completely, utterly yours, Riley."

She leaned her cheek into the palm I brought to her face, but her brows pinched with concern. "But I don't want to accidentally hurt Shiloh or anyone else."

"It's the full moon tonight," I reminded her. "Wolf instincts are dominant while our human sides take a backseat. Shiloh knows it too. That's why she took off while there was still plenty of daylight out. After tonight passes, you'll feel more in control. A little less growly."

"Hm." The tension left her face, a coy smirk replacing it. "I kind of like being growly."

"I like it too. It suits you." My touch slid from her cheek to run through the waves of her chestnut hair. I wondered what her wolf form would look like. Sometimes human coloring carried over but not always.

Riley grabbed my wrist and held it in front of my chest with a surprising amount of strength. "I want the bite, Sawyer. I want to be your mate completely. In both forms."

My wolf was so overjoyed, and a howl threatened to rise up my throat. Hell, any male would have been thrilled to hear those words. And while I was beyond happy to have found my perfect partner, I still had concerns.

"You should know that it's usually on the neck or the shoulder," I said.

Riley recoiled slightly, and that was all I needed to

know. She still had a bandage on her neck from the infected bite wounds and would need to take herbs for another month to boost her immune response.

Not to mention all the fucking mental trauma of being fed on by vampires until she was on the brink of death. Fuck that. I swore she'd never be harmed again and that included by me.

"Forget it." I swiped my thumb over her cheekbone and kissed her forehead. "There will be no biting, not until you're ready."

I started to pull away, but Riley grabbed my wrist again and held on. Her gaze locked onto me just as tightly as her hand. "You said you don't want to make decisions for me? Then don't. Give me your bite, Sawyer. Let me be who I really am."

"I will, sweetness. Just not yet. You're still recovering from being bitten too fucking much as it is."

"Don't you think *I* should decide that?"

Her voice took on that sexy growl again. And I had to admit, the way she was arguing with me was damn sexy too. Her wolf was just under the surface, probably clawing and howling to be released. The moon was making that beautiful animal side fire her up, giving her a backbone. She wasn't a meek little human anymore, and I fucking loved it.

"Are you absolutely sure you want it?" I stepped in closer until I was fully engulfed in the perfume of her scent. "The moon is calling to your wolf side. It's clouding your judgment right now. Dig deep and find your humanity, Riley. Because I don't want you to regret anything after tonight."

A single beat of silence passed. And then she pounced.

Her hands went to my shoulders, using me for leverage

as she jumped. I had no choice but to catch her, palms slamming into the round globes of her ass to anchor her against me. Then her mouth fell to mine, pressing and needy, tongue licking at me to get inside.

How could I refuse my mate?

I opened to her, locking our lips together as a flood of heat and desire overcame me like I'd been lit with a match. My fingers squeezed into her flesh and her hips rolled as she let out a soft whimper through our kiss. Her scent was everywhere and driving me fucking wild.

I turned to perch her ass on the island counter, just to free up my hands to explore her for a few moments. Riley seemed to have the same idea, releasing her hold around my neck to run her fingertips under my shirt. The thing was off in the breath before our next kiss. I was getting too damn hot, and clothes were so cumbersome, anyway.

Down, boy. Down, boy.

I repeated the silly mantra in my head to keep my head straight and my wolf calm, but the pull of the moon's magic made it especially difficult. Werewolves were not the most gentle lovers, but Riley was fragile and needed care. She needed more rest, food, and blood, not to be ravaged by a beast.

"What's wrong?" Her legs squeezed tighter around my waist, hands running up my back as she kissed my collarbone. "I don't want you to stop."

"I don't want to hurt you," I admitted, all the while running my mouth over the soft, unbroken skin at the top of her shoulder. My bite would fit so well there, the perfect spot to mark my beautiful mate.

"You won't," she insisted, lips pulling at my earlobe. "I trust you, Sawyer."

Hearing those four words was already more satisfying than any orgasm. What a gift it was to have this woman's trust, when it had been abused and trampled over so many times. After all she'd been through, I was determined to be worthy of that trust.

But to care for her properly, I needed my human mind in control, and that was a losing battle tonight.

My hands went to her hips and I pulled her flush to me, preparing to lift her off the counter. "I want you in my bed," I told her on another growl.

"No." She surprised me again, leaning back to stare at me with heat and need in her eyes. "Right here."

"Riley," I groaned through my teeth. "I'm trying to treat you right and be a gentleman about this."

"Well, don't." Her hand clasped around the back of my neck. "Be a wolf, Sawyer, and take your mate."

Those words became my undoing, the final unlocking of the cage in which I held my beast. I lunged in for my roughest, hungriest kiss yet, and she met me with equal ferocity. Lips, tongues, and teeth scraped with a friction that ignited the rest of our actions. I whipped off her T-shirt and sweater, then backed away to yank her pajama pants off before returning to that sweet place between her thighs.

Riley undid the button and zipper on my jeans, and this time, I let her. She reached inside my briefs and wrapped her palm around my length, then paused with a sudden gasp.

"You okay?" I asked with a kiss to her ear. It was all I could do to not thrust into the soft embrace of her hand, but my mate's comfort came before all else.

"Yeah," she breathed in a soft whisper, lips pulling into a smile. Her grip around me tightened slightly, and my resulting groan seemed to give her the green light to start stroking me. "You're just so...hard already."

"Have been since you said I was yours." I wrapped my hand around hers, guiding her into a rhythm that soon had me panting and leaking from the tip. She spread the pre-cum over my entire shaft, her palm slicking over me as she stroked me with more ease and confidence.

"Fuck, that's so good," I rasped, catching her wrist to slow her down. "Almost too good."

"Just returning the favor from last time," she said with a cheeky smile.

"That was no favor." My hand started up her inner thigh, gripping and kneading the flesh as I went. "That's how I want to make you feel every single fucking day."

I brushed my fingertips over her pussy, just the lightest touch to make her squirm. It worked, and she pinned me with a narrow-eyed glare. "If you're going to touch me, do it right."

"Now you're sounding like a wolf." I lowered my forehead to hers, grinning as I returned to stroking and playing with her.

She was so slick and ready for me. Her beautiful scent coated my fingers and I could not resist bringing them to my mouth for a taste. Our eyes locked as I sucked her wetness off my fingers and then returned them to her cunt. Her grip on my cock tightened as I pressed inside her, and I smothered her resulting moan with another hungry kiss.

"Bite me," Riley begged when we parted for a breath. "Please, Sawyer."

"Come for me first," I ordered. "Give me your last orgasm as a fully human woman."

She whined and whimpered, hips rising for more sensation from my fingers plunging in and out of her. My thumb swept over her clit, but I knew it wasn't enough to make her come, not yet. I wanted to draw this out a little more, make it good and memorable for her. I wanted her even more relaxed and ready for my cock when that time came. Anything to give her as little pain as possible.

"Stop fucking around," Riley growled, almost as if she was in pain. "I...I think I can feel my wolf, Sawyer. She's clawing at me, she's dying to come out."

"The full moon is drawing her out," I whispered in awe. "It's really happening."

"Sawyer, please..."

I pressed my thumb harder on her clit then, curling my fingers inside her to add more friction to her silky walls. My cock continued to pulse and leak pre-cum in Riley's grip. I was hard as iron and desperate to be inside her.

Riley's whole body shook when her orgasm finally squeezed around me. She exposed her long, beautiful throat column as her head fell back, and I felt my teeth shift to wolf-like canines.

Mark her. Claim our mate, my wolf howled.

It was like fighting against the pull of a chain wrapped around my neck, but I resisted, waiting for Riley to float back down from the high of her release. Her head came forward again, eyes dilated, sated, and feral.

Our mouths connected in another kiss, my hands gliding to her waist while hers drifted up my chest to my shoulders. I came forward until my cock nudged the center of her silky heat. Every instinct screamed at me to push forward, to sink in and finally be inside her, but I held on to my last thread of rational thinking and paused.

"Tell me again," I said, my lips grazing hers.

"Tell you what?" she breathed.

"You know what." My grip on her waist tightened. "Tell me."

Riley's hand slid up the side of my face, fingertips brushing the white patch of hair at my temple before wrapping around my neck. Her short nails bit into my skin like a pup's claws.

"You're mine, Sawyer," she said with a growl that was definitely not human. "My wolf. My mate."

I drove my hips forward, sheathing my length into her in one fluid thrust. "And you're mine, Riley."

Our bodies crashed together with a force that rattled the remaining dishes on the counter. Riley's nails dug into my back, pulling me closer, deeper into her. I held her hips in place as I drove into her, my mouth teasing along the uninjured side of her neck and shoulder. *So close, so soon. But not quite yet.*

"Sawyer..." Riley's mouth was against my shoulder, thighs squeezing around me as she took every one of my thrusts. "I don't think I can stop...it hurts. I need to..."

"Do it." I braced one arm against her back, holding her flush to me. "Don't fight it, sweetness. Let your instincts take over."

It only made sense that she bit me first. I would be claimed, but there would be no other changes on my end. She would have a lot more to deal with once I bit her.

Riley brushed a kiss over my shoulder muscle and then her teeth sank in. The pain flaring in my arm felt so fucking good, I nearly came. Flames licked like sensual hands all over my body, and everything I felt was amplified, like a dial had been turned all the way up.

Riley felt like utter heaven wrapped around my cock.

She was the most beautiful person I'd ever laid eyes on. I was completely, irrevocably in love with her, and there was no greater truth I'd ever known.

And then came the sensation of a great weight smothering me, threatening to flatten me into the floor. I could barely breathe, barely see. Of course, this mating bond was currently one-sided. I wasn't meant to handle all these feelings and sensations on my own. I needed to share them with my mate.

Now. I need to bite her now.

I couldn't speak, not with the feeling of my lungs being crushed. I could only look at Riley, only ask her with my expression one final time if she was absolutely certain she wanted this.

Maybe it was the effect of the bite, but I swore she had tears in her eyes. "Please, Sawyer," she mouthed. I couldn't hear her over the rushing of blood in my ears.

I held her upper arm, brought my mouth to her shoulder, and bit down hard.

CHAPTER 23

RILEY

I truly couldn't tell if it was an orgasm or an explosion of pain from Sawyer's bite. Thousands of sensations hit me at once.

A rush of heat came over me, and my body felt entirely too sensitive. I could feel my pulse in every blood vessel. And I could also feel him, Sawyer, like he was inside my skin with me.

He was still inside me, I knew that. I felt an offbeat pulsing between my legs like he had just orgasmed as well.

"Riley?" He sounded a million miles away, but I knew he was nearby because of how strongly his scent filled my nose. He was the very air I breathed.

"I'm so hot," I said, panting. But it felt good too, a thrumming, comforting kind of heat.

"CAN YOU HEAR ME?"

"Oh God!" I clapped my hands over my ears. "You don't need to yell so loud."

"WHAT? I'M NOT YELLING."

"Just give me some space, please!" I turned gingerly

onto my side, not entirely sure where I was. My legs kicked out, toes reaching in search of solid ground. But they just flailed through the air at strange angles and felt *wrong*.

"RILEY, YOU'RE GOING TO—"

Too late. I rolled off the kitchen island onto the floor. For some reason, my knees didn't bend to catch myself, so the floor slapped my stomach and chest, knocking the wind out of me. The whimper coming out of my mouth felt strange. Shit, everything felt weird and kind of hurt.

Something warm and soft nudged the top of my head, and I looked up to see Sawyer's wolf standing over me, gently licking and nuzzling at me.

Can you hear me, Riley?

His voice came through at normal volume...but not in my ears. I heard him directly in my head.

I'll take that shocked expression as a yes. He sounded amused, and I was endlessly fascinated that I could hear him this way. *You're halfway shifted, sweetness. The human side of you is probably confused and fighting for control. Just relax and let the wolf take over. It'll feel better, I promise you.*

It took a few extra seconds for his words to register. Shifted? *Me?*

I looked down at my hands, which were covered in gray fur ticked with bands of black and white and tipped with black claws instead of nails. The fur continued up my arms and over my chest. I could only imagine it covered my face too.

How bad do I look? I wondered, staring at Sawyer to see if he'd get the thought in his head.

The wolf's jaws parted in a smile and his tail started wagging. *Not bad, just uncomfortable. No one is meant to be stuck between forms. Take a deep breath and let the shift happen. The moon should make it easier.*

After taking a few moments to calm down, I looked past all the strange sensations and feelings in my body and introduced myself to the other presence who had been within me all this time.

Hello, I said. *You're my wolf.*

You're my human, she said back to me, not so much with words but with a deep, instinctual knowing. *Thank you for unbinding me.*

Thank you for choosing a good mate for us, I returned.

Oh, we did that together. Excitement lit up my spine, and I wanted to express it with a tail wag. *Shall we run?*

Yes, please.

I did the mental equivalent of taking a seat and letting someone else stand up. Immediately the discomfort left my body, and I rose to stand on all four legs, letting my tail wag.

Holy shit. Sawyer's voice in my head was filled with awe. *You're so, so beautiful.*

Am I? I turned in a circle, my ears flattening against my skull in self-consciousness.

You're gorgeous. I just...I can't... He walked forward, nuzzling his snout against mine. *I knew you would be, but the moon has blessed me with a mate who is just stunning beyond compare.*

You sure that's not just the mating bite talking?

It may be, but that doesn't make it any less true. He licked me, then took a nip at my ear before darting backwards like a playful puppy.

Can we go run? My front paws tapped eagerly against

the floor. I needed to feel the cool evening air on my fur and release these howls building in my throat.

I was hoping you'd say that. Follow me.

Sawyer headed for the front door and reared up on his hind legs to nudge a latch with his nose. The door swung open and I followed him through it, waiting with brimming energy as he pulled a braided leather rope on the outside of the door to close it. When the inside latch clicked into place, he returned to all fours and froze.

I copied him. Watching, waiting. Hardly daring to breathe.

Then, with a bark, he exploded into action, tearing off the front porch and through the trees. I went after him, shocked at my own running speed on four legs and all the smells and sounds pouring into my senses.

Catch up with me, pretty wolf, Sawyer teased.

His scent trail was easy to follow even when he was out of sight, which he never was for long. But the delicious scent of my mate always led me straight to him.

Sawyer had stopped several yards ahead of me, and I was horrified to realize I couldn't slow my momentum in time. I barreled into him, and then we were two yelping, furry masses rolling on the forest floor.

Shit, I'm sorry!

He let out a series of yips and barks that my wolf senses interpreted as laughter. *It's fine. You'll learn your wolf body in time.*

The next thing I knew, his large, dark wolf pounced on me, pinning me to the ground. Sawyer snapped his jaws, catching only the ends of my fur in his bite. I growled a warning and he just did it again, lips pulling back in a canine smile. When I snapped back at him, he jumped off of me and took off running.

Where are you going, big bad wolf? I hauled ass after him, focused on the target of his tail.

Just taking my mate on a tour of our territory, he answered. *If she can keep up, that is.*

I howled out a promise before picking up speed. When I crashed into him the second time, I did not apologize, and I even got a bit of his scruff when I bit him.

The full moon rose high and bright, lighting up the night sky while my mate and I spent the hours running and playing.

It was without a doubt the happiest night of my life.

))))) ❨❨❨❨❨❨❨❨

Sawyer covered me with his warm body. His naked, human body, that is.

"Cold?" The word was little more than a soft grunt, his face buried in the crook of my neck as he dragged lazy kisses up and down, focusing on the mating bite on my shoulder.

"Not so bad, actually." Even so, I wasn't about to refuse his kind gesture of warming me up with over six feet of dense muscle.

We were still outside in the woods, in the same soft patch of grass we'd finally collapsed in after spending the night running around as wolves.

Wolves. Plural. Together. Us. Me *and* him. I could barely wrap my head around it.

"Why you gigglin'?" he mumbled, lips against my skin.

"I'm a werewolf!" I declared with a laugh, wrapping my arms around his broad back. "I just can't believe this is real."

"Believe it." Sawyer nuzzled a kiss against the column of my throat. "Believe that you're mine. And in being so, you're safe, free, and cherished. Forever."

I traced the mark I had bitten into his shoulder. I knew I had bitten hard enough to draw blood, but the mark looked perfectly healed now. Two almost-symmetrical crescents of pale scars.

"Is mine healed?" I wondered aloud before pressing a kiss to the mark.

Sawyer pulled back to look, tracing my shoulder reverently as I had just done to him. "It is." He examined the other side of my neck. "Your vampire bites are pretty much gone too. How do you feel?"

"Incredible," I admitted. "I feel stronger and more alive than I ever have. Even though we ran all night, I feel like I have enough energy to stay up all day. And I can smell frost on the grass, but I'm not even that cold."

"Mm, perfect." Sawyer lowered a kiss to my mouth, loving and warm as his thighs nudged my legs apart.

"Thank you for giving me this," I whispered as a wave of emotion came over me. It was all because of him that I had this new life, this new strength and vitality. This new home. "You saved my life Sawyer, and you've given me...everything."

"I couldn't refuse you anything if I tried." He kissed me again deeper, a hand sliding under the back of my head to hold it up from the forest floor. "The moon knew you were meant to be mine. Our wolves knew. And now our stubborn human sides are no longer in the way."

He began a slow roll of his hips, his erection thickening as it dragged back and forth along my inner thighs. By the time he was fully hard and nudging that blunt head against my entrance, I was beyond wet and aching for him.

With no hands, he adjusted the angle and pressed through, filling me up in one long stroke that took my breath away.

"Good?" he asked, pausing with his lips hovering over mine.

I responded by lifting up to capture his mouth, nipping his bottom lip and squeezing my thighs around his waist. With a rough, sexy moan, he started to move, gliding through my body with the most delicious friction. It felt wonderful and was exactly what I'd craved last night on that kitchen island, when I'd been a human.

But I was a wolf now too, and I wanted a little more of an edge.

"Harder," I rasped in his ear. "You can be rough with me."

Sawyer's hips pistoned harder as he moaned, the drag of his cock making me see stars and claw at his back. Each crash of his body into me was more violent, every withdrawal more abrupt.

"Be careful what you ask for, sweet mate," he growled.

"Your mate can handle it," I returned. "I'm just as much a wild animal as you."

With that, he pulled out of me completely, and for a moment, I thought I'd said something wrong. Before I could say a word, he flipped me over to my belly. When he entered me again, the cry I let out sent birds flying from nearby trees. *Holy shit,* this position. This angle.

The next thing I felt was Sawyer's hand wrapping around the front of my throat, fingers holding the pulse points in a light squeeze.

"Still handling it?" he asked in my ear, deceptively calm while he fucked me at a brutal, punishing pace.

"Don't stop," I begged through a whimper, the pleasure building too fast for my breath to catch up. "Oh God, please don't stop."

"Fuck, Riley." He dragged a rough, biting kiss down my shoulder blade. "You were made for me."

Sawyer's fingers tightened on my throat just as I felt him swell inside me, turning up the building pleasure to an inferno I could no longer control, nor did I want to. My release shot off and dragged his along with it, sending us into a feedback loop of pulsing shockwaves, peaking and falling.

When it was over, Sawyer rolled to his side and hauled me to his chest. His scent was thick in the air, his skin feverishly warm despite the chill in the early morning air. I licked a bead of sweat from his neck, and he shivered with a soft moan.

"Feel this," he panted, slapping my palm over his heart.

It raced under my hand to the same tempo to my own, and I pressed a kiss to that spot with a smile. Sawyer brought a hand under my chin and lifted my lips to his, kissing me with a tenderness that spoke to how sensitive we both were from the sex and maybe something else.

"I love you, Riley," he whispered. "And before you say it, that is *not* the mating bite talking. I knew it before I marked you."

My breath felt stolen once again, and not because of the vigorous activity we'd just done. How many times had I heard those words before? Lots. Probably dozens. All said to play on my emotions, to make me feel important and let my guard down when I had just been a means to an end. Time and time again I had *hoped* they were true. That this time would be different. Sometimes I had even convinced myself that I believed them, that the men saying those words had meant it at the time but that feelings had changed.

This time though, in the arms of my werewolf, I didn't have to convince myself of anything. My mind was peacefully silent, no lingering doubts or warning bells going off because I *knew*.

He was telling the truth.

And this bond Sawyer and I had, tied together by the magic of the moon, would not change as easily as fleeting emotions. It was as solid as the ground beneath us.

We hadn't known each other long, even if we did count the last four weeks of being apart. But even in that short time, he showed me that I mattered simply because I was me. And in this strange world that felt so right for me, with this wild animal prowling under my skin, I found myself actually starting to like who I was.

All because of him.

"I love you too, Sawyer." My fingers ran through his hair on our next kiss. "Have I told you how much I love this?" I smiled against his lips, stroking the patch of white hair at his temple.

"My old man fuzz?" He chuckled through another kiss. "That's what the guys in the pack call it."

"Stop, it's beautiful. Even sexy on you." I lifted my

mouth to kiss those strands. "It's like you're kissed by moonlight."

Sawyer's laugh turned into a contented sigh, large hands skimming my body. "You're just making me think of you naked, nothing but moonlight on your skin."

"How about tonight?" I asked with a kiss to his neck.

He laughed again, turning us so I was flat on my back and he hovered on top of me again. "Anything for my insatiable mate."

The next kiss was deep, hungry. My legs slid apart and he nestled between them. "Who's the insatiable one?" I mumbled in the pause before he kissed me again. Sawyer just answered with a rumbling moan, hands roaming over my sides before catching my hips in a rough grip.

The anticipation sent my pulse fluttering. To take him inside me again minutes after we had just finished felt like such a treat.

Something changed in the air current, but I ignored it to focus on reaching between our bodies, taking Sawyer's length in my hand and stroking that hot, thickening organ.

Abruptly he tore his mouth from mine. "Wait, Riley."

I froze. "What's wrong?"

"Shh." He cocked his head, listening to, as well as scenting, our surroundings. "I don't think we're alone."

My pulse now raced for a very different reason as I slid out from under him, covering my chest as I sat up. Several yards away, the tall grass moved, and Sawyer darted in front of me, snarling.

Two massive wolves emerged from the waist-high grass, one clearly older with tears and scars mangling his ears. When they shifted to their human forms, the grass mostly covered their naked bodies from the waist down.

I recognized one of the immediately—Derric, Sawyer's alpha. He was the one with the scarred ears, which carried over to his human form and continued down the sides of his scowling face.

Derric's voice was pure venom when he spoke.

"What is *she* doing here, enforcer?"

CHAPTER 24

SAWYER

I knew this was coming but didn't expect it so soon after Riley's wolf had woken up. I would have loved at least one more blissful day with my mate before I had to face the music. But the moon's pull on all of us was nothing if not a precarious balance. She gave me Riley, and just as quickly, put me on the chopping block before the pack.

Riley's nails bit into my arm as Derric and Ruse continued staring me down, waiting for an explanation. There would be no leniency from them, I knew that straight away. Derric's eyes were murderous, and even in his human form, I could sense his wolf's desire to tear my throat out at my insubordination.

"Answer your alpha's question." Ruse stalked forward a few feet, his teeth still pointy and canine. "What is *she* doing *here*?"

"I went to Sanguine and got her out." Lying was pointless. And no matter what their decision would be, I respected these two wolves too much to be less than truthful with them.

Derric's growl of fury would have made the toughest human man shit his pants. "When did this happen?"

"Four days ago."

"And how long had you been planning to do this?"

Now it was me who bared my wolf teeth. "Since you made me turn her over to them."

"Sawyer!" The VP barked my name out in disbelief. "You *knew* the consequences! How could you do this?"

"Because she's my mate."

Riley pushed past my arm to get in front of me, and a snarl loosed from my throat, mainly because she was completely naked. It didn't matter to me, a newly-mated male, that nudity was common amongst our kind. My mate's body was only for me to see.

"Riley, don't—" I started, reaching for her waist to haul her back, but she batted me away.

"Sawyer saved my life, for the second time," she said to the two men, chin high. "And he had a hunch that I wasn't just a human, but a latent werewolf. One of *your* kind."

Derric and Ruse exchanged a narrow-eyed glance but otherwise said nothing in response.

"Turns out, he was right," Riley went on. "I'm not just a human after all. So your reason for sending me back doesn't hold water."

"Prove it then," Ruse bit out.

Riley didn't hesitate. The shift came over her smoothly, like she'd been doing it since she was a pup rather than just the last twelve hours. Her wolf had the most beautiful coat of white, gray, and black, and she let out a howl the moment she fell to all fours. Then she walked a tight circle around my legs, growling protectively while she gave Derric and Ruse the stink eye.

"So it's true. She's just like the Traveler's mate," Ruse muttered, rubbing his jaw as he stared at Riley. "Perhaps there are more latents in the human world than we thought."

"Perhaps." Derric didn't look, nor sound, anywhere near as impressed. His stony gaze returned to me. "This doesn't change anything, in spite of your mate's nature. Not only did you intentionally and methodically disobey me, you threatened every life in Vargmore the moment you crossed that border."

"I will own up to disobeying you, alpha, but I was careful," I said. "I used a potion, and made sure to be untraceable."

"It's still a great risk. One that I *never* condoned taking," he growled back. "Magic fails. Potions are volatile. Even if you went at high noon with a UV lamp strapped to your back, someone could have seen you."

Someone did, as the itching black scar on the back of my palm made sure to remind me. And not even just the dragon I was now in debt to. Fabian saw us leave while he was high as a kite and probably wrote it off at the time, but he definitely knew his pet was gone by now.

I just hoped my instincts were right, that he was too much of a pussy to rally Blood 'til Dawn to act for him again. No self-respecting vampire would survive the humiliation of losing a human blood pet. Twice.

None of that information was on a need-to-know basis with Derric, so I kept my mouth shut. Running my hand through Riley's fur, I stood tall before the werewolf who had given me place and purpose before I found my mate.

"You're right about all of it, alpha. I knew the risks, the consequences, and I went into enemy territory anyway." My fingers curled to scratch at the base of Riley's ears. "I will accept whatever judgment you choose for me."

Riley whipped around, barking loudly until she returned to human form. "Sawyer, what are you saying? You can't just accept this!"

"There's nothing else I *can* do." I took hold of her arms to gently maneuver her behind me again. The guys were tactful enough to not stare at her bare ass, but I didn't want to give them any opportunity.

"This is wrong!"

"No, sweetness. This is just how it is."

"Well then, I'm glad this comes as no surprise." Derric folded his arms over his scarred chest, all but ignoring Riley. "For willfully going against your alpha, and endangering all of Vargmore, you, Sawyer, once-enforcer of Howling Death MC, are now removed from both the pack and the club."

"No, you can't!" Riley started for him, but I held her back, bracing my arm around her.

"Furthermore, because you acted in your own self-interest against the pack and the territory," Derric continued, ignoring Riley. "You will forever be known and remembered as a traitor wolf."

I closed my eyes, wishing I could sink to the ground, but I still had a struggling, pissed-off Riley to hold back. Getting kicked out for disobeying orders, I could handle. But the traitor label was what I'd feared most and had, perhaps naively, hoped to avoid. Only the most shameful wolves carried that mark.

In the eyes of the pack, I was just as bad as those who

sold off our own kind to the vampires back during the war. If any of them were still alive, they were the stuff of nightmares now.

Elders told their pups ghost stories of the traitor wolves who went mad with no community, no contact with others for decades, if not centuries. With nowhere else to go, they slunk along the fringes of our territory like vermin. In the stories, they never shifted to human anymore, but they weren't accepted by non-shifter wolf packs either. So their human side atrophied while the bestial one took over. All the while, the human was still in there, their mental state slowly unraveling. Some said you could hear the anguished screams of traitor wolves in your head, deep in the forest. They had forgotten they were shifters at all and believed they were in hell, trapped in an animal's body for eternity.

Even with traitor wolf as my new title, I was lucky. I had Riley, which was all that mattered. At least, I had her as long as I could prevent her from tearing into Derric, which she seemed highly motivated to do.

"You can't do that to him!" she cried, still kicking out and fighting against my hold. "He was just doing the right thing! *You* sent me to die there, and he saved my life!"

With his judgment now cast in front of two witnesses, Derric dropped his arms to his sides and turned to leave. "I hope she's worth it, Sawyer."

In the next blink of an eye, two wolves slunk through the tall grass without a sound and disappeared.

A SHARP, lightly painful sensation pulled me out of my numbness, but just barely. My eyes felt like they weighed the same as two bowling balls as they searched the space in front of me. A slender, feminine shoulder with mating marks hovered just in front of my face.

My marks. This was *my* mate.

That was right. I felt adrift without a pack, but I still had my Riley. I had to remember that.

My head felt like a two-ton boulder on my neck as I lowered to kiss that shoulder. I couldn't allow myself to numb out like a zombie just because I didn't have a pack anymore. My mate needed me.

"You in there?" Riley's voice reached me, and I realized that sharp sensation was her nipping at my earlobe.

"Hm? Yeah."

Warm fingers caressed my beard, neck, and chest. "You haven't eaten all day, and you've barely said a word since this morning."

"Sorry." I accepted a kiss from her, knowing it was full of warmth, love, and support. But none of it could reach me. I felt as cold and impenetrable as a glacier.

"Sawyer." Riley's hands went to my face, and when I met her gaze, her eyes glittered with tears. "I hate this for you. What can I do?"

I tried to force a smile to reassure her, but it felt and probably looked like a pained grimace. "Nothing, sweetness. I just need...time to adjust, I think."

"I wish I could fix this." She curled up and leaned against my chest, arms going around me. "It's like the life has been sucked out of your eyes. How could they do that to you?"

"They did what they believed was best." I brought a

hand to her back and may as well have been touching a tree stump. I *knew* I loved her, but in that moment, I felt absolutely nothing. "But we have each other, and that's all that matters." It sounded like I was trying to convince myself.

"We're meant to have packs," Riley said. "I consider you my pack, but you've been with them your whole life. I can't imagine how devastating this is for you."

"I don't want to be dishonest with you, I'm completely numb. I feel cut off from you, from myself. My wolf is completely silent too. I'm sure this is some kind of shock. It might take some time, but I'm hoping it'll pass. And then we can start our new lives together."

Riley pulled away from my chest, and now the tears rolled freely down her cheeks. "They did this to you because of me," she said. "It's my fault."

That stirred up a little bit of feeling in me, and I hated that it was my mate's pain, not her love, that made me react. "Don't blame yourself. I chose to go back and get you, and I would do it again. These consequences are entirely my own."

She shook her head, refusing to hear me. "If it wasn't for me, you'd still have a pack."

"I don't care. I'd rather have you."

"You *do* care, though, look at you!" She flung a hand out in my direction. "You're a shadow of yourself without a pack. It breaks my heart to see you like this, Sawyer."

"My heart broke when I handed you off to a vampire," I snarled. "That was not something I was prepared to live with, Riley. I *am* prepared to live without a pack. This," I gestured at myself, "is just temporary."

A long silence passed between us before she asked quietly, "Are you sure?"

I released a heavy breath, and it still felt like a motorcycle was sitting on my chest. "I don't know," I admitted. "This hasn't happened to anyone recently." I shrugged. "But shit happens. Life goes on. And I have my sweet mate at my side. Lots of wolves don't have that." I drew her closer and kissed her, willing myself to break through this stony numbness so that I could feel her passion, her fire. Fuck, feel *anything*.

"I have to do something," she sniffed. "I can't just sit here and watch you suffer."

"You are doing something," I insisted. "It means the world to me that you're here and that you stood up to Derric like that." I tried for another smile, brushing my knuckles against her cheekbone. "My mate is beautiful and fierce. And I love her."

"I love you too." Riley turned her face and kissed my knuckles. "More than anything."

CHAPTER 25

RILEY

Sawyer's condition did not improve over the next week. Or the week after that. Even his vibrant, beautiful wolf form seemed to be deeply depressed or in mourning. He only picked at his food and barely spoke. As a wolf, his tail and head hung low, and the only sounds he made were mournful howls.

I tried everything, from distracting him with sex, running and playtime, even stupid jokes, to giving him space, to sitting and cuddling with him for comfort and support. All of it got the same reaction—nothing.

It made me realize how deeply intrinsic a pack was to a werewolf and how cruel it had been for Derric to rip it away. That was Sawyer's family, his community. And in the blink of an eye, it was gone.

Sawyer was a proud wolf and not one to wear his emotions on his sleeve. So his behavior was deeply concerning to me, and I could only wonder how deeply the hurt and numbness affected him.

Every time I remembered it was because of *me* this had happened, it felt like I'd been kicked in the chest.

He could shoulder the responsibility all he wanted, but the truth was that *I* had caused him this hurt, this loss. So I had to be the one to fix it, but how?

I laid awake for several nights wondering how I could bring a case to Derric. Maybe I could petition other werewolves in the territory, or even the residing witches and humans. Vargmore needed Howling Death MC's enforcer. Sawyer was the front line in keeping the territory safe. He couldn't easily be replaced.

Every idea I had was shot down by Sawyer. There were no options for him, aside from accepting his fate. And seeing him so defeated, so unwilling to fight for himself when he'd risked everything to save me, broke my heart even more. This sad shadow of the strong, protective wolf I met in Shiloh's apartment was not Sawyer. Not the wolf I fell in love with. Not my mate.

I was living with and sharing a bed with a stranger. A half-dead stranger, content to stare at the wall and slowly waste away.

"Sawyer, please," I sobbed one night. "Tell me how to help you. I miss you. I love you, and I want my mate back. I feel like I'm watching you die."

"I'm sorry," he told me in that same flat, emotionless tone. "I don't know why nothing has changed. I'm still just so...numb."

"Just talk to me then. I'm here for you. Whatever keeps spiraling in your brain, you can get it out and I'll listen. You felt better last time you vented, remember?"

He shook his head in a slow, stiff movement. "You started blaming yourself again. I won't have that."

"I...I'm sorry about that, but I..."

What a fucking mess we were. I wanted him to unburden himself and release some of his pain. The last thing I wanted was for him to feel responsible for *my* feelings too. I tried to swallow my guilt for putting him in this position, and most of the time, I was successful. But sometimes the guilt became too much to bear. I had excused myself from our conversation to go cry privately, but he had found me, and that sent *him* on another downward spiral. Now he was refusing to talk to me at all because he didn't want my guilt to consume me.

"But nothing," he said. "I'm making you feel shitty enough as it is."

"Who else are you going to talk to, though?" I demanded. "There's no one else, Sawyer."

"Then I'll talk to no one. I'll just deal with it on my own. But I won't hurt you."

"You're hurting me by *not* talking to me!"

The two of us stared at each other for a few moments of tense, painful silence. "I'm sorry," we said at the same time.

"I can't go on like this, Sawyer." My chest seemed to crack open when I admitted to what I'd been afraid to say for the last few days. "I'm your mate, your partner for life. It's my job to help you through tough times. But every day feels like you're slipping further and further away. I'm begging you to return to me, to let me carry some of what you're holding onto. I promise you I can handle it."

My goddamned stubborn wolf shook his head. "My job as your mate is to protect you from harm, no matter where it comes from, even me or you. And I will not put you in a state of mind in which you blame yourself for all this. I hate that look in your eyes and those tears on your face more than anything. So I'm begging you, Riley. Please respect me as your male, your protector, and let me shield you from that. Let me deal with this on my own, to spare you, because I love you."

"But you're not shielding me from anything. I'm hurting *right now* because you're shutting me out! Why don't you get that?"

"I'm sorry," he said again. I was getting really fucking tired of those two words on constant repeat between us. "I would rather be closed off to you than burden you with more pain. That's just my nature. I'm sorry."

We were at a fucking standstill, having the same argument over and over. Something *had* to change. Something drastic needed to be done or neither of us would survive this.

"Let's go to Shiloh tomorrow," I said. "Maybe she has an herbal remedy that can help. Or you can just talk to her maybe, if not me. A neutral third party might be better."

Sawyer shook his head again, and I wanted to scream.

"No one in Vargmore is permitted to associate with traitor wolves," he said. "By now, they've spread the word and everyone knows of Derric's judgment. And you can't go to her on my behalf. She could be punished if she's found out trying to help me in any way."

"So...what?" I threw my hands in the air before letting them slap violently to my sides. "We do nothing? Just keep carrying on like this?"

Sawyer pulled in a deep breath like he was having trouble getting enough air. "I'm sorry, sweetness. I'll...I'll keep trying to shake this. More than anything, I wish I could. All I want is to be happy with you." His gaze went to my shoulder, where his mating mark was. "I'm sorry I chained you to me like this. I'd do anything to hear you laugh again. Fuck." His head rolled slowly on his neck like it was another burden to carry. "I wish I *wanted* to hear you laugh again. I wish I could feel...anything."

We climbed into bed silently after that. I waited until he was deeply asleep to turn away on my side and let the pillow muffle the sounds of my sobbing.

I knew what I had to do. And it made my heart break all over again.

)))) 🌓🌑🌑🌑((((((

I COULDN'T SLEEP A WINK, so it was easy to get up before dawn the next morning. Sawyer continued to sleep soundly. He slept well over ten hours per night after becoming a traitor wolf and still seemed to have no energy during the day. I watched him as I shifted, grateful that my wolf couldn't cry like a human did.

She would have plenty to howl about though, soon enough.

After padding quietly down from the loft bedroom, I unlatched the front door with my nose as I'd seen Sawyer do. Then, once outside, I pulled it closed until I heard the latch click into place.

It was cold, the chill even penetrating my dense fur. A whine escaped my throat while I lingered on the front porch. All I wanted to do was run back inside and curl up next to my mate's warm body.

Even though I knew there would be no warmth waiting

for me in that bed. Everything I loved about Sawyer was a memory now.

I forced myself off of the front porch, away from the house. It had rained overnight and the ground was cool and muddy.

Perfect for what I needed to do, even though it felt my chest was carved open and I was bleeding onto the ground.

I headed for the woods—paws dragging, tail and head hanging low. When I came to a mud puddle that would fit my wolf-sized body, I whined and whimpered the whole time I walked into it and set my belly down.

With Sawyer, maybe on a warm day after a spring rain, this would have been fun. Rolling around in mud without a care in the world, then washing off in the stream before getting dirty the human way. But the cold, wet dirt seeping into my fur was utter misery.

It's misery you deserve, some dark voice inside me said. *You did this to him.*

I even rubbed my face and snout into the mud, then shook my head rapidly to get the cold, dripping sensation out of my ears. As I kept rolling around and coating myself in mud, I resisted the urge to shake my entire body. I needed it to stay on me for as long as possible.

Once covered from nose to tail and shivering, I emerged from the mud puddle and headed deeper into the woods. The humidity in the air and clouds overhead indicated more rain was coming soon, so I had to become untraceable before the mud washed off. Once I got out of sight, the rain would also help to wash away my scent and any mud trail I left behind.

Where would I go? Who the hell knew.

I couldn't entirely figure out if I was doing this more for

myself or for Sawyer. It killed me to be in the cabin over the last couple of weeks, watching him float through the days like a ghost. But it couldn't have helped to have me, the reason for his exile, hovering around him all the time.

Maybe I was giving into cowardice by no longer standing by him. Maybe I was doing him a kindness.

I believed that Sawyer loved me. With my whole heart, I even believed we were destined to be mates. But I had ruined his life. I was no good for him.

I didn't know what the outcome of this would be, if it would even change anything for him. All I knew was that we couldn't go on as we were.

He had given up everything for me. How could I just sit by and selfishly take his generosity without sacrificing anything in return?

So, this was my sacrifice. Me. Us.

I was leaving my mate and making sure he couldn't track me down.

CHAPTER 26

SAWYER

I roused slowly, like I usually did these days. Pushing the blanket down was like shoving away a stone slab. I was always so tired. Maybe this was the madness of being a traitor wolf, feeling like your body and mind had turned to stone. Simply moving around was a monumental task, but if I didn't, it felt like I'd be locked in that position forever.

Turning to my side, I reached across the bed to Riley's side. It took a moment for me to register the mattress as cold and empty. She had gotten up, and not recently. I scented the air, not finding any smells of coffee, breakfast, or the moisture from a shower.

"Riley?" I called. No answer came except for the light pattering of rain on the windows and roof.

She had been upset last night. Maybe she went for a run to clear her head. After having the same argument again, she probably needed some space.

I got out of bed, unnerved by the silence in my house. It was funny how I used to crave this solitude. But Riley's presence had filled it up with a bright liveliness I loved, even after being found a traitor. She was the one thing keeping me going, the reason why I still had hope for a new day. A day when I would no longer feel like a cold statue.

"I should tell her that," I muttered to myself, filling a glass of water from the sink.

Shit, after last night, she probably thought I had no hope left at all. Riley only wanted to help me, and like an asshole, I kept shooting down her attempts. It was hard to have a positive outlook when mentally and physically I felt stuck in sludge all the time, but for her, I needed to do better. I needed to get past this funk and *be* better.

I needed to apologize and let her know how appreciative I was that she was still here at my side, despite everything. If anything, female wolves were even more pack-oriented than males, so anyone else would have dropped me the moment they heard I went against Derric's orders. Riley was truly special, and I was the damn luckiest wolf to call her mine.

Fuck the pack. I didn't need them when I had her.

I should make coffee for when she gets back. And omelets, I realized, feeling a fresh surge of energy at the thought of serving my mate.

We would eat first, and then talk. This time, I would be receptive to what she said, and it wouldn't be an argument but two partners figuring out how to move forward. She was completely right when she said we couldn't go on like this. Hopefully this would be the first in several steps toward positive change.

I made the omelets and brewed the coffee without much difficulty and almost felt like my old self again. When Riley came home and saw what I'd made, I knew the look on her face would make me feel even better. A wolf provided for his mate, and there was satisfaction in doing these simple tasks for her again.

There was still no sign of her by the time I set the plates out on the island, so I went to quickly wash up, making sure I looked and smelled decent.

When the food started getting cold and the light drizzle of rain became a full-on downpour, I started to worry. Riley didn't know the woods as well as I did, and what if she got lost? The rain could wash away scents that were familiar enough to lead her back home.

I shucked off my clothing, the thought of my mate cold and lost spurring a determination I hadn't felt since venturing into Sanguine to rescue her.

The cold rain barely registered on my skin as I went out the front door. It didn't even penetrate my thick fur when I shifted. I was singularly focused on getting my mate back.

Riley's scent was faint, a soft undertone of all the water falling from the sky, but I quickly found her paw prints in the ground. Her tracks had nearly disappeared with the rain, so it was a good thing I didn't wait any longer to go searching.

Something was odd about her tracks, though. They kept zigzagging across wide areas that made no sense and went through areas that were difficult to follow, like ground covered in leaves, rocks clustered together, or jumping over fallen logs. It was almost like she was trying to throw me off her trail.

A frustrated *whuff* left my mouth, though it wasn't aimed at her. She had been so upset at me that she didn't want me following her. That was fair enough if she wanted space, but she had to be miserable out in this weather.

I put my nose back to the ground, refusing to be deterred. She had hours of space to herself this morning, but now it was time for my mate to come back. I'd drag her home by her scruff like a pup if I had to.

Or if she was, for some reason, in human form out in this weather, I'd throw her over my shoulder like a caveman and carry her home that way.

I let out an amused yip as I found more of her tracks to follow. *Now* I was feeling more like myself. All it took was my mate triggering these instincts to protect and provide for her.

You should run into the woods more often, sweetness, I thought hungrily. *Because I will always chase you. Maybe we can make a sexy game out of it.*

Riley's tracks abruptly stopped. And so did her scent.

The mud was slicker here, creating the shore of a puddle that was nearing the size of a small pond. Any tracks she left here had likely been washed away. But why would she...

I walked up and down the edges of the puddle, even walking around to the other side, scenting everything that I could. No sign of her, like she had just disappeared.

My head fell back with a brief howl, calling to her in case she was nearby. No answer came after howling a few more times, and then I started to panic.

Anxious whines and frustrated barks filled the air as I circled the puddle again and again, sniffing every leaf and twig and square inch of mud for the tiniest whiff of my mate's scent. I couldn't face it, couldn't let my brain arrive at the conclusion that was right in front of me. It simply couldn't be true.

I tried to backtrack, wondering if I had followed the

wrong trail somewhere, but the rainfall had erased all traces of Riley's scent and tracks. So I circled that damn pond again, searching beyond it to see if I could pick up her trail on the other side, and came up with nothing.

I howled until my throat was hoarse, called out her name telepathically, ran myself in fucking circles until I had no choice but to face it. She didn't just want me to not follow her. She didn't want me to find her at all.

The sky darkened even as the angry storm clouds rolled away, which meant that I had been out here for hours. Nearly the entire day.

I was numb and cold again. It had nothing to do with the weather or being a traitor.

My mate was gone.

And she wasn't coming back.

CHAPTER 27
RILEY

I thought I heard Sawyer's howls over the next few days, and it was physically painful to not run straight to those sad, haunting sounds. Being away from him only got more difficult with each day, not easier.

It turned out, I sucked at being a wolf. I sucked even harder at being a lone wolf.

Hunting for food was a failure more often than not, and I was constantly hungry. Sawyer had said hunting was a skill and that he would teach me. While I scrounged the forest floor for rodents, fruit, mushrooms, *anything*, my heart was heavy with all the memories we'd never gotten to make.

The yearning for a pack hit me hard on my first night out in the wild. My instincts screamed at me that this was both unwise and unsafe. No wolf was meant to live alone. Having my mate would be satisfactory enough, but an entire pack? That would be ideal.

I came across a pack of werewolves living deep in the woods in my third day on my own. They looked like nomads, their homes simple yurts rather than permanent structures.

These wolves were wary of me, naturally, but gave me a meal and a space by their fire for one night. All the while, they watched me like hawks and barely said a word. After finishing a meal, I muttered a thanks and proceeded to slink away, despite my instincts to find my new home with this pack. I had a feeling that even if they were open to me, joining a new pack wouldn't be easy.

They probably had reasons to be suspicious of outsiders, and besides, the only place I considered home was with Sawyer.

Maybe I've been gone long enough, I thought. *Maybe he'll be willing to work with me if I head back now.*

But what if he wasn't? What if I returned to that cabin, full of heartache at how badly I missed him, only to find that nothing had changed at all? I could only go back if I was willing to face that, and I wasn't sure that I was.

Even so, I missed the simplest companionship. I missed just being in the presence of other people.

And thankfully, my fourth day was a bright, sunny one. I stepped out into a clearing and relished in the sun's warmth on my fur. My time with the vampires felt like so long ago, but I would never take the sun's rays for granted again.

I ran at a leisurely pace along a rocky ridge, catching as much sunlight as I could. My mood had been dour since leaving Sawyer, but today I had a small spring in my step. I was heading toward Stout & Spirit at the southern end of Vargmore. The thought of seeing Shiloh and talking to her made my heart ache something fierce. I was desperate for her warm company and kind words. Hopefully she could lend me some clothes for when I shifted to human and wouldn't be too busy with the bar.

And if she was, that was okay too. Hell, maybe I could jump in and help her. I wondered if her offer of a bartending job still stood after everything that had happened.

Or was I subject to the same judgment as Sawyer? For being his mate and the reason for his going against the alpha.

The thought stopped me in my tracks. Maybe this wasn't such a good idea. I still wanted to see Shiloh, but maybe doing so privately was better. I didn't want to cause a stir among the other wolves and citizens.

With a whine, I sat my haunches down and looked out over the territory. Stout & Spirit was a short run away, its brick chimney sticking out among the treetops. Gentle plumes of smoke released from the top, and I could practically smell the wood-burning pizzas from the small kitchen.

This ridge was high enough that I could just *barely* see past the southern edge of the territory. As the trees and hills thinned out into flat plains and then into desert, I knew the Shadowburn Cliffs, the dragon's territory, were somewhere beyond the horizon.

It had been mighty tempting to plan an escape to the dragons' home after Aran had made that offer to me by the bonfire. I thought of it often while I was awake in Fabian's captivity. I didn't know if dragons kept human pets, but it probably was a trap. Still, it couldn't have been much worse, right? I had just been too weak to make any kind of escape attempt. Fabian had made sure of that.

Thinking back on that whole ordeal made my heart

ache for Sawyer again. He'd planned on rescuing me for weeks, in spite of the consequences, and for what? To lose his pack *and* his mate.

That sent my head back in a long, anguished howl, and when I finished the song, I'd made up my mind.

I was going back to him. And we would figure this out. Together.

Despite not being in my human skin, I was fully aware of his mating bite on my shoulder. The spot felt warmer than anywhere else on my body, like the first sign of a sunburn that was not yet painful. Even after days and miles of separation, I felt the pull of longing for my mate.

Now, I was finally ready to return.

I started to turn around, heading for the direction of Sawyer's cabin, when movement near the bar caught my eye. I didn't know what urged me to stay and watch, but looking back, I would be forever glad that I did.

Someone was walking through the woods with intention while also making an effort to stay hidden behind tree trunks. At first, I almost wrote them off as a human going about their business, but I kept my gaze on the figure moving through the trees. Something set off my instincts like alarm bells, and my entire body went stiff, ears pricked and all senses focused.

The figure was too close to the border between Vargmore and Sanguine to just be going about their business. And the way they kept trying to stay out of sight was fishy.

After a moment of deliberation, I turned and ran down the side of the ridge, leaping into a sprint toward the bar once I hit the ground. My wolf eyesight was poor from far away, and I couldn't get a good look at the figure's face. I needed to get closer to use my better senses—smell and hearing.

It would be several minutes of hard running before I reached the bar though, and the urgency in my instincts pushed me onward. Something about this was suspicious at best, and dangerous at worst.

Once I was a few hundred yards from the bar, a mix of scents that were familiar and disturbing hit my nose so hard, I nearly tripped in my run.

Vampire and draitrium.

I smelled *a lot* of draitrium, to the point where it burned the inside of my nose. It was even stronger than the vampire smell, which meant the figure in question had to be an extremely heavy user.

I knew one person who fit that profile.

Screams hit my ears next, and then the scent of fresh blood being spilled.

No! A terrified howl burst from my mouth. *He's attacking the bar!*

Still, I kept running, my focus locked on that structure only a hundred paces away, coming closer.

"Someone call Howling Death!" I heard someone scream.

"No one's calling those mutts to save you!" My heart froze at the sound of Fabian's voice, the familiar rage-filled tone striking fear in every part of my body. "I want my pet back! I know she's here."

"We don't know what you're talking about!"

Popping sounds rang in my ears and then more screams. Holy shit, he had a *gun?!*

"I'm not leaving until I have her!"

"Please! We don't know who you mean!"

"Then you dogs better start rounding up your humans, because until I have mine, you're stuck with me."

More gunshots. More screams.

I reached the back of the bar and slunk along the exterior side wall. Looking around the corner, I saw that the front door was wide open. No one was outside, so everyone could only be trapped within.

That left me no choice.

Knowing every second counted, I shifted to my human form and simply walked inside. "I'm right here, Fabian. Leave everyone else alone."

As he turned around, my eyes darted around the bar to assess the damage. It was too early in the day for the rowdy bar crowd, so it was mostly families and a few small groups gathered for drinks. Everyone was on the ground or taking shelter under tables. One man had his back against a wall, looking pale as he and Shiloh pressed their hands over a bleeding wound in his shoulder. A few bullet holes made dark spots in the walls.

Once Fabian faced me, he was almost unrecognizable. Not only were his eyes yellow, but so was his skin. Unfocused and glassy as his gaze was, he also looked downright murderous, with his brows pulled down tight and his fangs so long they extended past his lower lip. I glanced down to the handgun he had, pointing outward at his side.

"You..." He didn't seem to notice or care that I was naked. "You got me kicked out of my club, bitch. I've lost everything 'cause of you!"

"I'm sorry. I'll go with you. I'll do whatever you want." I clasped my hands in front of me and looked downward, trying to play the part of the meek, helpless human that he loved to mistreat.

"I want to watch the light leave your eyes as I drain you 'til you're nothing but a husk," Fabian hissed. "You're fucking worthless. Look what you've done to me!"

"I know. Take me, then." I took one step backward, holding my palm out in his direction. "Let's go outside."

"No!"

He spun in an unsteady circle, waving his gun around as everyone else flinched and braced themselves. I spotted one guy sliding a cell phone into his pocket, and while there was no lost love between that alpha and me, I prayed that Derric and his wolves were on their way.

"These dumb fucking dogs need to pay for what they did!" Fabian yelled at the top of their lungs. "They stole you from me! Where's that enforcer? I need to drain him too, then make a coat out of his fur."

"Come with me." I stuck my hand out farther to him, urging him to follow. "I know where he is. I'll take you to him, and you can have us both."

Fabian stared at me for several long seconds, units of time that hopefully meant help was coming closer and closer. His drug-and-sunshine addled brain was probably having trouble making sense of my offer. At least, that's what I was banking on.

"You're lying!" Gasps rose from the bar patrons as he leveled that handgun right at my chest. "You've never made it easy for me. You think I'm stupid, bitch?"

"Yeah, I do."

Actually, I was the stupid one right then, choosing the moment my captor and torturer had a gun pointed at me to antagonize him. Maybe it was adrenaline pumping through me, maybe it was a tactic to keep him distracted while we waited for help. I couldn't place the *why* exactly, but everything I'd been holding onto decided to unload right then and there.

For the moment, though, it worked. Fabian blinked dumbly at what I'd said.

"You're stupid enough to let your blood pet escape. Twice. Stupid enough that you had to manipulate a home-less human with food and shelter to get a blood pet in the first place instead of making a consensual arrangement like other vampires." Once it all started pouring out of me, I just couldn't stop. "Stupid enough to lie to your president about your drug usage. Stupid enough to blame everyone but yourself for what happens to you."

"Shut up!" The gun barrel shook as he kept it trained on me. "I'd have fired this at you already if your blood didn't taste so good."

"You can still drink from me." My palm remained raised and held out to him. "Let's do this outside. You like to feed from me in the sunlight, remember?"

"Where Howling Death can spot me from a mile away? I don't think so." Fabian looked down to where a woman huddled on the floor with a young child in her arms. She shrieked, shielding her pup with her body when his arm swung to point his gun at her. "I'm dead either way, so I might as well take a few fucking werewolves out with me."

The shift came over me the moment his finger curled around the trigger. There was no thought, only action as I collided with him. The gun went off before we hit the ground, and I could only hope the bullet went through a wall, not someone's body.

Fabian's head bounced on the hard floorboards with a satisfying thunk. Sadly, it didn't kill him. In the next instant, my front paws braced against his shoulders, pinning him to the floor while I stuck my muzzle full of teeth right in his face.

He didn't seem to comprehend it at first, then his drugged-out yellow eyes went wide with surprise. "So you're one of the mutts too, huh?"

I growled and snapped my jaws within an inch of his nose. I was content to sit on his chest until Howling Death came to deal with him, but if he tried anything, I was beyond ready to tear his throat open.

"No wonder your blood tasted so damn good." Fabian's expression hardened into one of pure hatred. "Killing you and your kind will only be more satisfying then."

I barked a warning right in his face, making sure he saw all my teeth.

"Too bad for you, I don't want a mouthful of fur with my last meal."

Something pressed against my stomach, and a loud pop hurt my sensitive ears. I knew what had happened before the burst of pain spread across my abdomen like a third-degree burn.

So I did the only thing I could do, which was lunge forward with my jaws open. My mouth closed around soft flesh and bit down hard, forcing past the resistance of the windpipe. I closed my jaws into that vampire's throat and shook him, wrenching back and forth with the last of my flagging strength.

I thought of everything he did to me—every lie he said and every feeding session that he'd purposely made painful —and shook even harder. I thought of Sawyer, everything he went through so I could be safe, so we could be together, only for this bastard to shoot up a place full of innocent werewolves and then me. I released Fabian's throat, barely aware of him flopping to the floor like a rag doll, then bit into him again, making sure I punctured the big blood vessels in his neck before thrashing him again.

Blood filled my nose, my mouth. It covered my paws and the fur on my belly. Mine, his, who knew? I wanted to keep tearing into him, keep killing him, but I was starting to feel *so* heavy...

My vision started going in and out, and then nothing was in my jaws anymore. The bar's ceiling looked fuzzy, kinda spotty. I just wanted to go to sleep.

Something touched the side of my face, gently stroking the base of my ear. I turned my head with a whine and licked the gentle hand.

"...you hear me...?"

That sounded like Shiloh, and I howled for her, asking my fellow wolves if she was okay. Then her face appeared in my vision, long black hair falling over shoulders, her expression pinched with fear.

"...need you...stay awake for me, okay?"

I howled again, and it turned into a yelp as I felt a cold, aching, pain in my abdomen. Yeah, that hurt like a bitch and was definitely going to keep me awake.

"...hit with a silver bullet..."

Whoever said that made it sound like a dire situation, worse than a regular lead slug. I was trying to recall some old legends from the human world, something about silver and werewolves, when infinite blackness pulled me under.

CHAPTER 28

SAWYER

2 8. Sawyer

MY BIKE PROTESTED under the stress I put it under, some metallic screeching noise alerting me to something running too hot, and still I pushed on.

My heart was in my throat and it was moments away from choking me for good.

Tryn had just made an unexpected visit to my cabin and he only had to say a few words to get my ass moving.

Vampire attack. Riley had been shot with a silver bullet.

It was especially heinous that a vampire had shot her. Silver was poisonous to both of our species. Fabian must have procured it from the dragons, who loved their shiny metals.

I didn't know if the bloodsucker was alive, dead,

imprisoned, or had gotten away, and didn't give a fuck. Seeing to Riley was my first and only priority.

Hell, I hadn't stuck around to listen to Tryn long enough to know if *she* was alive. He could have come to give me his condolences for all I knew.

It wouldn't matter either way. I needed to see her for myself.

I should have killed Fabian the moment I left that place with her. He wouldn't have seen me coming, and it probably would have done Thorne a favor too.

All kinds of should-have scenarios ran through my mind as I tore across the landscape, burning rubber and fuel like my life depended on it. I should have killed that bastard, should have kept looking for her after she left me, should have actually listened when she told me *to my fucking face* that I was breaking her heart.

Only the heat in my shoulder prevented me from totally losing my shit, the feel of her mating bite in my flesh. I could always feel it, an ever-present sensation. That connection and vow to her kept me focused.

It felt like years before I pulled up to the Howling Death lodge. Vargmore didn't have a formal hospital. The witches with healing magic usually made house calls. If someone needed a safe, comfortable place to recover, the lodge was where they were usually taken. There, they would be guarded by the fiercest wolves in the territory, which, at one point, was me. The pack protected our vulnerable, and everyone must have known Riley's shifter status by now. That was the only place she could be.

Moments after shutting off my bike, I crossed the porch and crashed into the meeting hall like a bull in a china shop. Nothing got me moving, got me feeling, like knowing my mate had been injured. And it was my biggest regret, that it had come to this before I could see her again.

"Where is she?" I demanded, pressing against the forearm braced across my chest. Someone's face was in front of me, but I didn't know or care who. "Let me see my mate."

"You're not supposed to be here, traitor," sneered the person holding me back.

I focused on the face in front of me, baring my teeth when I recognized Ruse. "I won't hesitate to rip off one of your ears, or even your throat, VP. Riley is my mate. You can't keep me from seeing her."

"Have you forgotten what you are?" he growled back. "Who *I* am? You've got balls the size of the moon to show your face around here."

"She's in my room."

We both turned to see Derric making his way down the stairs, his posture casual but no less authoritative.

"Why?" I hissed, my vision turning red at the implication of *my* mate in *his* room.

"Because it's the biggest and most comfortable, and she's a hero to Vargmore." He paused a few feet away, regarding the two of us. "We called in an angel healer, who's with her now. So you can't see her yet, but you may stay if you behave."

Ruse snarled in frustration toward his alpha. "He's a traitor, Derric. He shouldn't be here at all."

"I'm aware," Derric said lightly. "But they are a mated pair, and it's natural for Sawyer to fight and claw his way through any obstacles to be at his mate's side." The alpha's gaze landed on me. "I'm willing to allow it, so long as no trouble is caused."

"Fine," I bit out. "When can I see her?"

"When the angel is done working on her." Derric angled his head. "Let him go, Ruse."

There was a moment of hesitation before the forearm came away from my chest. Ruse glared at me and I returned the stare. He wasn't a bad guy, but he so single-mindedly followed Derric's commands that he didn't see the big picture in every situation.

A figure coming out of a side door pulled our attention away from each other. A male angel with glossy, black wings so large that he had to duck slightly and come through the door sideways emerged from the lodge's kitchen.

"Camael," I said by way of greeting the Broken Wings MC's president. "Are you the healer for my mate?"

The angel looked like he was made of glass but not in a fragile way. Everything about him was sharp and shiny, from his slicked back dark hair, to the leather jacket that fit him like a glove. His whole look, from his clothes to the feathers in his wings, was perfect and polished, making us wolves look rough and ragtag by comparison.

Stuck-up bastards, these angels were. Good thing they were on our side.

"No, my sister Laylah is," Camael said. "I'm just her chaperone."

I kept my expression neutral, not revealing how weird it was that single angel women had to be escorted everywhere by a family member until they were mated. What I loved about being a wolf was that we always had our community to look out for each other, but as individuals? Adults were free to go and do as they pleased. Chaperoning was for children.

"How long have you two been here?" I asked, just to pass time and make conversation.

"Since Derric called us early this morning. Laylah's been at it for a few hours."

"The witch healers removed the bullet and closed up her wound, but were unable to stop the silver from poisoning her bloodstream," Derric said. "We called in Laylah when she took a turn for the worse."

"How do you know it wasn't too late?" I growled.

"My sister wouldn't still be in there if there was nothing she could do." Camael put a hand on my shoulder and his chiseled face actually looked genuinely sympathetic. "She's the best we have when it comes to purifying magic. Your mate is in good hands, enforcer."

"He's not the enforcer anymore," Ruse muttered under his breath, still glaring at me.

"Ah. Seems I'm out of the loop." Camael apparently didn't care to be brought in the loop as he made his way to an armchair with his procured prize from the kitchen—a cheese Danish. Rather than sit in the chair, he perched on one of the arms. "Derric, you really should consider getting some backless chairs. It'd be way more hospitable toward visits from my kind."

"You mean, like, stools?" Derric waved his arm toward the bar, tucked away next to the kitchen, all the barstools empty for the time being. "Or benches, maybe?" He used his other arm to indicate the picnic-style dining tables with their bench seats in the dining area.

"I mean *chairs,*" Camael clarified helpfully. "Look, I'll have my craftsman in HC make a few and send them over. You lot will probably enjoy them too, they're like elevated dog beds."

Derric shrugged. "As long as it's on your dime."

A door opened moments later, and we all looked to the sound coming from the top of the stairs. From Derric's bedroom emerged a beautiful, red-haired woman with brilliant white wings. She wasn't as tall as Camael but still had to do a side-step shuffle thing to get the tops of her wings through the door.

Laylah floated down the stairs gracefully, smiling warmly at those of us down below. "Riley is resting. You may see her now, but for the sake of her recovery, I suggest you do not wake her up."

The female angel wore a simple white dress with a black leather jacket, similar but with an obviously more feminine cut than Camael's, over it.

"How is she?" I asked eagerly, turning to face her. Laylah was easily the most stunning creature in the room, if not the entire territory, but the mated male in me only wanted my Riley.

"She is well." Laylah smiled easily at me and a tiny bit of tension left my shoulders. "I'm confident Riley will make a full recovery. She only needs plenty of rest."

More tension drained out of my body. This woman had none of her brother's arrogance. I sensed only pure kindness from her as I lowered my head, dropping my gaze to her feet in a show of gratitude.

"Thank you for saving my mate," I said through a tight throat.

"She is strong, both in her body and her will to live," Laylah said. "I just helped to guide the light already within her."

When I lifted my gaze, my eyes landed on Laylah's neck for some reason. The scars I noticed were faint, but unmistakable. Puncture wounds. Made from fangs sinking over and over again into the same spot right over her carotid artery.

Laylah had been fed on by vampires? When?

It was practically unthinkable. Angels were a high and mighty sort and had pretty strict customs about "purity". They wouldn't be caught dead in one of those underground caverns, hidden away from the sun. Wolves had reason to hate the vamps, given our bloody history, but angels never associated with them, to my knowledge.

For one of their own to have been a vampire's meal was unheard of.

Laylah locked eyes with me for a moment, and a delicate flush crept into her cheeks. She subtly adjusted the collar of her jacket over the scars and gave me another warm smile.

"Will you be needing anything else from us?" Camael came over to stand by his sister, offering her elbow for him to take. "Aside from those chairs."

"No. Thank you again for coming out." Derric gave a slight bow to the angels, which was strange to see. Not only because he was an alpha, but his hands were shoved in the front pockets of his jeans and the movement was stiff. "We'll see you at the next alliance meeting."

"You definitely will." Camael turned to the front door, guiding Laylah along with him. "We'll have lots to talk about, I'm sure. Those scaled lizards to the south seem to be overstepping their boundaries lately."

I nodded in agreement while clasping my palms in front of me, making sure to cover the one marked by Aran's claw.

"And from what I've heard regarding Sawyer's injured

mate," Camael went on, nodding toward me, "so are the vampires."

"We've got the bloodsuckers handled," Derric assured.

"I certainly hope so." Camael gave us a curt nod while Laylah waved her goodbye. "'Til next time, *friends*."

Yeah, that was a loaded word if I ever heard one. Angels believed themselves above everyone else. They always made it sound like allying with us was doing us a favor, throwing a bone to the four-legged shifters stuck to the ground.

We were allies, on the same side when it came to conflicts with vampires and dragons. But friends? Hardly.

Camael and Laylah went out the front door, then I heard a soft *whoosh* of beating wings as they took flight. It was a much softer sound than dragon wings.

Once they were gone, I whipped around to face Derric. "What do you mean it's handled? Where's the vampire that attacked?"

His answer was only a wolfish smirk. "You should ask your mate when she wakes up."

CHAPTER 29
RILEY

It felt like I'd been sleeping deeply for days. I roused with stiff limbs, but that was the worst of it. The intense pain and icy-cold sensations were completely gone.

The room was dark, illuminated only by moonlight pouring through a window. The moon wasn't full tonight but she was bright and lovely all the same.

My eyes blinked a few times before focusing on the high vaulted ceiling with dark beams meeting in the center. I started to sit up, my heart racing at the memory of a ceiling just like this one—Sawyer's. But no, this wasn't Sawyer's house. This place was different.

"Riley?"

I looked toward the deep, rough voice that spoke my name and couldn't choke back the emotion flooding my chest. "Sawyer!"

We rushed at each other, or at least I tried to. I was tucked firmly into this wide, comfy bed, so Sawyer practically leaped from the bedside to crush me in a desperate embrace.

"I came as soon as I heard what happened," he whispered. "Fuck. I'm so sorry, Riley. I should have listened. I should have been a better mate to you."

"I'm sorry too," I answered, clinging to his shoulder. "I think we were both too stubborn to see the other person's point of view. I'm sorry I left like that."

Was I sorry I left at all? To be honest, no. Sawyer and I needed the space to think clearly about our situation. And if I hadn't been away, I never would have been at Stout & Spirit in time to help.

Oh God, the bar...

I pulled back from Sawyer, dread tightening up my throat. "Where's Shiloh? Is everyone okay? I know at least one other person got shot. What happened after I passed out?"

Sawyer pushed back a lock of my hair, his expression serene. "All injuries were minor, except yours. We almost lost you and had to call in an angel healer."

"Angel?" Damn, I wish I would have been awake to see that.

"Was it Fabian who attacked the bar?" Sawyer asked, rather than answer me.

"Yes. He was high on that drug, ranting and raving about getting kicked out of Blood 'til Dawn. Threatening everyone and demanding they hand me over."

My wolf growled, and I loved seeing him so alive. He had returned to me. With a smile, I ran my fingers through his hair, stroking his moonlight-kissed strands. "What did you do?" he asked, his growl softening under my touch.

"I showed myself to him as a human and just...talked to

him. I was stalling, hoping someone would call your pack for help while I had him distracted. Then he started waving his gun around again, and I couldn't let anyone else get hurt. So I shifted and pinned him to the floor."

Sawyer's lips brushed my shoulder, trailing over the bite marks he'd left there. A delicious shiver went down my spine, and my wolf let out a jubilant howl. The two halves of me melted at the sensual contact from our mate.

"What happened then, Riley?" he murmured.

I swallowed, steeling myself with a breath, and realized I had no lingering fear. Rather than traumatize me, the event made me feel proud. Powerful. I had been injured, yes, but the last year of my life before Sawyer was one long, festering wound. What was one more? Not only that, but I had gotten my ultimate revenge and killed the one responsible for my year of torment.

"I felt his gun barrel in my stomach," I said. "I didn't know about the silver. I just knew I could only do one thing in that moment, which was to stop him for good." Sawyer kissed my shoulder again, waiting patiently for what I'd say next.

"I almost want to say my wolf took over, but she didn't," I said. "It was all me, the human Riley. My wolf just gave me the tools. Her jaws, teeth, and her physical strength. But I was the one who crushed his windpipe and shook him with all the fury of what he did to me."

Sawyer pulled me against his chest, and I happily fell into that warm, protective space. "I'm so proud of you, my mate," he purred into my hair. "I would have loved to have killed him for you, but I'm so glad you took that vengeance for yourself. You're the bravest, most beautiful woman and wolf I've ever met."

I curled up tighter against him, burying my nose in the hollow of his throat to inhale more of his delicious scent while I clutched tightly to his shirt. After being without him for days, I didn't want us to leave this bed for a week, whoever's it was.

"I'll be a better mate to you from this day forward. You can handle yourself, but I'll still protect you *without* being bullheaded about it. I'll listen to you. I'll pay attention when you tell me you're hurting. I'm so sorry I was too stubborn to put aside my own wallowing to hear you."

"If I ever need space from you again," I kissed under his chin, "I'll leave a note. I don't think I really wanted to leave you for good, but I just...couldn't take it anymore."

"I know." He kissed the bridge of my nose. "I'm sorry."

I smiled against his neck. "Water under the bridge, my love."

We sat quietly for a while, content to just bask in the presence of each other again.

"What happens to us now?" I asked after a while. "Are you still...?"

"A traitor? Yes," he said. "That's kind of a lifetime thing."

"But Derric still let you come see me?" I lifted my head, looking around at the room that appeared to be a master suite in a luxury cabin. "Where am I, anyway?"

"Derric's bedroom," Sawyer grumbled like he was unhappy about it. "At the HDMC lodge."

My wolf barked with laughter inside my chest, amused at the jealousy she sensed in him. "So he *did* permit you to see me."

"Not without some resistance from the VP, but yes." He

nudged another kiss at my temple. "The alpha knew even he couldn't keep me away from you."

I leaned my head on his broad shoulder just as a knock came to the door. It swung open before Sawyer and I could respond, and the flick of a light switch brought a gentle glow to the room that thankfully wasn't too bright.

"There she is," the Howling Death alpha said from the doorway with a hint of a smile. "I heard voices and figured you'd woken up. You're looking much better, Riley."

"Thank you." A timidness had come over me now that I had a better picture of Derric's strength and authority. Inside, my wolf wanted to lower her head and tail, eager to not present a threat or challenge to this alpha.

"She's not ready for company," Sawyer growled, squeezing around me tighter.

"That's up to her, don't you think?" Derric swung his gaze to me. "Riley, would it be alright if I spoke to you for a moment?" His eyes flicked to Sawyer. "Alone?"

"No," my mate answered for me, and Derric's eyes started to roll like he was already sick of this shit.

"I'm feeling okay to talk," I said. "But anything you say to me can be said in front of Sawyer."

"Alright." Derric closed the door behind him and approached the foot of the bed, stopping just short of it. "You risked your life to save several others yesterday. It was incredibly brave of you to stand up to a vampire, who I understand had held you captive before."

"When you believed she was human and worth less than a wolf," Sawyer cut in. "The captor who *you* ordered her to be sent back to."

"Right, I was getting to that." Derric ran a hand through his long hair, temporarily exposing his mutilated ears and the scarring at his temples. "I misjudged you, Riley. And probably humans in general. I understand now why Sawyer went against my order to get you back." The alpha's eyes locked on my mate. "Not that I'm excusing what you did. By all our laws, you're still a traitor."

"Fine, whatever. It's not about me." Sawyer nudged his temple against mine. "But don't punish her for what I did."

"I'm not punishing her, I'm honoring her." Derric returned to addressing me. "Riley, you're already considered a hero in Vargmore. So many of our people want to meet you and thank you personally."

"Oh, wow." I shrank back against Sawyer's chest. "I'm not sure if I'm ready for that."

"I figured you wouldn't be." Derric gave me an easy smile. "So keep my room for as long as you'd like. Lay low and recover until you're ready to face the world."

"Oh no, I couldn't keep you out of your own room—"

"Yes, you can," Sawyer scoffed. "Staying in a guest room in his own house is the least he can do."

"Not only that," Derric added. "It's not enough. A heroine of Vargmore deserves more." The alpha spread his hands, palms open. "I would like to offer you an official membership into the Howling Death pack, plus anything else you desire. My wolves will be your family, which is essential for a young wolf. And this pack is the strongest, fiercest community in the territory."

Stunned and completely clueless on how to respond, I looked up at Sawyer.

"Accept," he said simply. "He's right. You need a pack, and there's no better one than Howling Death."

I didn't miss the note of sadness in his voice. The offer was only extended to me, not him. He would still be a traitor, packless and alone. How would that work if I was part of the pack and we were mates?

"You will be subject to me as alpha and must make a pledge of your loyalty if you do accept," Derric said. "But like I said, I will also grant you anything else you desire." His gaze was intense on me as he said that, like he was leading me somewhere.

"Anything?" I asked tentatively.

"Anything at all, given that you accept the terms of pack membership."

It hit me right then what he was doing, and I almost laughed out loud. I still didn't *like* Derric, but I respected his craftiness. Maybe, after some time, having him as an alpha wouldn't be so bad after all.

"Then I accept. I would love to be part of Howling Death."

"Excellent." Derric grinned broadly. "We'll have an induction ceremony as soon as you're feeling up to it. Do you know what you would like in addition?"

"I do."

"Then name it."

I brought my hands around Sawyer's forearm which was draped over my torso. "I want Sawyer's traitor status removed and for him to be reinstated as Howling Death's enforcer."

My mate's shocked breath pressed against my back, as did his racing heart.

"My, what a completely unexpected surprise." Derric didn't sound surprised at all as he crossed his arms over his chest. "Traitors are usually forbidden from returning to the fold, but sadly for me, I didn't place any restrictions on your request. And because you are a hero who we all owe our lives to, I cannot refuse you."

"How unfortunate," Sawyer coughed, still in apparent disbelief.

Derric turned to him. "Do you accept being reinstated as my enforcer?"

Sawyer swallowed, then said thickly, "If you will have me, alpha."

I lifted a hand. "Alpha, I would also like to request an apology from you to him."

"To me?" Sawyer echoed. "He should apologize to *you.*"

Derric rubbed his temples and sighed. "You only get one request, dear hero. But fine. It's overdue, and I know I'm not infallible." He placed a hand over his heart. "I'm sorry to you both. My decisions caused you both suffering that was unwarranted. I deeply regret that." He paused, looking to a distant corner of the room as he took a deep breath. "I have a lot to think about, especially with regards to humans and how far mates will go to stay together. I accept that I'm imperfect and may fuck up decisions again in the future, but I swear to you both, I will never send an innocent back to a place of suffering again. And I will never cast anyone out as a traitor when their only intention is to save the one they love. May the moon's light reveal my hypocrisy if I break this vow."

He ended there, letting his hand fall to his side.

Sawyer made a *hmm* sound as he nuzzled his rough cheek against mine. "That work for you?"

I took a moment to absorb everything Derric had said. I wanted to be sure, because he was now my community leader. If he gave me orders, I would have to obey him. I listened to my wolf, looking deep inside to see how she felt.

Her response was positive, tail thumping with restrained excitement. She was happy to be part of a pack, and she felt this alpha was sincere. He wasn't perfect, but he did his best to lead fairly and owned up to his mistakes.

My wolf's feelings aligned with my human ones, and I was relieved. Plus, I was beyond ready to start my new life with the past behind me and my best foot forward.

I lifted my chin, meeting Derric's eyes. "I accept your apology, alpha."

"I do as well," Sawyer echoed.

"Thank you both." Derric bowed his head slightly. "You are gracious and proud wolves." He started backing up toward the doorway. "I'll leave you alone to rest now."

No sooner had he turned the knob and opened the door than panicked noise and commotion filled the room from downstairs. Shouts of, "What the fuck is *he* doing here?" and, "Go back to your hole in the ground, bloodsucker!" floated up into the room.

"Stay here," Sawyer commanded, leaping up from the bed and following Derric out through the door. In his rush, he didn't fully close it behind him.

I got out of bed, my legs a little wobbly but sturdy enough to hold me, then went to peek through the gap in the door.

In the large room below, surrounded by a growling semicircle of werewolves, stood Thorne, the Blood 'til Dawn president.

CHAPTER 30
SAWYER

Derric took the stairs, but I jumped down from the top landing halfway shifted and ready to tear the vampire apart.

"Is stupidity something of great value to your people?" I asked through my elongating jaws. "Because I can't imagine any other reason why you'd come here."

"He says he comes peacefully," said Tryn, his expression betraying just how much he believed that statement, which was not at all. "He was waiting at the border for us to escort him. Says he's alone and unarmed."

"State your business, vampire." Derric's shift was also riding him, his eyes flashing and his canines long. "And make it quick."

To his credit, Thorne wasted no time. "I've come to request the body of the vampire who died in your territory. He was removed from my club but is still one of my kind. I would like to bury him on his own soil."

"How do you know he died here?" snarled Ruse.

"My vampires are brought into Blood 'til Dawn with a blood pact," Thorne said. If he was unnerved or even the tiniest bit afraid being here, surrounded by enemies, he didn't show it. He was cool as a cucumber, ruby eyes alert but steady. "His blood is in me and I felt when he died, we all did. I could also sense that he didn't die at home. Given his obsession with that former blood pet of his, I could only deduce that he had met his end here."

I got up in his face the moment he referred to Riley. "That former blood pet is my mate, and she has a name."

He met my gaze, neither flinching nor standing down. A good thing, otherwise he'd be a shitty excuse for a MC president. "I never got her name. My apologies."

"It's Riley."

The voice that spoke was feminine and came from above us. Every head turned and looked up. Derric's door was open but no one stood on the threshold. Moments later, a beautiful wolf with gray, white, and black fur emerged and started down the stairs. Riley's eyes were bright, determined, as her paws took the steps with a dainty, animal grace, her tail swishing calmly from side to side.

"I see," Thorne mused, understanding creeping into his tone. "Riley. I wish we could've met under...less violent circumstances."

Tell him what happened, Riley said as she came to sit at my side. *I want him to know what I did.*

Derric gave a subtle nod, indicating that he heard her. "The vampire came in broad daylight, high on draitrium, and attacked a bar full of our people. Riley confronted him, killed him, and saved at least a dozen lives in the process." The alpha crossed his arms and stepped up to

Thorne, right next to me. "And if she hadn't been there, nothing would have stopped Howling Death from coming down on you like the beasts we are. Thanks to her, we have no dead to avenge. So consider yourself lucky, vampire."

"I understand." Thorne let out a weary sigh and rubbed his face. "I should have seen this coming with Fabian, honestly. He always had issues with addiction, but I never thought he'd be so bold—er, stupid." He lifted his eyes, meeting Derric's gaze again. "You have my word that I've only come to request the remains. If you grant me that, I'll happily be out of your fur."

"Take the body and leave," Derric spat. "And this better be the last we see of any of your kind in our territory. Otherwise, we *will* retaliate."

"Trust me, I wouldn't have come if it wasn't absolutely necessary," Thorne returned. "For all of Fabian's faults, he deserves a proper burial on his home ground."

"We certainly don't want him poisoning our soil," I remarked.

The vampire's red gaze flicked in my direction for a moment before he gave a small jerk of his head. "I recognize and am grateful for this kind gesture, werewolves. Hopefully we never meet again."

"Likewise." Derric nodded at Orson and Ruse, who flanked Thorne on either side to escort him to wherever the body was being kept.

Once the vampire was gone, it was like the whole room had been holding its breath and let it all out in a huge, collective sigh of relief.

"Those dudes are so creepy." Tryn gave a visible shudder.

"Did you see anything about him?" I asked, mainly for my own curiosity.

Tryn shrugged. "Not much. He was telling the truth, at least. Oh, and his fate thread is intertwined with one that's completely different from his. Not sure what that means." He gave another shrug before holding out a palm toward me. "By the way, welcome back, enforcer."

"You really do have a sense about these things, huh?" I clasped the offered palm with a grin.

"I do. But I also might've been eavesdropping at Derric's door." He turned to Riley, still in her wolf form, and spread his arms wide. "Welcome to the family, young lady!"

She reared up on her hind legs, bringing her front paws to Tryn's chest as her tail wagged furiously. He laughed and hugged around her neck. It was so endearing to see my mate already being accepted into the pack that not even my ultra-possessive wolf could be jealous.

"I see both of your fate threads now too," Tryn added, looking at the space between Riley and I. "Beautifully intertwined. You two will have a long, happy life together."

Nothing could stop the grin on my face or the happiness threatening to burst from my chest as he said that. "Thanks, Tryn. That's the plan, anyway."

He leaned in closer to me. "You know what else I see?"

"What's that?" Riley returned to my side, pressing the length of her body against my legs as I stroked down her back.

"Your armor, remember when I said it was cracking?"

"Yeah, what about it?"

"It's all gone now." Tryn smiled broadly. "Your strength is still there, but you've no longer got a protective cage around yourself."

Tryn's riddles and vision usually were nonsensical to me, but this time, looking back at my own imperfections and mistakes, they made perfect sense to me.

"Yeah," I agreed, running my fingers over Riley's delicate ears. "It just took the right person to get past it."

EPILOGUE
RILEY

My initiation ceremony was held at the next full moon, and I was on the verge of panicking upon realizing how much of a Big Deal it was. As the reigning pack in Vargmore, all of Howling Death would be there. Not only that, but so would all the smaller packs in the area, meaning around 100 werewolves would watch me get brought into the pack officially.

"There's really nothing to it," Sawyer assured me the night before. "Derric will ask you a bunch of questions in front of everyone, you'll answer everything with, 'yes, alpha' and 'I will, alpha'. Then you and the moon will have a moment alone together at the lake, and when you're ready, you'll join the rest of us for a pack run."

I made a fist on his chest and propped my chin on it to look at him. "What do you mean 'the moon and I will have a moment alone together'?"

"Well, you'll have privacy. So it can be whatever you want." Warm fingertips made lazy circles on my shoulder blade. "The moon's magic is what triggers the change in us, so many of us see her as a deity. Some people foster a very close connection to her and communicate with her often. Others are more casual about it or don't have much of a connection with her at all except during the full moon shift."

"I see. So there's this understanding among your kind—"

"*Our* kind," he chided me gently.

"Sorry, I'm still getting used to this. But there's an understanding that everyone's relationship with the moon is very personal?"

"Yes, exactly. So you can do a full-on howl song or have a few moments of silence just to enjoy the moon's light. Whatever feels right to you."

By the next sunset, as I prepared to present myself before the pack, I still had no idea what I'd do during that 'alone with the moon' time. I hadn't exactly thought about what my relationship with the moon was. Adjusting to the presence of my wolf inside me, plus just learning *how* to be a wolf, felt like a full-time job sometimes.

I still had moments of being overwhelmed that this was *my* life. I had a mate and community who loved me. No other shoe was going to drop. No one had ulterior motives. I wondered if I would ever fully get used to it.

"You look beautiful." Sawyer came up behind me and kissed the crown of my head, careful not to mess up the braids I had running along the sides of my head. His inky blue eyes were hungry in the mirror. "I can't wait until you and I can sneak off during the run."

"Is that what we're doing?" I grinned at his reflection.

"At the first fucking opportunity," he growled.

We walked hand-in-hand to the ceremony site, a clearing in the woods not far from where Derric and Ruse had caught us together. Ruse had also apologized to me not long after Derric had said his, which I accepted tentatively. Only time and any future interactions with humans would tell if he was sincere.

Werewolves were already crowding the space, some chatting in small groups as humans, others in their wolf forms. Sawyer and I made our way through, smiling and greeting people, many of whom returned with congratulations to me.

It made my heart swell. I wasn't even officially part of the pack and they were already treating me as though I was.

We broke through the crowd and Sawyer hung back with the others, giving a small squeeze to my hand before releasing me to continue forward alone into the clearing with Derric.

The alpha had pants on but was bare-chested, moonlight giving an ethereal shine to the multitude of scars criss-crossing over him. He looked formidable, powerful. Every bit the leader of these gathered people, and a stab of anxiety halted my feet.

But Derric gave me an easy smile and reached his hand out to me. "Come forward, Riley."

I looked over my shoulder at Sawyer, whose lips twitched as he held back a proud grin. He nodded once, encouraging me onward. When I looked at Derric again, anticipation and excitement sparked inside me, not fear. I crossed the distance to my soon-to-be alpha and placed my hand in his.

"Will you please kneel, Riley?" Derric took a step back, allowing space for my knees to touch down to the soft grass.

I did as asked, and the next few minutes were a blur. Derric asked me questions and the human side of me answered, but I could already feel that side of me stepping back. The full moon was approaching its peak in the sky and drawing out the wild animal in me that had been dormant for so long. The shifting process would be impossible to stop and would overtake me at any moment, the moon's magic prickling at my skin like an itchy sweater.

Eventually, Derric placed a kiss on the top of my head and crouched to meet my eyes. "Welcome to Howling Death pack." His grin revealed long rows of wolf teeth. "*And Howling Death MC.*"

Instead of giddy laughter, a howl burst forth from my throat. A chorus of wolves joined moments later, and I wiggled out of my loose dress just in time, right before the shift took over and I ripped it.

Sawyer loped over to me with long powerful strides, dark fur glossy in the moonlight. He licked my face and jumped all around me, yipping in excitement. *You can have your moment with the moon now,* he said. *We'll wait for you as long as you need.*

It felt like the moon had a spotlight on us right then, turning the grass, trees, and even the gray in Sawyer's fur a beautiful silver color.

You know what? This is all I need. I nuzzled him and licked his snout. *The moon led me to you, led me to find out who I really was. I just want to spend the rest of my days and nights with you, under her light.*

Sawyer was completely still for a moment, like he was

dumbfounded, before rubbing his forehead hard against my face and neck. *I could not have asked the moon for a more brave, resilient, beautiful mate. You've shown me what true strength is, and I'm endlessly amazed by you. I love you, Riley, and I promise every day to be a mate worthy of you.*

I love you too. And I'll hold you to that promise. I nipped playfully at his ear before licking him there.

Please do. And if I fuck up, tell me and I'll listen.

I will. I rubbed my forehead into the side of his neck. *We both learned some hard lessons, didn't we?*

I'm sure we have plenty more to learn. He leaned into me. *But now we can do so together.*

Can't wait. I licked his snout. *So how is a group of over a hundred wolves supposed to run together?*

Sawyer's lips pulled back in a wolfish grin. *Oh, that's easy. You'll get into the flow of it. Just follow me.*

Always, my mate.

He took off, and I narrowly missed catching his tail between my teeth. As he went to join the gathered wolves, I gave chase, blending in seamlessly with my new pack, my new family.

My future.

Thank you so much for reading Traitor Wolf!
If you'd like to read what Sawyer & Riley get up to when they finally have some alone time (wink wink), grab their bonus scene here: https://BookHip.com/DAFALQP

))))))●●●(((((

Ready to see our girl Shiloh get a love story? Her and Orson's book is up next! You can pre-order Enemy Wolf now: https://books2read.com/enemywolf

Hey, thank you so much for reading my first ever Shyftworld novel! I truly hope you enjoyed Sawyer and Riley's story.

Since you made it this far, you probably have a few questions. When and why is Aran going to call on Sawyer with the scratch he made? What's up with the vampire bites on Laylah's neck? And is bad boy Thorne going to get some love?

All of these questions will be answered in upcoming books! There are so many characters and conflicts to explore in this world, and I'm just getting started. Be sure to let me know whose story you want to see next!

Until next time! Happy reading,
    Sophie

Also by Sophie Ash

<u>Gods and Myths</u>

The Minotaur

<u>Howling Death MC</u>

Traitor Wolf

Enemy Wolf

Interested in my reverse harem books?

Check out my catalog as Crystal Ash

ABOUT THE AUTHOR

Sophie Ash is a USA Today Bestselling Author from California who also writes as Crystal Ash. As Sophie, she writes steamy, romantic variations of classical myths and folklore, as well as paranormal motorcycle clubs with plenty of bite.

When she's not writing, she's probably drinking craft beer with her husband or trying to coax her feral cat into accepting affection.

crystalashbooks.com

facebook.com/Crystal.Sophie.Ash.Books

instagram.com/crystalsophieash

amazon.com/author/sophieash

bookbub.com/profile/sophie-ash